Dead Wrong

Lynn Emery

Lazy River Publishing
Baton Rouge, Louisiana

Lynn Emery/Lazy River Publishing
P.O. Box 74833
Baton Rouge, La 70874
www.lynnemery.com

Publisher's Note: This is a work of fiction. Names, characters, places, and incidents are a product of the author's imagination. Locales and public names are sometimes used for atmospheric purposes. Any resemblance to actual people, living or dead, or to businesses, companies, events, institutions, or locales is completely coincidental.

Book Layout & Design ©2013 - BookDesignTemplates.com

Dead Wrong/ Lynn Emery. -- 1st ed.
ISBN 978-0-9965272-9-3

<u>*Joliet Sisters Psychic Detectives Titles in*</u>
<u>*Paperback*</u>

Spirited Sisters – (Two Novellas)
Smooth Operator & Hunting Spirits

1.

Estate of Confusion

Charmaine closed her eyes and inhaled southern Louisiana, the scent of magnolias in bloom. Even in mid-October, the subtropical climate resulted in flowers in abundance and green all around. Then she opened her eyes to take in another view of the garden. Behind her, a huge tree wore big creamy white flowers nestled among deep green leaves like a southern debutante decked out for her first ball. Rows of rose bushes grew in a section to her left. A stone path snaked through more flowering shrubs of gardenias. The heavy perfume reminded her of long, lazy hours on a front porch with sweating glasses of sweet tea. Charmaine's pleasant reverie ended when Jessi plopped down next to her on the stone bench.

"This place is creepy as shit," Jessi said. She poked Charmaine's arm and then pointed to a stone statue on a pedestal. "I mean really, woman? A lawn jockey."

"That's a cherub," Charmaine replied mildly. Then she squinted at the worn figure and saw outlines of a jacket. "Or maybe it's a stable boy."

"Magnolia Grove Estate, a perfect symbol of the evils of slavery. Lookit." Jessi held up a tourist brochure given to them by their new client and read aloud. "The gardens were lovingly established in 1806 and improved upon by a succession of plantation owners."

Charmaine sighed and stood. Her moment of tranquility was over. "So?"

"First off, they changed the name, trying to disguise that this was a plantation. Artie calls it sanitizing the past to make it palatable." Jessi once again quoted her history professor at the University of New Orleans.

"Whatever. And since when does a student call her college professor by a cutesy nickname?" Charmaine walked toward a fountain. One of three groundskeepers cleaned leaves out of it.

Jessi caught up with her. "Artie isn't stuffy like some of those guys. He likes having an easy-going kinda vibe with his students."

"Uh-huh."

Dr. Arthur W. Marigny was a distinguished member of the history faculty at the University of New Orleans. His family was so "old New Orleans" that Charmaine imagined he smelled like dusty antiques. In fact, he lived up to the stereotype. His eccentricities were legend, and he lived in a grand house off Magazine Street in the heart of the city.

Charmaine suspected her sister was getting more than history lessons from "Artie".

"Anyway," Jessi said, breaking into Charmaine's thoughts. "These flowers are fertilized with the blood and flesh of our people. I can't believe you dragged me here. You shouldn't even consider dealing with these *people*. Our ancestors are crying out against this travesty."

Charmaine stopped in her tracks to face her sister. "Did you just say 'travesty'? And lower your voice; they'll hear you."

They both glanced around at one blonde woman who had paused from pulling weeds to stare at them. She gave them a tentative smile, then bent back to attacking stubborn crabgrass.

"I don't care." Jessi had lowered her voice even so. "We shouldn't be here, much less having this discussion."

"I'll tell you a real travesty, acting like we don't need the money Mrs. Villiers is willing to pay us to fix her spooky problems." Charmaine crossed her arms. "I don't have my own version of an Artie financing my habits."

"I don't know what you mean." Jessi sniffed and lifted her nose in the air.

"I'm sorry you had to wait," Mrs. Villiers called out, ending their debate.

The seventy-year-old mistress of the manor descended the steps of the grand gallerie, Louisiana Creole French for porch. She moved with the energy of a woman half her age. Impeccable in her pale pink silk blouse and gray linen slacks, she smiled at them. Her short cut silver hair lay in neat waves away from her face. Her perfect pale pink lips smiled at them warmly.

"No problem at all. I was enjoying this fabulous garden." Charmaine smiled back at her.

"Chyle, please," Jessi mumbled from behind her.

Charmaine ignored her baby sister's petulant commentary. "Hard to believe anything could disturb such a setting as this."

Mrs. Villiers blinked fast a few times. Her smile wilted at the edges. "Looks can be quite deceiving." Then she started back toward the house. "I have tea and finger sandwiches on the veranda since it's getting close to lunch time. The least we could do for holding you girls so long."

"Girls?" Jessi hissed under her breath.

"Charmaine spun around causing Jessi to jump back. She gave Jessi her death-ray stare. "Smile and act like somebody just offered you premium weed."

Mrs. Villiers stood poised with one foot on the first step up to the luxurious front porch. "Is everything all right?"

"Just fine," Charmaine replied in a cheerful tone. "Right, sis?"

Jessi transformed into the charmer that had gotten her into and out of trouble most of her life. She beamed at their new customer. "Thank you so much. I could use a bite to eat, come to think of it."

Charmaine let out a huff and rolled her eyes at the change. Fortunately, Mrs. Villiers didn't notice the too sugary tone. Instead, the older woman continued on filling in facts about the architecture of the mansion. Thanks to a land grant from France, the first owner moved to what would become Magnolia Plantation in seventeen eighty-seven. Located thirty-eight miles from New Orleans along River Road, the plantation was originally two hundred acres. The current property was less than ten.

"You know, sugar farming is what really led to our family's first true wealth. Our fortunes waxed and waned more than a few times." Mrs. Villiers settled into one of four comfy wicker chairs around a matching table. The sunroom was on the north side of the house. Jessi and Charmaine sat as well. "The Civil War especially took a toll. Glory days were destroyed back then."

"Such a pity," Jessi said. She sighed, sipped from her glass of tea, and avoided looking at Charmaine.

"I'm not defending slavery, of course," Mrs. Villiers replied. She blinked at Jessi.

"Of course." Jessi nodded to her.

"It's just, well, change is so hard. I'm thinking of today really. My family insists on selling off parts of our heritage to land speculators." Mrs. Villiers wore a dainty frown of repugnance.

Charmaine smothered a giggle as she finished chewing a tasty pimento cheese sandwich. She suspected Mrs. Villiers really wanted to call them common trash rascals. "So maybe the problems you're having are because of a disgruntled relative who wants to sell."

"No," Mrs. Villiers said and shook her head. "We have ghosts prowling the house, even the gardens. I'm convinced that they're disturbed by all this talk of building strip malls. Not to mention those awful cookie cutter brick boxes."

"You mean like the subdivision Magnolia Estates Phase I," Jessi replied. She picked up a finger sandwich and nibbled on it for a few seconds. "Hmm, these are tasty."

Mrs. Villiers wore a proud smile. "Our Yolanda makes the best chicken salad in the south. She's like a member of the family."

"Compliments to the cook then," Charmaine broke in before Jessi could reply. She stared at her sister, a warning against social observations about class and race.

Instead, Jessi nodded in sympathy. "I know what you mean about those houses. Row after row of blandness."

"Exactly. Oh, I know my oldest daughter and her husband would be happy to sign on the dotted line so to speak. But they wouldn't stoop to pulling pranks. Besides, the house has supernatural history." Mrs. Villiers sat back and stared at them in turn, as if her statement made it official. "No family shenanigans involved but ghosts and poltergeists."

Charmaine wiped her fingers on a napkin, took one last swig of sweet tea, and took out her notepad. "Okay, so give me an exact description of when it started."

"As I said, the incidents go back generations. Nothing sinister though. The occasional footsteps when no one is there. Things being moved around. Once or twice, house guests swore they saw a woman dressed in the fashion popular in the early nineteenth-century."

"Right, routine haunting," Jessi said dryly.

"Well, dear, this is Louisiana. Life wouldn't be normal if dead relatives didn't turn up every once in a while," Mrs. Villiers replied with a giggle. Then her humor vanished. "But almost a year ago, the episodes took a rather alarming turn."

"When was this exactly, as in month if you can remember," Charmaine said.

"Right around the holidays, so maybe mid-October or early November. Honestly, I didn't mark it on the calendar. Oh my, do you think sinister spirits set loose on Halloween could be the cause? Yolanda is always against our Spirits on the River Halloween week tours. I told her our ghosts were harmless. Now..."

"Ghouls and goblins don't operate by the calendar, ma'am. That's just superstitious nonsense," Jessi blurted out before Charmaine could stop her.

"Yes, that's what my children said. They dismissed it as Yolanda being a "holy roller". But I'm not so sure. Simpler folks than us have a down-to-earth wisdom. My grandmother always said so. She put a lot of stock in her housekeeper's advice on certain things."

"Another family member, right?" Jessi shifted her gaze from the matriarch to her sister.

"Annabelle served us with such devotion for over thirty years. I remember eating in the kitchen with her. Those biscuits were melt-in-your-mouth wonderful." Mrs. Villiers sighed at the happy memory.

"Uh-huh." Jessi slurped more tea to cover her lip curl.

Charmaine gave Jessi a brief squint, then turned to Mrs. Villiers. "So around maybe late October might be more accurate?"

"Yes, though I will admit nothing unusual happened during the Halloween Mystery Weekend. That culminates a week of special events. We decorate and everything, all period of course. Though my eldest grandson has incorporated modern technology. We have a mist machine for one thing. He even outfitted the porch with a device that makes fake cobwebs and spiders descend from the ceiling. Teenagers are so clever these days. He'll attend Vanderbilt this fall. Most of the boys in our family do. I'll get his photo for you." Mrs. Villiers started to get up but stopped when Charmaine put a gentle restraining hand on her arm.

"Maybe in a bit. Back to the ghosts." Charmaine wore a restrained smile. She wanted to avoid going down the "these are my wonderful grandchildren" rabbit hole. They'd be listening for hours.

"Of course. I tend to test the patience of guests, raving about my seven sources of pride and joy." Mrs. Villiers sank back onto the cabbage rose designed chair cushion.

"You were about to tell us what's been happening, an example or two," Jessi prompted.

"Yes. Oh it was awful. Yolanda was in the kitchen, and I heard a loud crash. She insisted a copper pot on the top shelf above her head had been thrown at her, aimed like a cannonball she said. A week later, one of our bed and breakfast guests came screaming to the house just before midnight. She said icy cold hands had grabbed her by the throat. The noises increased as well." Mrs. Villiers took a sip of sweet tea and shook her head. "Horrible. Yolanda won't work alone in the house anymore. Such a nuisance, too. But we love her dearly, so we indulge her."

Charmaine made notes. "Can you tell us if there are any milestone events or tragedies associated with the house?"

"My goodness, let me think. People have died in their own beds at home many times over the decades. Most were treated at home when ill," Mrs. Villiers replied.

"Any rumors that one or more were helped on their way?" Jessi leaned forward.

"Natural causes were most common." Mrs. Villiers cleared her throat and glanced out of the window. "We're a very private household traditionally."

"Check with our former clients. They'll tell you we treat all of our cases with extreme discretion," Charmaine said.

"Our lips are sealed when it comes to the skeletons in your family's closets," Jessi added.

Mrs. Villiers glanced at Jessi. Then she gave a short nod as if making a decision. "I like your plainspoken manner, young lady. I'm relying on you to keep that promise. What you're about to hear may shock you."

"Us, be shocked. That's cute. Okay, let's get to the real deal about the fam." Jessi looked interested for the first time.

Mrs. Villiers fortified herself with another two sips of sweet tea, daintily dabbed her lips without smudging her pink lipstick, and sighed. Charmaine resisted the urge to glance at her watch. They'd been rambling around Magnolia Grove since ten o'clock that morning. She silently willed Mrs. Villiers to get a move on.

"I may not have been entirely forthcoming. Yes, it's true that I wanted you to investigate the spirits here. But there are several family accounts that we don't speak of to those on the outside. The bloodiest deaths occurred during the Slave Revolt of 1811. The mistress of the house and her oldest son were both killed. Her husband survived, but never fully recovered physically."

"Yes, we learned about it in class. The 1811 uprising was the largest slave revolt in American history. As many as five hundred slaves meant to take over New Orleans." Jessi let out a low whistle. "They made it here."

"Yes, with horrific results. They hacked the family with machetes. Monsieur Pinchot was said to have been a benevolent master by all accounts," Mrs. Villiers replied and shook her head.

"There is no such thing as a *good* slave master. Would that make you feel better?" Jessi retorted.

"I spoke without thinking. As I said, different times and change can be hard to navigate. When you're raised a certain way..." Mrs. Villiers waved a hand around at the house and gardens.

"Yeah, for generations." Jessi pressed her lips closed and went silent.

"Exactly," Mrs. Villiers agreed.

Charmaine glanced between the two women, then pushed on. "So the bumps in the night, things being moved around, increased. Plus actual physical contact with the living happened. Tell us about other tragedies."

Mrs. Villiers fidgeted with the fancy napkin in her lap. "During the Civil War, one of our ancestors went mad when New Orleans came under union control. There were allegations that he killed three slaves in a rage. He shouted that they were his property, and he'd destroy what he owned before bowing to Yankees. Journals from the time indicate he'd never been mentally stable at the best of times."

"You said allegations. He either killed them, or he didn't," Jessi said.

"His brother put forth a self-defense argument. They claimed the slaves, three women, were emboldened by the prospect of a Union victory. They attacked him and planned to kill his wife and two daughters. That, along with attitudes of the times, meant he didn't face any kind of legal repercussions."

"Big surprise," Jessi murmured. Before she continued, a loud crash startled them all. "What the hell?"

Yolanda, the cook/housekeeper, rushed down a path of crushed stone from the side of the house and onto the veranda. The short plump woman had cinnamon brown skin, her hair in neat cornrows, and looked to be around sixty years old. She wore a terrified frown.

"It's starting again, Miz Vee. Somethin' is ramblin' around in the house. I come out the back door and around. I'm not walking through those rooms. No ma'am." As she spoke, more thumps and bumps sounded in the house.

"What a damn racket." Jessi stood and stared through the open antique French doors to the house's interior.

"See what I been sayin'? A big soup bowl moving a few inches in the china cabinet is one thing. But this is too much. Lord knows I need my job, but—"

"Calm down, Yolanda. I'm sure it's nothing to get all in a tizzy about, right ladies? It's probably a strong wind. Look how the leaves are swaying in the old oak tree." Mrs. Villiers patted Yolanda's shoulder. She gave Charmaine a frantic look pleading for support.

"Wind hell," Jessi shot back before Charmaine could at least try. Another crash seemed to confirm Jessi's terse assessment. "I'm going in."

"Maybe we should wai..."

Charmaine bit off the rest of her sentence because Jessi had already crossed the threshold. She watched her sister stride without hesitation toward the noise. She sighed and turned to the two wide-eyed older women. Yolanda had one hand clamped over her mouth. Mrs. Villiers had turned pale, making her pink lipstick stand out even more.

"Everything is going to be okay." Another thump seemed to make her assurance ring false. Charmaine forced a smile. "I mean, as you said Mrs. Villiers. I'm sure there's a simple explanation."

The tinkle of what sounded like breaking glass interrupted Charmaine's attempt at reassurance. The women transferred twin panicked gazes from the house back to Charmaine. Jessi's yelp punctuated another crash.

"Um, excuse us a minute. Be right back. Don't go anywhere," Charmaine stammered.

She hurried inside following the path Jessi had taken. Stuffed chairs, antique tables, and other fine furnishings were a blur as Charmaine raced through two rooms. She slid along the polished hardwood floor of the wide foyer.

"Get in here," Jessi yelled.

"Shit, Jess, where is 'here'?" Charmaine pushed down fright to focus.

Jessi yanked open lovely double wooden doors. "The damn library. Hell, I thought you could read minds."

Charmaine let go of the breath she'd held. "I thought you were... Are you hurt?"

"Stop playing around and get in here." Jessi spun on her heels and disappeared from the doorway.

"Playing—" Charmaine bit back a scream of outrage. She marched into the library.

The room was long and wide, taking up half of the east side of the first floor. The other half was the formal dining room. One wall was a floor to ceiling bookcase. A polished oak ladder, original to the house, allowed users to reach the upper shelves. An imposing eighteenth-century oak desk sat to one side. A large fireplace with a gray marble mantle was set in another wall. The room was a beauty, filled with antiques that reflected the travels and interests of several generations of Villiers men. All rich, cultured, southern gents. Yet Charmaine didn't examine the decor. She scanned for signs of malevolent spirits.

Leather bound tomes scattered the floor. A couple of Queen Anne chairs lay on their sides. Clues that the crashes and bumps originated in that room. Jessi glared at one of three portraits on the wall. She pointed a forefinger at the dour looking man from another era. He seemed to glare back at her with disdain.

"This asshole here? He got what he deserved. Yeah, I'm talking to you," Jessi snapped.

She marched over to another oil painting, a woman with her hand on the shoulder of a young boy. An infant girl dressed in a pretty lace dress sat in her lap. All were dressed in fancy clothes popular in the early 1800s.

"Jessi—"

"Boo-hoo, you had to put up with a lot of crap back in your day. But you took it out on your slaves. Bitch." Jessi crossed her arms. "Nah, I got no sympathy for ya."

Charmaine raced back to doors and pulled them shut. "Those old ladies are about to keel over with matching heart attacks. Keep your voice down. Now explain what the fu— what's going on."

"I'm not sure. Now this dude..." Jessi wound up for another rant.

"Never mind the history lesson. Switch to the flying objects in the present," Charmaine hissed. She started to pick up two books.

"We need to take pictures. Luckily, I have video of some of the action." Jessi held up the compact digital camera in her hand and gave a satisfied nod.

Charmaine thought about the seven-hundred dollar charge on her credit card and winced. "Those images better be full-color HD perfection."

"Whatever."

Jessi got busy taking a series of photos around the room. Charmaine retraced Jessi's steps, putting items back in place once she got the signal. She called out to Mrs. Villiers to give them more time twice.

"Okay. I think we're ready. Dang, this stuff is heavier than it looks." Charmaine huffed and wiped sweat from her face.

"I don't know why you bothered. They have 'the help' you know." Jessi swiped the three-inch screen of the digital camera reviewing her results.

"We want them to know we're in control of the situation." Charmaine started to go on but the library doors flew open.

"I demand an explanation for what's going on in here. Who are these people, and why are they marching around in our home? Good Lord, mother. We deserve at least a small amount of privacy."

Her face flushed red with anger, the newcomer glared at Charmaine and Jessi in turn. A tall blonde man stood right behind her. He looked at Charmaine and Jessi with interest but said nothing.

"My daughter Evelyn," Mrs. Villiers said with an apologetic smile. She followed Evelyn into the room. "And Tanner Gladstone."

Evelyn stood at least five feet eight inches, towering over her petite mother by at least five inches. Her thick brunette ponytail bounced as she scanned the room. Charmaine guessed the cream-colored front-button shirt tucked into brown slacks cost more than Jessi's beloved camera. In other words, she could buy and sell the pair of them. No doubt Evelyn could communicate just that with a look. When she faced Charmaine and Jessi again, her expression confirmed it.

"Well, mother?" Evelyn cocked her head to one side.

"These are the private investigators I've hired to solve the mystery of what's going on around here. Not the least of which is almost one million dollars' worth of missing art objects and antiques."

"You admitted you haven't seen most of those things for years. You assumed they were in the attic. Our grandparents probably sold or gave them away. At any rate, you forced us to hire Tanner to head up our security team." Evelyn spoke in a level tone. She plastered on a tight smile. "Remember? No need to worry about it."

"Thanks for the vote of confidence, Ev," Tanner Gladstone said and extended a large hand to them. He beamed as Jessi first and seemed amused when she only nodded. His bright smile turned to Charmaine when she accepted the handshake.

No need to read minds. Evelyn's posture and words screamed she resented the man. Figuring out why interested Charmaine. She sensed that the answer was important. Tanner's voice pitched low, but he spoke loudly enough for Jessi and Charmaine to hear him. Mrs. Villiers frowned at Evelyn.

"My parents would never have frittered away our family legacy. There are other forces at work. These ladies specialize in paranormal phenomena.

Our spirits are turning quite hostile." Mrs. Villiers glanced around the room as if expecting a sprite to confirm her statement.

"Ladies, I'm the chief security officer at VSI, Inc. My duties have expanded to include all holdings, not just the main business branches. I have two section coordinators. We've pretty much had our hands full with... other matters." Tanner smoothed down his silk tie. "But we're going to work with the police."

"Robert and I met with Tanner this morning. We'll discuss our decisions in private, mother," Evelyn said, her lips stretched tight as though maintaining the smile took effort.

Mrs. Villiers blinked at her daughter. "Evelyn, listen to me—"

"I don't know what kind of sales pitch you gave my mother, but we don't need your services. I'll be happy to pay you for the time you've spent so far, provided it's reasonable." Evelyn swung her leather purse from one shoulder, opened it, and pulled out a check. I don't suppose you take debit cards."

"Wait." Charmaine held up a hand.

"No, I suppose not." Evelyn strode to the desk and sat down in the leather chair behind it. She proceeded to write a check without paying attention to them. Then she held it out. "I'm sure that should be more than enough."

Jessi walked over to her casually, took it and smiled at the amount. "Oh yeah, it takes the edge off being fired."

Charmaine ignored her sister's minor celebration. "Excuse me, but you're not our client. Last time I checked, she was grown and fully capable of making her own decisions."

"Mother gets over excited about the least little thing. Old houses make noises, Ms.," Evelyn paused.

"Joliet, and this is my sister Jessi." Charmaine crossed her arms.

"I heard the racket, too," Yolanda said. She stood in the hallway just outside the door. She peered around the library but didn't move to enter.

Evelyn sucked in a deep breath and blew it out. You're in the kitchen banging pots and pans all the time. Don't let your imagination fill in perfectly commonplace cracks and creaks."

"I know what I heard. I'm going back to the kitchen." Yolanda looked around as if inspecting her surroundings for threats. Then she took a few tentative steps. When nothing moved, she vanished down the long hall toward the addition that included the modern kitchen.

"Mother, you and Yolanda feed into each other with this foolishness. I swear." Evelyn pursed her lips in displeasure.

"Hello, what's happened?" Another woman, her hair a reddish blonde color, entered the room. She looked at Evelyn with both finely arched eyebrows raised.

"My younger daughter Laura Villiers Mandeville. I'm sure you've heard of that fine old family name. Quite a colorful history that connects to some of the events to this house," Mrs. Villiers spoke to Jessi and took her by the arm.

Evelyn stood. "Mother, those are family matters. This is exactly what I've been talking about, Laura."

"Don't be ridiculous. I haven't told them anything they can't learn reading a copy of St. Charles Avenue magazine. Or find in the library after some digging. But you won't have to do that, Jessi. I hope you don't mind the familiarity. I feel like we're friends already. I'll give you as much background as I can. Fortunately, my ancestors kept journals. They got quite chatty on paper." Mrs. Villiers chuckled.

"These days we can find out about people from their Facebook, Instagram, or Snapchat pages. You'd think they'd know better. Me? I just post cute kitten videos and stuff." Jessi grinned at the older woman as if they were officially BFFs.

"She's hired these 'paranormal investigators'," Evelyn replied, gazing at her sister. Then she performed the upper-class version of rolling her eyes.

"Ghostbusters?" Laura strolled over to a sofa in rich brown leather and took a seat. "Really, mother, I thought we'd settled this."

"Don't take such a casual attitude, Laura," Evelyn snapped. "We have too much at stake."

"Interesting. Tell us about these high stakes. Maybe we could help," Charmaine said.

"I doubt it. You've been paid, so I'll show you out." Evelyn gave a curt nod in the general direction of the nearest exit.

Mrs. Villiers let go of Jessi's arm and walked over to her daughter, who still stood behind the desk. She glanced at the checkbook and picked it up. "I'll keep this."

"Mother." Evelyn huffed.

"The estate accounts are under my signature. I allowed you access to help manage the business, not to assume you could dictate to me." Mrs. Villiers lifted her chin to stare at her oldest child.

"From delicate southern belle to steel magnolia in five seconds flat. My girl." Jessi looked at Evelyn. "Your move."

"Please, Evelyn, mother, not in front of strangers," Laura said and stood. "As fun as this has been to watch, we really must ask you to take your check and go."

"Hello, everyone. You're having a lunch party and didn't invite me?"

The tall man speaking strolled into the room. Dark wavy hair framed his face to perfection, and what a face. He had the good looks of a male model who'd stepped out of the pages of GQ magazine. Charmaine and Jessi gasped in sync as he turned his magical blue-eyed gaze on them.

"My son Nicholas," Mrs. Villiers said, a curt wave at the newcomer. "This is Ms. Charmaine and Jessi Joliet, private investigators I've hired."

"Two sexy young sisters who track down bumps in the night. I like it." Nicholas transferred his intense blue gaze from Charmaine to Jessi, and back again. Then he grinned at Tanner Gladstone. "What's up, Tanner?"

"The usual. Keeping busy." Tanner Gladstone nodded to him.

"Keep Evelyn and Robert on their toes, my man." Nicholas Villiers winked at him and ignored his sister's hiss of irritation. Then he looked at Charmaine again.

Charmaine felt a familiar hum go through her body. Nicholas's mind had fast-forwarded from the introductions to an X-rated list of things he'd like to do to Charmaine. In response, she bit her lower lip. Charmaine adjusted the collar of her striped shirt to let him see more of her cleavage. He sucked in a short breath. The reaction implied he could live up to her expectations. The explicit images that flashed in his head confirmed he had the right ideas.

"Focus on business," Jessi whispered aside to Charmaine.

"The circle is complete. All of my living children have arrived. Two to interfere and the one to no doubt ask for another advance on his inheritance." Mrs. Villiers gave her son a sour look.

"Mother, really. These people..." Evelyn broke off at the dark look Jessi shot at her. "I'm sorry. I've been rude."

"Yeah, very," Jessi retorted.

Charmaine forced her heated gaze and imagination away from the delectable rich boy. She faced the three Villiers women. "Listen, we've obviously stepped into delicate family matters. You folks discuss if and how you want to proceed, and get back to us. Meantime, this check will adequately compensate us for our time."

"You're not going anywhere," Mrs. Villiers said. She faced her daughters.

Laura and Evelyn launched into rants at the same time, with Mrs. Villiers countering every argument. Then they lowered their voices, no doubt remembering they were genteel southern ladies. Yet the intensity of the exchange remained high. Evelyn flapped her hands in agitation as she made her case. Laura tried the soft, rational approach laced with honey. Charmaine heard the words "be reasonable", "don't be ridiculous" pass back and forth.

"Girl, I vote we take the check and run. We don't need this drama," Jessi mumbled. She looked at her camera's LCD display again. "Sweet pics though. We can use them in our marketing."

"Yeah, but we do need the kind of money this job will bring in: One hundred fifty dollars an hour," Charmaine whispered back. She glanced at the women, and then felt a psychic jerk. Nicholas's erotic thoughts pulled at her like a powerful magnet.

"Damn. We could rack up serious cash flow in no time. I... be back in a few." Jessi darted off to the other side of the huge library before Charmaine could question why.

Nicholas wet his thin lips as he looked at Charmaine. He walked over to her. "I'll help in any way I can: waiting in dark rooms for a sign, hours in the haunted attic after midnight..."

"But will I be able to do my job with you so close by?" Charmaine replied, her voice low. She looked at his mother and sisters. They were too caught up in their squabble to notice them for now.

"Put your camera on a timer. We'll need hours of uninterrupted consultation," he whispered back.

"I'm wondering if you can meet my price." Charmaine's breath caught at the image that flashed in her head. Nicholas pictured them on a certain antique settee, her naked astride him bucking wildly.

"I'll do my best." Nicholas swallowed hard.

Charmaine smiled up at him. "You've just given me a verbal contract. I expect you to comply fully, no holding back."

"Damn girl." Nicholas lifted a hand to touch her hair, but Evelyn's sharp voice made him freeze.

"Nicholas, we need to talk," his older sister snapped.

He winked at Charmaine and then faced his sisters. He put on a sober expression for their benefit. "Sure."

"The discussion is over. My decision is final. The Joliets are on the case," Mrs. Villiers said. She scowled at her adult children then beamed at

Charmaine. "I want you to get started immediate-ly."

"If you're sure." Charmaine nodded toward the three Villiers offspring huddled in an opposite corner.

"Despite what Evelyn and Laura think, I'm in charge. Give me a plan of how you will proceed within the next seventy-two hours. Include all fees, and what you expect to deliver." Mrs. Villiers tilted her silver-haired head to one side. "Acceptable?"

"Yes." Charmaine blinked at her. Mrs. Villiers had dropped the gardenias and old lace façade.

"Good."

Mrs. Villiers marched off like a general intent on whipping her troops into shape. She waded right in the middle of the three Villiers heirs. Angry gesticulating followed, along with discordant restrained upper-crust voices. Mrs. Villiers alone seemed calm. She wore a granite hard expression in the face of their wrath.

Jessi rejoined Charmaine. "We need to leave. There's more going on here than the old lady told us."

"Tell me something I hadn't figured out." Charmaine shook her head.

"I don't mean family feud over there. She didn't mention the damn family murders." Jessi nodded slowly at Charmaine's gasp of shock.

2.
Lies and Half-truths

The next day, Jessi sat across from Charmaine at her home office, which also doubled as the headquarters for 1-800-Spirits. The tidy cottage just on the edge of the ruined Ninth Ward of New Orleans perfectly reflected the post-Katrina city. With help from state grants and FEMA, Charmaine had rebuilt the family home. Gone was the shotgun styled home her great-grandfather had built in nineteen-twenty. The house had slowly gone to ruin, like portions of the neighborhood. Unlike most of the Ninth Ward, her street featured several homes with neat front yards. All of them had big dogs or security systems that included cameras. And guns. They all owned guns. There was history, culture, and a fierce love for their old neighborhood. There was also danger.

Charmaine stood over Jessi's shoulder watching her edit the video footage she'd taken. The computer app represented another unpaid three hundred dollars on her credit card balance. The Apple iMac desktop also added to the debt.

"The crazy ghost says there were murders in the house. No surprise. Mrs. Villiers sort of mentioned bad stuff happened there over the years."

"Yeah, but she didn't mention her late husband and her uncle were among them. She talked about killings like a hundred years ago. So, why didn't she say, 'My husband might be one of the restless ghosts in the big house'? Maybe she already knows. Maybe she killed him." Jessi executed a couple of key strokes.

"You've jumped to a big set of theories on not enough information. I read the obituary. Natural causes written all over it. He died at his home after a brief illness. Age fifty-five is kinda young, I agree. But it happens."

"Doesn't say what kind of illness though," Jessi countered.

"Probably heart problems helped along by high blood pressure. We've met his wife and kids, remember?" Charmaine retorted. "Marguerite de Gravelles Villiers came off all sweet and cuddly at first. Then a hot minute later, she turned into dragon lady."

Diamond, Jessi's best friend and frequent co-conspirator in mischief, came holding a bowl and smacking her lips. "Hey, y'all. I'ma bounce up outta here."

"I must be outta food if you're leaving so soon," Charmaine retorted. "And you better not have eaten all my Aunt Judy's apple and walnuts salad."

"Uh." Diamond put the bowl behind her back. "It was only a little bit left."

"I swear," Charmaine huffed out. "To top it off, you don't gain weight. I'd at least feel some revenge if you got fat eating up all my food."

"My baby ate some before her daddy picked her up. I mixed it in her oatmeal, and she gobbled it right up. Indyah loves visiting Auntie Charmaine." Diamond beamed at her and sat down.

"Uh-huh. At least Andre is doing something for his child. Taking her to pre-school isn't as good as paying regular child support though."

"He's tryin' to get back on his feet after jail. It's hard, ya know. Hmm, Miss Judy makes the best—" Diamond broke off at the scowl Charmaine aimed her way. "Sorry. We were hungry."

Charmaine squinted at her. "You get away with a lot because of that little rug rat. But one of these days..."

"Hey, look at this," Jessi said, poking Charmaine in the side with an elbow.

Charmaine turned back to frown at her sister. "I don't see anything other than the outline of the second spirit. You already showed me that one."

"Y'all trip me out. Talk about ghosts and stuff like it's no big shit." Diamond shook her head. "My grand-mama came back to me and fussed because I was on the pole. Then I told her how much money guys paid me to get naked, and that shut her up. Madea Lucy loved herself some money. She..."

"I thought you were heading off to your new job?" Charmaine cut in.

"Bobby doesn't mind if I'm a little late every now and then. I'm a single mother after all."

"Will you focus?" Jessi broke in. "Look at that shadow there. By the door. Somebody was listening in to us talking."

"Okay, so Yolanda eavesdropped on her employers. Servants have been snooping on their bosses for thousands of years." Charmaine stretched, yawned, and frowned at Diamond again. "I suppose you drank up the last of my morning coffee."

"I made a fresh pot. Oh, and I baked some biscuits. Since there's no more apple and walnuts salad," Diamond mumbled as an addendum.

"You know your way around my kitchen and food pantry way too good," Charmaine retorted without much heat. She sniffed the air for the first time, noticing the smell coming from the kitchen.

Diamond nodded. "Yeah, I cooked some sausage, too. Warming in the toaster oven."

Whatever mild annoyance Charmaine had faded when her stomach rumbled approval. "Well at least you make yourself useful every now and then."

"You're welcome." Diamond stuck her tongue out at her. "Y'all up real early working."

"My bill collectors don't sleep in, believe me." Charmaine turned back to Jessi. "Which brings me back to Mrs. Marguerite de Gravelles Villiers. Okay, so she's not the sweetie pie we first thought. We've worked jerks plenty of times."

"Yeah, but that old saying is hella wrong. What we don't know will bite us on the ass. She's lying about something."

"Again, not new. Do I have to list the number of cases we've had where the client lied? Not to mention shorted us on payment," Charmaine said.

"Don't even start. You were the one who let that old lady in Belle Chase gives us chickens and mustard greens instead of cash. Who does that?" Jessi gave a snort.

"Sounds great to me," Diamond piped up. "Bet she can cook, too."

"Mrs. Gordon worked for little or nothing all her life. Now her pension is teeny-tiny. I couldn't take her what little savings she had. Seeing her tears of joy when we found her son was payment enough." Charmaine smiled at the memory of one of a few satisfying cases she'd had.

"Her no-good son who couldn't be bothered to call his mother. Laid up with some just as no-good woman drinking his days away. Yeah, touching reunion. I'll bet they're both mooching off her now." Jessi turned back to the computer screen.

Charmaine's smile faded. "I'm going to check up on Mrs. G., just to see how she's feeling these days."

"Before you jump into another non-paying family mess, do some research on ol' Marguerite and her peeps. I'll ask Artie for leads on their history. Bet he won't even have to crack a book to tell me all about 'em. He's got the scoop on all the fancy bloodlines." Jessi executed a series of mouse clicks and keystrokes as she talked.

"You two are so way too cozy with your teachers." Charmaine looked from Jessi to Diamond.

"They're happy to help two struggling young women of color trying to better themselves," Diamond popped out in a sing-song voice. Then she winked at Charmaine.

"So, this guy teaching you at the Newcomb College Institute got you a job in the admissions department because he's kind." Charmaine cocked her head to one side. "Yeah, sure."

"A single mother needs a steady source of income. Stripping isn't a safe occupation," Diamond replied. She mimicked a cultured accent from uptown New Orleans.

"Y'all still working games to get by." Charmaine shook her head.

She trudged to the kitchen with Diamond following close behind. True to her word, a small pan with biscuits and sausage links warmed in the oven. Charmaine took it out. She inhaled the aroma of spices coming from the meat. The biscuits came from a frozen package, but it didn't matter. They tasted like homemade. Though not as good as her aunt's melt-in-your-mouth fluffy version.

By habit, Charmaine loaded two plates, one for Jessi. Her sister appeared seconds later carrying her lap top, and they all sat down to eat. Diamond munched on a sausage link making happy noises.

"I thought you ate with the baby." Jessi glanced at her friend.

"Yeah, but this smells too good to let pass." Diamond dug her cellphone out of her cross-body purse. She dropped it back in and wrapped up two sausage links and a biscuit into a paper towel. "Gonna be late. I'll take mine to go."

"I'm sure Professor Sugar Daddy will understand." Charmaine pursed her lips and shot a sideways glance at Jessi.

"Well yeah, I do him every now and then. No biggie." Diamond shrugged. "I'm taking courses in their 'help the po-folks' program. They get to feel all liberal and shit, and I get some benefits."

"Sex greases the wheels of life," Jessi wisecracked.

"Wonder if Dr. Artie's wife is so open about you and her husband." Charmaine looked at her sister.

"Hey, she's busy selling houses to out-of-town hipsters, pretending she's got a career. With her full social calendar, she doesn't notice Artie's not bugging her for nookie." Jessi giggled.

"Probably doesn't care. Most of the women in their circle marry money. Sometimes they care more about the fine old family name." Diamond licked her fingers and stood. "Let me know if I can help."

"Good idea. Your prof is younger than Artie. He can fill us in on the under forty high society crowd." Jessi nodded at Diamond.

"I'll pump him for info. Talk to y'all later." Diamond started to leave, darted back to snag a second biscuit, and then headed for the back door. "Extra snack for later."

"Hit up your mark for some grocery money," Charmaine yelled at her retreating back.

"Girl, you so crazy," Diamond called over her shoulder without stopping. The door banged shut. A click signaled she'd locked it on her way out.

Charmaine turned to Jessi. She watched her sister work on a biscuit stuffed with sausage for a few seconds. "Listen, we don't need new drama."

Jessi mumbled around a chunk of food, fingers still tapping the keyboard. Then she chewed, gulped from Charmaine's mug of coffee, and cleared her throat. "Now what are you naggin' me about?"

"We don't need trouble from well-connected outraged wives. Let's concentrate on building our business. Then Diamond gets hooked up with this Bobby dude. Also married."

"Engaged. Not the same thing," Jessi broke in.

"No trouble, no explosions," Charmaine shot back.

"You're never satisfied. Me and Diamond haven't been arrested for almost a year. We only work the poles during convention season now days."

Charmaine stared at her. "Make sure dancing is all you do."

"If I want to do sex work, it's my business. My body, my choice," Jessi said, repeating the motto of SWU, Sex Workers United. The organization advocated for decriminalization of prostitution.

"I don't care what fancy slogans y'all come up with. It's dangerous and dirty work," Charmaine countered.

"Oh, so you having one-niters for free is somehow different. I'm not judging." Jessi held up a palm when Charmaine started to object. "You like to get freaky. Cool. But don't make out like it's somehow better than me and Diamond getting paid."

Charmaine pressed her lips together. Matching bad childhoods left both with issues. Both had been sexually molested by a series of their mother's shady boyfriends who drifted through their lives. Her reaction was to use sex for commerce. By her own admission, Jessi had trouble finding any pleasure in the act. What she enjoyed was feeling in control. Charmaine by contrast craved erotic encounters as recreation. A succession of therapists explained that Charmaine associated closeness, affection, even friendship with sexual activity.

"I'm way more selective. Not just any guy with a roll of cash gets in," Charmaine grumbled.

"Enough of the family therapy replay." Jessi waved a hand. She slurped up the last of Charmaine's coffee. Then she went back to reading on her laptop.

"Get your own damn cup." Charmaine snatched her mug out of reach.

Jessi's only response was a disinterested grunt. Charmaine refilled it despite grumbling. She also washed up the dishes, including those Diamond dirtied cooking. The story of her life—cleaning Jessi and Diamond's messes. More insight from therapy. Charmaine had taken on the role of protector. She was a fixer with a need to repair broken things and people. She'd had no success in one area.

"Mama called yesterday," Charmaine said casually over her shoulder as she scrubbed the pan Diamond had used to bake biscuits.

"And you know what I'm going to say," Jessi replied without emotion. "No, I don't want to know what she said, or what she's been up to."

"She's thinking about moving back from Missouri City. You know she's never been crazy about the Houston area or Texas. Her husband—"

"What part of, I. don't. give. a. shit, confuses you, Charmaine?" Jessi cut in.

"Ernest is actually a nice person. I think he's been good for her. She's in church now," Charmaine pressed on.

Jessi heaved a sigh and turned to face her. "Okay, let's get this over with. You were more than happy to cut her off. Now she's a holy roller, which means you both believe in some non-existent dude in the sky who will make everything wonderful. Except he doesn't. Bad shit happens. Tell her to stay in Texas."

"Okay, fine. Don't get all worked up about it," Charmaine said, her voice even.

Her hand shook a little as she put a plate in the drainer. Jessi tended to turn to dangerous behavior, like drugs and prostitution, to numb pain. Charmaine silently cursed her current therapist once again. Sometimes "confronting the problem" was a bad idea.

"Hey," Jessi spoke loud to get Charmaine's attention. "I'm good."

Charmaine faced Jessi. She studied her sister's expression, probed to get a read of her emotions and thoughts. Blank slate. She let out a slow breath. "I said okay."

"Then we're all 'okay'." Jessi went back to working.

Charmaine bit her tongue to keep from retorting they were far from it. Instead, she dried the dishes. "I've got two appointments at the clinic today, so at least I'll be getting paid."

"Thought you didn't like working at the Central City Community Clinic? This job with the Villiers is going to pay some bills for a minute."

"At this point, I won't turn down any source of income. Besides, I love helping mentally ill patients. It's the executive director who pisses me off daily." Charmaine frowned just thinking about the man.

"Hmmm." Jessi seemed intent on reading the web page displayed on the screen.

"You know, Jessi. I think one of my clients may not be psychotic at all. I think he's actually hearing the dead like you." Charmaine put away plates and coffee mugs as she talked. "In fact, I'm almost sure of it."

"Um-hum."

Charmaine became enthusiastic at the prospect of helping the twenty-year old. The hollow feeling that came from talking about their past got pushed aside. "I was thinking you could talk to him and..."

"Yeah, yeah. Let me know. But look at this. Mr. Villiers' obituary. They had another son who died back in nineteen-eighty eight. He was just eighteen years old. That's a lot of tragedy for one family. Damn, it goes back generations." Jessi swiped the pad to scroll to another page. "Wow, he was one fine guy. He would be forty-six if he'd lived."

Charmaine walked over while drying her hands on a dish towel. "So, he wasn't one of the spirits you saw at the mansion, and neither was his father. That's odd."

"Who knows why some hang around and others don't. If we figure that one out, we'll make a fortune." Jessi studied the old photo of the handsome firstborn Villiers son, Matthew.

"Let me guess. You're working on it."

"Emotion is a form of energy. See, Logan thinks we'll eventually be able to explain most paranormal phenomena. After all, pre-historic people thought fire and lightning were magical." Jessi's face lit up.

"Logan, another one of your collections." Charmaine gave a snort. She went back to cleaning up the grease spatters Diamond had left all over her stove. "Your study group discusses the supernatural. This should be interesting."

Logan Broderick, a twenty-one-year-old fellow student, was a scientist who didn't believe in God or religion. He and Jessi met in a physics class, mutual skeptics who became buddies almost immediately. Their friends, Kirsten (the agnostic) and Thi, rounded out Jessi's college crew. Thi practiced Buddhism in a perfunctory manner to satisfy her Vietnamese parents and grandparents.

"Logan is a major physics nerd, from a long line of geeks. His grandfather was one of the first black astrophysicists at NASA. Don't be so sure we won't hack a lot of the unknown."

Charmaine smiled, though she didn't let Jessi see it. Anything that distracted Jessi from her penchant for street life was a good thing. "No doubt. Just keep our cases confidential."

"I know," Jessi shot back with irritation. Then her expression cleared again. "No details on what killed Andrew Villiers. His obit just says he 'succumbed after a brief illness'. Sounds fishy."

"With forensics these days, I don't think a suspicious death would have been overlooked. On the other hand..." Charmaine hung the damp dishtowel up to dry on a rack. "They're influential. He's known to have health problems."

"Autopsies aren't routinely performed when someone dies. He's over fifty, and his doctor says the guy had a crap heart. The cops or DA wouldn't question it." Jessi looked at Charmaine. "I know what you're thinking, it's not a lot to go on."

"It would help if the old man popped in to give you a clue," Charmaine replied. "So how do we handle the case? We're getting paid to clear out troublesome ghoulies."

"I need uninterrupted time in the house. All that squabbling and Yolanda listening through door cracks gets in my way," Jessi said.

"Okay, here's the plan. Mrs. Villiers can make sure you have time in the house alone. I'll talk to her away from Magnolia Grove, maybe at the family's office building."

"Shut up," Jessi blurted out. "They own an entire office building?"

"Yep, a thirty-story building on Common Street. Mrs. Villiers and the oldest daughter sit on the board of Villiers and Sons Industries, VSI."

"Really? Bet Evelyn doesn't like that 'and Sons' part," Jessi joked. She went back to looking at her laptop. "I better get on my assignment for Artie's class. We might be pals, but he will flunk my ass if I don't do the work."

"You make a good point. When I talk to Evelyn, I can look for tension about her place running the family firms. She wants to be in control for sure. Laura I haven't figured out yet. Nicholas likes to party." Charmaine felt warmth in intimate places at the memory of what was on his mind.

"Yeah, I'm sure you'll enjoy exploring Nicholas. And the other way around," Jessi said with a snicker.

Charmaine flinched. She indeed was thinking of Nicholas in very explicit poses. "I'm going to interview members of the family. I'll set up a day with Mrs. Villiers for us to go back to the house."

"Preferably when Yolanda has the day off." Jessi stood and picked up her laptop. "I can't wait to hear about your interview with sexy Nicky boy."

"Oh shut up," Charmaine shot back.

"What does God have to say about your sexual appetite by the way?" Jessi jabbed again at Charmaine's sore spot.

"I'm working on it. Besides, sex isn't forbidden. It's a natural part of life. Christianity is all about forgiveness." Charmaine bit off the rest her jumble of justifications.

Jessi let out a snort. "Forgiveness huh? Mighty convenient Plan B. I say screw who you want and stop feeling guilty about it."

"I like going to church," Charmaine mumbled.

"Uh-huh." Jessi started to say more but stopped when Charmaine glared at her.

"Like I said, shut up."

Jessi tucked the laptop under one arm. "I'll talk to Artie about our new clients and get back to you. I'm sure you'll enjoy your assignment more than I will."

"Didn't I just say—"

"Not another word." Jessi grinned back at her and gave a last goodbye wave as she headed out.

"Humph." Charmaine knew better.

****

Charmaine finished up with her last client at the Central City Clinic. She managed to avoid her obnoxious boss most of the day. However, the weekly staff meetings had been excruciating per usual. Her friend Scotty's bar and grill offered just the right antidote. By that evening, Charmaine relaxed at her favorite end-of-the-day hangout with a glass of whiskey. Just one, three at the most. Another area she had to work on. So maybe she had a long way to go in the good Christian department.

"Hey, girl. Long time since I've seen you up in here. Backsliding from the church girl gig, huh?" Scotty wore an impish grin from the other side of the bar.

"Don't you start on me, too." Charmaine pointed a forefinger at his nose.

Scotty laughed. "Jessi on you 'bout the holy roller lifestyle."

"Quit calling them holy rollers," Charmaine grumbled. "You done made me need another drink."

"Yeah, you gonna tell Bishop Whats-His-Face it's my fault." Scotty poured two fingers of brandy in Charmaine's tumbler.

"What are friends for, right?" Charmaine lifted her glass in a toast to him.

Charmaine felt a measure of comfort being with Scotty, unlike other men. Their relationship remained blissfully free of complications. They'd wisely decided even no-strings sex was a bad idea for them. He was a friend, her "got-your-back" guy who knew how to handle himself on means streets with even meaner people. He was her enforcer and hit man if needed. Scotty Minor, a handy man to have around.

"Some people's children," Scotty quipped.

"Be quiet and do your job." Charmaine gave him a frown that melted into a crooked grin. She raised the glass to him, and he winked at her.

"Just like you to come in my own damn place and order me around."

Scotty ambled off to check-in with his bartender. Then he checked the bottles to see if they needed more stock. He disappeared through a door leading to his back rooms. Charmaine concentrated on her drink and ignored the lean man eyeing her from a booth nearby. He looked like a hungry yard dog eyeing steak someone left unattended. She inwardly heaved a sigh of resignation, composing a line to make clear she wasn't interested.

Scotty's female bartender came over. Rochelle had been working at Mellow for just over a year. She rubbed a glass until it sparkled. "Don't worry. Scotty will take care of him."

"Hmm." Charmaine tried not to dislike Rochelle and always failed.

"Regulars know better than to mess with you up in here." Rochelle glanced at the man. "Guess playa over there gotta learn like everybody else."

"Rochelle, for the umpteenth time. Scotty is not my man, not even part-time," Charmaine said dryly.

"I'm not even talkin' 'bout that. I got me somebody." Rochelle made an unconvincing tsk sound.

"Okay." Charmaine hid her smirk by lifting the thick crystal tumbler to her mouth.

"Scotty is nothin' but a boss to me. Whatever."

Rochelle went off to ask a newly arrived couple what they wanted to drink. Charmaine gave a snort of amusement. The woman would whip off her skinny jeans and wrap her legs around Scotty in a hot minute. All he had to do was ask. Too bad Scotty had a strict rule against sleeping with his staff. Rochelle kept working but slid her gaze over at Charmaine from time to time. Scotty returned, swapped out an almost empty bottle for a full one, and headed straight to Charmaine. Rochelle's expression tightened before she turned away.

"Rochelle didn't miss me one damn bit. Guess not coming around gave her hope," Charmaine said.

"Hmm..." Scotty got busy arranging a tray of bartending tools.

"What?" Charmaine leaned forward as she eyed him.

"Nothing. Drink your drink." Scotty waved to two men leaving together. "I told Tyrone to be honest with Myeisha. I ain't judging him for liking other dudes, but lying to his woman is wrong. And they got two babies, too. Just accept who you are is what I say."

"Uh-huh. Tyrone wrong. Now back to you and Rochelle." Charmaine wiggled her eyebrows.

"I'm just saying..." Scotty broke off. "Jessi say y'all got a new case."

"Oh hell to the naw-naw," Charmaine whispered dramatically. She pursed her lips.

"What is wrong with you, girl? You gonna scare off my customers acting all crazy." Scotty polished a stainless steel cocktail shaker until Charmaine could herself in it.

"You broke the golden rule," Charmaine said low. She gaped at him.

"Shush," Scotty blurted out.

Rochelle and several other patrons turned to look at them sharply. He waved at the bartender. Rochelle sniffed and marched off to wait on other customers at the other end of the long bar. Scotty gave a quick smile to the customers. Then he came back around the bar and hustled Charmaine to a booth.

"What's the big secret anyway? You're both single and..." Charmaine settled into the dark green imitation leather bench. Then she sat straight, mouth open. She allowed Scotty to get situated across from her. "She's got a husband. Where's she been hiding him?"

"You might as well grab the stage mic and make an announcement," Scotty hissed at her, and he looked over one shoulder to see if anyone paid attention. He scowled at the skinny dude, who lifted a glass as if he hadn't noticed.

"So now you gotta fend her off, because I know she wants seconds." Charmaine gave a tiny hoot.

Scotty rolled his eyes. "Oh shut the hell up. I went through something for a minute. She stayed late to help clean up after a big private party a couple of months ago, listened to my troubles. We had a drink and... ended up bouncing on that old cot in one of the back rooms."

"Yeah, but there was no sleeping that night." Charmaine chuckled. Then she got serious. "You didn't tell me about having troubles. You coulda called me."

"Buddy I was with in Iraq hung himself. Nothing you could have done. No sense bringing you down with it." Scotty traced an invisible line on the table top between them.

"Still." Charmaine sighed. "I've been through enough to be able to handle troubles."

"Like you just said, you been through enough. That kinda news takes it out of a person, even though you didn't know Larry." Scotty, not prone to emotion, avoided her gaze.

"Okay. Okay." Charmaine patted his arm. "You alright?"

"I'm dealing. Me and the guys, we talk." Scotty sank back into the seat. He'd never call his circle of war vets a support group.

"Good. Real good." Charmaine didn't press. She counted it a huge win that Scotty had taken her advice about the VA counseling center. Then she sat straight. Without turning her head, her gaze shifted.

Scotty's gaze followed Charmaine's up to one of two security mirrors. Mounted in corners where two walls met, they gave staff a view of the entire bar. Both concealed security cameras. They blended so well reflecting the décor, few noticed them. Mr. Thin Man, as Charmaine dubbed him, lazily flirted with a trio of ladies at a nearby table. Laughter burst from the group from time to time.

"I need to handle him?" Scotty didn't look around. They'd always been in sync, since their days as kids on the street.

"Uh-uh. He's connected to my new client." Charmaine's voice went so low that Scotty leaned across the table. Rochelle glared at them, but Charmaine ignored her.

"How?" Scotty maintained his casual pose and took a drink.

"Not sure yet. I'm getting some kinda interference." Charmaine looked at him with interest and made sure he saw her.

"Probably from all that cackling," Scotty wise-cracked. "Guy's a regular comedy show. The girls' night out crew eating up his act."

"Just a cover. He's watching me."

Pencil thin, and not bad looking, he could be a runway model. His smooth looks made him almost too perfect. He wasn't pretty boy good looking, but he'd do. Other beefier men might mistake him as being easy to beat. They'd be wrong. Charmaine concluded that he had a hard wiry kind of strength. She gave him a brief smile, then looked back to Scotty. Mr. Thin Man favored her with a slight nod as if they understood each other.

"Time for me to go." Scotty made a show of getting up. He smoothed down the front of his button front G-Star designer shirt. "Enjoy the rest of the evening, Charmaine. I gotta get back to work. Don't take so long to come around next time."

"I won't." Charmaine gave him a reserved smile and lifted her glass. "Thanks for the free refill."

"Anytime." Scotty bent forward and brushed her temple with his lips. He smothered a chuckle when Charmaine turned her head a bit. Then whispered, "How you gonna diss me in my own place?"

With his back to Mr. Thin Man, he gave Charmaine one last amused grin before he strolled away. Minutes later he disappeared through the door leading to his rear office. When two waitresses popped out with food and drinks, Rochelle followed him. No psychic skills needed to know Scotty would be looking for a new bartender soon. Shame. Rochelle had serious mixology skills. Mr. Thin Man stood, and Charmaine's attention snapped back to her target. His female audience looked disappointed. Game on.

"If you don't mind..." He pointed to the padded bench across from her in the booth.

"You may." Charmaine waved a hand granting him permission.

"Thank you. I've been wondering about you." Mr. Skinny sat. He crossed his long legs sideways, as they wouldn't comfortably fit beneath the table.

Charmaine sipped the brandy. Her body thrummed at the sexual vibe swirling around them. "Oh?"

"I figure you choose to be alone. A beauty like you would have any number of dudes eager to be in my place."

"I see." Charmaine's sixth sense told him being coy would excite him more. He liked a mystery and being the one to solve it.

"Kadeem Hardy." He held out a large hand and smiled when Charmaine took it for a few seconds before letting go.

"Charmaine Joliet."

"I like your style." Kadeem settled in to begin what he decided would be his eventual conquest.

"You've watched me for a grand total of twenty minutes, and you already know my style." Charmaine raised both eyebrows at him. She heard his thought. The jerk actually thought, "Gotcha."

"Ah, you know how long I've been watching you. Which means you've been keeping an eye on me." Kadeem pressed his lips together for a few seconds as he gazed at her.

"You're hard to miss." Charmaine tilted her head back to examine him. "I guess six feet five. Dressed head-to-toe in SeanJohn. No wonder you got a fan club." She nodded to the group of women, who laughed less now that Kadeem had left them.

Kadeem let loose a deep throaty laugh. "Six-four actually. And the boots are Timberlands."

"Consider me corrected," Charmaine replied.

"You allowed me to sit like the sweet brown queen you are, and I'm grateful."

Charmaine laughed, surprised at the cheesy line. His game wasn't as tight as he thought. Playing along, she inclined her head in a regal manner. "You're most welcome."

Kadeem lifted his glass to her in salute, drank, and lifted a finger. When the waitress floated over, he ordered another beer. Twenty-year-old Latreece looked ridiculously happy to serve his every need. Guess cheesy still works, Charmaine mused.

"I'm going to be honest with you, Charmaine. I intended to meet you tonight."

Kadeem broke off when Latreece returned with a tall glass. She also brought two small bowls of mixed nuts and extra napkins. Charmaine got a flash of Latreece's heated hopes to get her hands on Kadeem before she left. Then Charmaine returned her attention to Kadeem.

"Honesty from a man in a club. What a refreshing change." Charmaine put on a sassy smile and aimed her breasts at him. His black coffee eyes widened a bit. He stared at her nipples, visible beneath the soft red sweater she wore over denim leggings. The guy actually gulped. Who's got who?

Kadeem worked to regain, in his mind, control of the situation. He blinked hard. "You're not the kind of woman who gets easily played."

Charmaine knew he thought the opposite. Playing him in return would be all the sweeter. "I can't wait to hear it."

"It's not a line, Charmaine." Kadeem glanced around and leaned toward her. "I work for VSI, Inc. You recognize the name?"

"Damn right I do. They hired you to follow me around and report back to them." Charmaine adopted a false irritated frown. "Well, you tell them..."

"Calm down baby," Kadeem said.

"Don't 'baby' me, slick. Tell your boss, I don't deal with clients who can't trust the work I do for them," Charmaine retorted, continuing her act. In truth, clients regularly checked her and Jessi out. She took it in stride, unlike Jessi.

"We're Ninth Ward. Stick together like rice and red beans, right?" Kadeem winked at her. "I wasn't supposed to tell you I work for VSI."

"So why did you?" Charmaine didn't have to feign being intrigued by his unique tactic.

"Call it me giving a homie the heads-up. You know how these rich white folks be, all nervous when they're faced with smart sisters like you." Kadeem wore a satisfied expression.

Charmaine studied his lean face with more care. His full mouth promised good times. She'd been too quick to dismiss his attractiveness as ordinary. "Okay, but what if I tell them?"

"Then we'll lose our mutual advantage." Kadeem sat back, content to let Charmaine digest his words.

"You're willing to give me the inside story on what moves they make." Charmaine gazed back at him in frank admiration.

"I knew you had brains inside that beautiful head." Kadeem beamed back at her.

"You're a greedy man, Kadeem. Getting paid by the Villiers mob, and you expect me to pay you, too. Ain't happening." Charmaine gave a flick of her wrist to dismiss him.

"You're missing the big picture, baby," Kadeem replied in a mild tone.

"Don't. call. me. baby. I won't tell you again. Damn condescending." Charmaine didn't have to force the edge in her voice.

"My sincere apologies." Kadeem held up both large palms when Charmaine rolled her eyes. "Okay, I'll drop the dollar-store approach. I can see you're one of those rare women who see through it."

"Thank you," Charmaine shot back and gave him the stinky-eye. Another cheesy come-on, but of course she would let it pass.

"Cards on the table. We can both profit if we approach the way you handle your investigation right. Mrs. Villiers is smart, but she's superstitious as hell."

"I'm listening."

"The old lady wants you to figure out if some ghosts from the past are really causing them problems, and get rid of them. But she doesn't want the family's dirty laundry pulled out the history books."

"Such as?"

"No clue. They're experts at keeping secrets. I figure we're talking some seriously rotten shit, pardon my language."

"I kinda like dirty talk." Charmaine ran her tongue over her bottom lip.

"Then we need to schedule a private party sometime," Kadeem murmured. His smoky gaze smoldered for a second, and then he went back to business. "Look, I know what you're thinking."

"I am psychic," Charmaine quipped. She wiggled her eyebrows at him.

"Yeah sure." Kadeem laughed with her, two scam artists in on the joke. "Anyway, you're probably thinking, 'If he turned on his meal ticket then this dude will turn on me'. Right?"

"Crossed my mind," Charmaine said dryly.

"Except you could bust me, get me fired and worse. They're vicious when you cross 'em. So, I'm taking a big chance here." Kadeem studied Charmaine's face for a reaction.

Charmaine waved a hand to get another drink. Scotty got Latreece's attention and sent Charmaine another tumbler of brandy. The waitress bounced over, for Kadeem's benefit no doubt. One more button on her blouse had been undone. She leaned forward to remove Charmaine's empty glass with one hand and set the new one down. Kadeem made Latreece happy by flirting with her. Meanwhile, Charmaine let him think she was taking some time to consider his proposal.

Kadeem drank the rest of his beer in one long pull. Then he looked at Charmaine. "Well?"

"You mentioned something about a private party. Scotty has rooms next door. The Crescent Arms Hotel. They have a vacancy. Get a beer to go." Charmaine let her gaze drift down his body then back up to his face.

"Girl, lead the way. I'm good and ready," Kadeem breathed.

Kadeem followed Charmaine next door to the small boutique hotel Scotty owned. She knew Rochelle would delight in throwing up Charmaine's liaison in Scotty's face. Latreece and the women Kadeem had flirted with watched them leave. Sorry girls, Charmaine mused. Then switched her focus back to Kadeem.

Once they entered the third-floor room, Charmaine took a sip of her drink and set the tumbler on the dresser. She watched Kadeem bring the frosty beer glass to his mouth. His throat worked as the smooth lager went down. He then put it in the mini-fridge.

"Wanna keep it cold ya know," Kadeem said as he opened his belt and then his jeans. He slid them down over narrow hips and kicked them out of the way.

"While you keep me hot?"

Charmaine pulled a condom from her purse and tossed it to him. Kadeem caught the small square foil in one hand, undressed and put it on. Then she threw the bag onto the chair next to the bed. Her sweater came off in one quick motion. Seconds later, her red lace bra, leggings, and panties were on the floor next to his jeans. Before he could speak, Charmaine was on him. His reply was muffled by her mouth. She pinned him to the wall. Kadeem proved her theory about his strength. He lifted her with ease and she wrapped her legs around him. She made a mental note to compliment Scotty on the sturdy walls and quality furnishings. They gave them all a vigorous workout for hours. She didn't learn much more from Kadeem's thoughts though. His focus remained on pleasure, not business. That was   okay   with   Charmaine.

3.
Plots Thick As Grandma's Gumbo

The next day Charmaine met Laura Villiers Mandeville at the Lakeside Oyster House in Metairie. The stylish woman had waited for her outside, cigarette in hand. Charmaine blinked at her in surprise but said nothing. Once inside, they traded small talk while the waiter attended to them. Charmaine ordered a diet cola. Laura asked after their cocktail menu then changed her mind.

"I don't need it after all. Bring me a Rosa Mae." Laura pursed her lips as she swept a gaze around the dining room.

"You start early. Not that I'm judging." Charmaine lifted a shoulder. She studied Laura closely. The flush to her cheeks told Charmaine she'd already had a drink, or two.

"Looks like tea if any of mother's gossipy lady friends happen to see us." Laura's thin mouth lifted at one corner.

Charmaine smiled at her. "Thanks for agreeing to meet me for lunch, Mrs. Mandeville."

"I'm in town on business, so it wasn't out of my way." Laura broke off when the waiter returned with a tray that held their drinks. He took their food orders. When he left, she looked at Charmaine. "So, you're here to pump me for information?"

"It helps to get a variety of perspectives when I take a case. Honestly, the friction between y'all kind of..." Charmaine let the words trail off.

"We're not the rich man's version of The Brady Bunch. My sister Evelyn has always been bossy, demanding. I don't think she ever got over the nerve of mother having more children." Laura gave a short laugh.

"Sibling rivalry is common," Charmaine said in a mild tone.

"Humph, nothing common at all about us. Evelyn delighted in making life miserable for me." Laura's expression turned sour. She seemed to become the angry little girl in a hostile environment again. "My brothers weren't much better. Mother was busy with her social events. Daddy worked all the time."

"They expected you all to buck up and deal with whatever. No patience with childish whining." Charmaine spoke on auto pilot as the impressions poured over her. "Your father thought it was enough he satisfied expensive tastes. Your mother enjoyed having children to show off, but not to raise."

The color drained from Laura's face. She stared at Charmaine in silence for a good fifteen seconds. "Yolanda talks too much."

"Your mother's housekeeper didn't tell me any-thing. I haven't seen her since the first visit to Magnolia Grove," Charmaine replied. She drank down half of the diet.

"I read up on you and your sister. Don't you just love this electronic age?" Laura favored Charmaine with a superior smile.

"And?" Charmaine was content to let her think they were evenly matched. They weren't.

"NOPD detectives grudgingly admitted you helped them resolve a couple of sordid cases. My family isn't like those people." Laura sniffed. She stopped when the waiter arrived with her Cobb salad.

"Shrimp and corn soup for you," the waiter said to Charmaine. "Can I get you ladies anything else?"

"No thanks," Charmaine said. She watched the man stride off to help another table. "The Forstall family is quite prominent."

"Never liked them. Mother always questioned if their lineage was quite as pristine as they claimed. Especially on the wife's side. I think there's more Irish Channel in them than they'll admit." Laura took a refined bite of salad from the tip of her fork.

Charmaine gazed at the woman. "Really?"

Something in her tone must have caught Laura's attention. She took a sip of Rosa Mae and sighed with happiness. "I don't claim to be psychic, but I know what you're thinking. What a snooty thing to say. Most people who count in Orleans and Jefferson Parishes are bowled over by the Forstall name. Even after that distasteful situation."

"Yes, very uncouth of them to die in such a messy way and get their names in the news," Charmaine said, one eyebrow cocked. She lifted a pinky finger as she sipped a spoonful of soup.

Laura looked at Charmaine in mild shock for a few seconds. Then she burst into laughter. "Coming to lunch with you is proving to be an unexpected treat."

"Hmmm." Charmaine refrained from stating she didn't feel the same.

"I happen to know not all of the most colorful details came out. I think the police and media were uncharacteristically discreet. For the sake of their children of course. Poor kids." Laura's expression softened.

"You have two sons," Charmaine murmured without thinking. She could feel the woman's genuine maternal sensitivity.

"Yes." Laura looked off for a few seconds. "They're delightfully normal. Spoiled rotten thanks to their paternal grandparents. Okay, I confess. Me, too."

"I'll bet."

"They're sweet boys though, very kind and thoughtful. Have no idea where they get it. Definitely not from the Villiers gene pool," Laura joked. Then her expression hardened. "We're not here to talk about my children."

Charmaine winced when Laura's mind clicked shut like a steel vault. But not before Kadeem's name flashed. Interesting. "Relax, Mrs. Mandeville. I'm just trying to get background information that will help me address your mother's problems."

"Employee pilfering, nothing more. Did mother mention she hires catering and cleaning companies for special events? Yes, I thought not." Laura shook her head and gulped down more of her cocktail. "Since we've expanded special themed weekends, Yolanda and the regular groundskeepers can't handle the extra load."

"Your mother's assistant emailed me a description of the missing items." Charmaine pulled out the page she'd printed from her purse and handed it to Laura.

"Hmm." Laura pursed her lips as she scanned the list, then handed it back seconds later. "I'll bet mother hasn't seen most of those things in twenty years or more. You know Magnolia Grove has huge attics in two sections of the house. Nothing ghostly about sloppy record keeping."

"How would you explain the attack on a guest and moving objects?" Charmaine ate more of her soup before it went cold.

Laura waved a hand. A large diamond flashed from her wedding set. "Too much wine and one too many ghost stories told over dinner at the mansion. I'll tell you the real case you should be on."

Charmaine stopped mid slurp of the delicious dish. Sensing another intriguing twist from the lovely Laura, she put down her soup spoon. "Oh?"

"I agree with my sister on one subject, and trust me, it doesn't happen often. There aren't any ghosts involved in Mama's troubles. Not that I don't believe in the supernatural. I'm a Louisiana girl after all." Laura raised a perfect golden brown eyebrow. "But my brother and I are more concerned that... We can rely on your keeping this in strict confidence, right?"

"Our business would be ruined if we couldn't keep our mouths shut," Charmaine replied.

Laura nodded as if making a final decision. "Evelyn is ambitious and eager to run the company. Even at her age, Mother has been unwilling to give up control. Honestly, she was the brains behind the man. Daddy was the firstborn. Our grandfather believed in the old-school succession custom."

"Oldest son always inherits the bigger piece of the pie. Yeah." Charmaine studied her.

"I know it doesn't make sense. But tradition meant everything to grandfather. I certainly can't complain since my daddy got the company." Laura shrugged.

Charmaine watched her eat for a few minutes. "Any resentment from his brother?"

"Brothers, two. In fact, daddy was a twin. Born a scant two minutes before Uncle Anthony. Tension doesn't describe it. All out war. Grandfather built on what his father achieved, and great-grandfather was no slouch. A huge fortune and profitable business were on the line." Charmaine patted her lips. "Thank goodness this restaurant came back after the hurricane."

"Yes. So, other family members are still angry?" Charmaine replied, steering her back on topic.

"The youngest son took it in stride eventually. Accepted a position with my great-uncle's law firm. Became a partner, built up his own wealth. Uncle Anthony and daddy never really made up though. We don't see much of our cousins, three girls and a son. Drayton is all right. But his sisters? Awful snobs." Laura shoved more salad into her mouth. She sighed in approval.

"Yeah, don't ya just hate pretentious folks?" Charmaine murmured.

Laura blinked at Charmaine a few times. "My cousins and their mother take it to a whole new level. Aunt Victoria makes us look like hippies by comparison. Talk about stuck in the past. I have to admit it worked. My cousins married well."

"Into money you mean." Charmaine controlled the urge to roll her eyes.

"Family lineage matters, too. All parents want the best for their children. Didn't your mother have rules about the people you played with as a little girl?" Laura cocked her head to one side.

"Not as many as she should have," Charmaine retorted.

"Tough childhood?" Laura probed.

Charmaine gazed back at her. No doubt Kadeem had given Tanner Gladstone background information on her and Jessi. But Charmaine was there to pump Laura, not the other way around. "I meant, it's too bad I didn't bag a rich husband."

"I don't want to make us sound too cold-blooded. We believe in romance and love."

"Sure," Charmaine replied. She ate the remaining soup, chewing on a last plump shrimp.

"You managed to contain your sarcasm quite well," Laura quipped. Then she grew serious again. "The point is, mother is from the same kind of tradition. She's made it clear that Nick is the CEO. But he'd be propped up by my husband."

"Evelyn's husband Robert has kept the company profitable, from business reports we've read," Charmaine added when Laura's nostrils flared.

"I suppose he's contributed in his own plodding way." Laura took a swig of her cocktail.

"You're saying your brother doesn't have the skills to run VSI on his own?" Charmaine suspected Nick's other gifts were of more interest but put her libido in check.

"My brother takes after daddy in more ways than one," Laura replied, her tone heavy with unspoken family truths. "Nicholas does fine following my husband's guidance, but..."

"What you do mean by 'the real investigation'." Charmaine at forward in anticipation.

"We suspect Evelyn is encouraging mother to think something other-worldly is happening. Mother has always been smart, but somewhat eccentric as well. She had Ouija board parties as a teenager. One time she claimed a spirit became attached to her. She ended up making her father hire a local voodoo priest to get rid of it. He indulged her, as usual, to keep the peace." Laura shrugged at her mother's peculiar inclination.

Charmaine drank cola to cover her grin. She peered at Laura over the edge of the glass. To her relief, Laura gave more interest to ordering another Rosa Mae. "Evelyn set up some of these spirit activities to rattle your mother so she could..."

"I think Evelyn wants mother to get so upset that she lets her run the company, the whole works, including Magnolia Grove. Mother won't allow any filming on the property, a huge income stream. They've clashed on other business decisions as well." Laura sat back after making her case. "Evelyn has an iron will to match mother's."

"Hmm." Charmaine could have remarked that Laura got her share in the iron will department as well. "Sounds like a stretch. There's no guarantee Mrs. Villiers would be so upset that she'd want to retire, chuck off to her second home in Manalapan, Florida."

"You have done your research," Laura said with genuine admiration. "But mother doesn't want to live there. Not since Hurricanes Katrina and Rita. She wants to sell our family estate there and move to Austin, Texas. Can you believe it?"

"You and your husband want the house in Florida," Charmaine replied in a dry tone.

"What's important is stopping Evelyn. She wants to shove the rest of us to the back row. Lord knows her husband shouldn't run the family businesses. Robert has no imagination." Laura snorted in her high-class way.

"So, you want me to pretend I'm working for your mother, but really work for you."

Laura dropped her voice to a confidential whisper. "I propose that you protect your client from the real threat."

"Evelyn and her husband, the one with no imagination." Charmaine marveled at the twists and turns she was being asked to navigate. First Kadeem, and now Laura.

"Nick would be content to let Robert really run the business. Robert is fine letting Nick pretend he's in control, but Evelyn isn't. I'm not looking to cut Evelyn out completely. Just limit the damage she does until... Well for the time being." Laura paused. "Mother hired you to look after her interests, and I want to help."

"Thanks. Why don't you tell Mrs. Villiers what you suspect?" Charmaine said.

"Mother wouldn't believe me," Laura blurted out.

"But why—"

Laura broke in with a scowl of impatience. "Look, I've given you valuable information. Mother is very generous to those who deliver. If you report these findings, discovered during your investigation, she'll see the truth."

Charmaine affected a thoughtful expression for several moments. The waiter returned, giving her even more time while the dishes were cleared away. The waiter chattered on, no doubt to improve his chances for a generous tip. Charmaine exchanged friendly banter with him. Her lunch companion, used to being served, treated him like a non-entity.

"Can I get you ladies anything else? Refills maybe?" The young man smiled at them.

"No, thanks. The food was delicious," Charmaine returned his smile.

"The check please," Laura said. She continued to eye Charmaine. When the waiter left, she leaned forward. "Well?"

"You're right. Mrs. Villiers paid me to act on her behalf. I'll go wherever the facts lead me and advise her based on what I find out. If I discover the ghostly stuff is a hoax, I'll tell her."

"That Evelyn is behind it?" Laura couldn't quite keep the excitement out of her voice.

"I'll give Mrs. Villiers a full explanation," Charmaine countered.

"Good."

Charmaine let Laura assume she'd accomplished the goal of sticking it to Evelyn. The waiter popped back into view. He placed the lunch checks on the table between them. Laura insisted on paying for both meals. Charmaine put up token resistance.

Laura dabbed the corners of her mouth. She wore a slight grin. "More advice. My sister can be persuasive. She has a very strong personality. Be on guard when you take her to lunch."

"I'm meeting Mrs. Harmon at her office. She declined my lunch invitation, too busy," Charmaine replied. In fact, she hadn't invited the formidable Evelyn to lunch at all. But Charmaine decided to let Laura think she had her figured out.

"Into the lioness' den. Every move Evelyn makes is thought out." Laura picked up her designer purse and stood.

"Meaning?"

"She'll play up the home advantage for all it's worth. Check in with me after. I'll be able to dissect and translate what she says. When do you meet with her?" Laura took a compact mirror from a pocket of her leather handbag. She checked the state of her lipstick.

"Thursday."

"Two days should give you plenty of time to be ready. Check Magnolia Grove for hidden devices, like speakers. You know, anything to..."

"I know what to look for, but thanks for the tips," Charmaine broke in. She pushed down the urge to tell the woman off.

"But don't confront her just yet. Talk to me first. I know how to handle big sister. Yes, indeed." Laura seemed wrapped up in revenge fantasies for a few seconds. Then she offered Charmaine a cool smile. "Goodbye."

"Bye-bye. And thanks again for all of the great information. So helpful," Charmaine clipped.

Laura nodded like the lady of the house satisfied her maid had the instructions down. She strolled to the exit. Charmaine heaved a long sigh. The last thing she needed, a case complicated by family backstabbing. What she most wanted was a quick wrap and nice payday. Domestic disputes tended to get ugly. The Villiers family had clout and bad tempers beneath the society polish. A battle of the giants could lead to the little guys getting flattened. She and Jessi needed to up their fancy footwork to avoid being collateral damage.

****

At four o'clock that afternoon, Jessi met Charmaine at Magnolia Grove. Mrs. Villiers had been more than willing to let them come over on short notice. Once they shooed her and Yolanda out of the way, they got to work. Jessi kept an eye out. Sure enough, she caught Yolanda spying on them twice. The second time, Yolanda gave up pretending she was dusting furniture. Charmaine heard their voices and left the library. They stood in the foyer at the foot of the curved main staircase.

"You ain't even good at snooping. I keep catching you. I thought you had the day off anyway." Jessi crossed her arms.

"Y'all need to listen to me. There's a lot going on around here that you don't understand." Yolanda glanced around before she continued. "This family got more skeletons than St. Louis Cemetery."

"So Mrs. Villiers told us," Charmaine said.

"Yeah, well some of them bones still got meat on 'em," Yolanda said low. She glanced over her shoulder again.

"Huh?" Jessi exchanged a glance with Charmaine.

Yolanda blew out a puff of air. "Look, do one of your little hokum-pokum ceremonies, tell her you got rid of the bad spirits, then get the hell outta dodge. You girls don't want to get pulled into their mess."

"We done rolled with liars, thieves and murderers. And I ain't even got to the ghosts and zombie yet," Jessi replied.

"Then you're gonna feel right at home. That Forstall couple you dealt with? They were Sunday school teachers compared to this crew," Yolanda said with force.

"So how you stayed with 'em for so long?" Jessi said before Charmaine could speak.

"I got a lotta practice knowing when to speak up and when to keep quiet; when to be around, and when to disappear. This ain't about me anyway. I'm telling y'all to get to your act, get paid, and get moving." Yolanda looked from one to the other with a frown.

"We're not a couple of fake psychics waving gris-gris bags and mumbling bogus spells," Charmaine hissed at her.

"Yeah, right. Don't listen to any nonsense Kadeem told you. He—"

"Hold on. You know Kadeem Hardy?" Charmaine stepped closer to Yolanda.

"He's my nephew. I helped him get a job in the mailroom. He's worked his way up the food chain with his slick ways. Now he's working in the security department under Tanner. I told him not to get involved with this nest of vipers. Thinks he knows it all. Just like you two." Yolanda squinted at them.

Jessi gave a low whistle as she looked at Charmaine. "Her nephew."

"Me being here for all these years ain't no accident. I don't need y'all causing trouble. Do your little dance and clear out." Yolanda looked less and less like the subdued housemaid.

"So that 'I's scared of them dere spirits, Missy Vee' is an act. You've got an angle playing up the ghost sightings. What is it?" Jessi gazed at her with a sideways grin.

"Like I said, think you know so damn much. I don't have to pretend. Magnolia Grove got all kinds of ghosts. You need to be more worried about the living." Yolanda stabbed a finger at them.

"Charmaine, I think she's threatening us," Jessi said. She gave a dramatic shiver. "Should we run now or later?"

"You got no idea who I am, Miss Thang," the older woman snapped. "You little rejects from the projects don't scare me. If you don't know about Yolanda Dawson, you better ask somebody."

"Oh, we sure as hell will." Jessi bristled at the challenge, her eyes sparkling with eagerness.

"Hey, hey. Everybody take a breath and cool off." Charmaine pulled Jessi away from Yolanda. Then she positioned herself between them. "We know there are a lot of scam artists around, but we're the real deal. We were hired to find out what's going on here and stop valuable antiques from disappearing like the ghosts. Only reason you should worry about us is if you're involved."

Yolanda turned her glare from Jessi to Charmaine. "You sayin' I'm a thief?"

"You pretty much said so yourself," Jessi shot back.

Charmaine blocked Yolanda from going at Jessi. "Uh-uh, no."

"Let her come on. I'll mop these pretty hardwood floors with her old ass." Jessi removed her large silver hoop earrings as she spoke.

"Baby, I was street fightin' before you was born," Yolanda spat.

Charmaine gave the heavyset middle-ager a shove away from Jessi. Then she huffed to catch a breath after the effort. Still, Yolanda didn't go after Jessi, and Jessi stayed in her corner as well. "Throw fists and we'll all be out of a well-paying gig," Charmaine yelled.

Mrs. Villiers scurried into the foyer. She wore a pretty lace poncho over a pink blouse and tan wool skirt. Eyes wide, she looked around. "What's happened? Good Lord, if the spirits are showing up so early we're going to have a lot of trouble. The Bloombergs are coming from New York this weekend. The Green family from Wisconsin are still in three cottages. They'll be terrified if..."

"Mrs. Villiers." Charmaine tried to head off her panicked stream and failed.

"Not to mention if word gets out our All Hollow's Eve Month bookings will be canceled. People only want to be scared in theory, not in real life." Mrs. Villiers flailed her arms as she spoke.

Jessi strode over to her. "Calm down, we got it under control. Yolanda heard us bumping around and freaked out. She didn't know we were in here. She let out a yell before we could come downstairs. Right, Yolanda?"

Yolanda still puffed from going into fight mode. After several seconds, she looked at Jessi, Charmaine and last, Mrs. Villiers. "I was in the dining room dusting and I heard... something. Y'all need to watch yourselves around here."

Jessi squinted at her. "You, too."

Charmaine put a restraining hand on Jessi's arm. "We'll make sure everyone knows we're in the house next time."

"Yolanda, I told you several days ago they would be in and out. They have run of the place. I've never known you to be so jumpy." Mrs. Villiers gazed at the housekeeper, lips pursed.

"All this talk about spirits, murder mysteries, and Halloween. Who wouldn't have bad nerves?"

"You insisted on working your usual day off. Go home if you're stressed," Mrs. Villiers replied.

"Yeah, go rest your bad nerves," Jessi added.

"You just said we got a lot going on. I don't wanna come back to a pile of work left undone. Let me finish up." Yolanda darted a mean glance at Jessi and turned to leave.

"And why were you dusting in the dining room? The house is clean. The Green family left early for a French Quarter tour. Betty just arrived, so help her straighten their rooms." Mrs. Villiers continued to study Yolanda.

Yolanda's tight expression relaxed under her employer's scrutiny. "We'll have the rooms in shape in no time. Me and Betty work fast. Best thing you did was hire her part-time."

"Hmmm." Mrs. Villiers nodded. She looked at Yolanda. "Remember The Crescent City Tour Company will be here shortly with a group. I want their visit to be memorable in a good way. Thank you, Yolanda. That's all." The dismissal rang out loud and clear.

Yolanda glanced at Charmaine and Jessi, then left without saying more. Mrs. Villiers stared after her for a few seconds before she faced Charmaine and Jessi again.

"Sorry again. We got so caught up in investigating that we might have made too much noise," Charmaine said.

"Follow me to the library," Mrs. Villiers replied.

Charmaine exchanged a silent message with Jessi using only her eyes. "Sure."

Once they were in the spacious room, Mrs. Villiers pulled the doors shut with a solid thump. "Yolanda has been with our family a long time. Since the early eighties in fact. Her aunt worked for my late husband's grandmother. So you see, our families have a connection."

"Yes." Charmaine thought of Kadeem but decided against mentioning Yolanda's nephew.

"Sometimes she gets a bit too comfortable commenting on matters she shouldn't. Do you understand?" Mrs. Villiers gazed at Charmaine.

"She gossips you mean?" Charmaine replied with care. "Yolanda hasn't been telling tales about your family. She's only talked about the house."

Mrs. Villiers pursed her lips. "It's more complicated."

There was a knock on the door before she could go on. Yolanda pulled the sliding doors open. "Mrs. Villiers, I made lemonade and some of my own roasted nut mix you love. I figured the young ladies might want some. I could serve y'all in here while you meet."

"I'll call you when we're finished. Thank you." Mrs. Villiers waited until the doors closed, and turned to the sisters. "See? She can get overprotective to the point of interfering."

Charmaine cut a sharp look at Jessi, who clamped her lips together instead of offering commentary. "We've dealt with our clients' employees before. It's okay."

"Yes, well." Mrs. Villiers sighed. She walked to a seating area near the windows and sank onto a plush leather chair "I..."

Jessi followed and sat in the chair closest to her. "You don't trust Yolanda. Do you?"

"You have to understand how things work." Mrs. Villiers seemed to search for words. "Complete confidentiality."

"No worries. Click, lock, not talking no matter what," Jessi said firmly.

"Except we can't hide crimes. We're licensed private investigators and—"

"Only if we think somebody is about to be killed. We're very flexible about what we tell the police," Jessi broke in.

"I'll try not to put you in a difficult position, Charmaine." Mrs. Villiers shared a conspiratorial grin with Jessi.

"Uh, thanks." Charmaine suppressed a sigh at the sign she should expect the opposite.

"So, there's a lot more to Yolanda than you told us already." Jessi hitched her chair closer to Mrs. Villiers.

"Yolanda's family has worked for the Villiers for a long time. I sort of inherited her as a housekeeper here at Magnolia Grove. I have a small home in the Garden District."

"You don't live here full-time then?" Charmaine raised an eyebrow.

"My sister inherited an aunt's house. Nothing big. Five bedrooms, a sun room. You know." Mrs. Villiers waved a hand.

"Yeah, small," Jessi said and looked at Charmaine.

"Hmm." Mrs. Villiers didn't notice. "My sister passed away a year after Hurricane Katrina. Her daughter's family decided they didn't want to live in New Orleans anymore. The chaos after the storm, crime. You understand."

"Sure. A lot of people just decided to stay put after the evacuation," Jessi said.

"To keep the house in our family, they sold it to me. Lovely garden. One of my nephews lived there with his family for years. He took a transfer to Spain. He's the vice president of—" Mrs. Villiers started to go on but stopped when Jessi tapped her hand.

"Back to Yolanda?"

"Yes. Yes. Yolanda worked for my late husband's mother briefly. When she died, Andrew hired her to work in our home. They were... close." Mrs. Villiers wore a taut expression. The lines around her mouth multiplied as she stared ahead.

"You mean?" Charmaine gaped at her, mouth open.

"Yes, I mean they had sex. The affair, if you can call it that, lasted only a few months. Andrew grew bored with her." Mrs. Villiers avoided looking at either of the sisters.

"Why in the... world didn't you fire her?" Jessi said.

"My husband refused, wouldn't budge. We had our own home in Metairie. My sister-in-law managed Magnolia Grove at the time, so she took her on here. Andrew swore to me it was over, and I had to be satisfied with that. He told me the truth, I'm sure of it," Mrs. Villiers said with force. She turned to them, a challenge in her blue-eyed gaze.

"Okay. You knew him. We didn't." Jessi held up both palms.

Mrs. Villiers sighed. "My husband and I grew distant, but we always got along fairly well. Years went by and it didn't matter to me as much. Then not at all. When he died, it seemed silly to hold on to the past. Yolanda and I actually get along well most of the time. We have something in common, you see. And she really does manage things well at the estate."

"Ah." Charmaine decided the fuzzy logic might be a rich woman's thing.

"My sister-in-law grew too ill to deal with Magnolia Grove. Andrew was too busy with the company, so I took over in 2007. Estelle died a year after Andrew. Her children had no interest in the estate, and here we are." Mrs. Villiers sighed once more.

"Okay, but I don't get it. You can get rid of her now," Jessi pressed.

"My husband's set up a trust to maintain Magnolia Plantation. It includes instructions that Yolanda remain as housekeeper at Magnolia Grove until she retires, or in case extraordinary circumstances occur," Mrs. Villiers replied. The tightness returned to her mouth.

"Good thing she's good at her job," Charmaine murmured.

"When does she retire?" Jessi asked.

"Whenever she decides," Mrs. Villiers said.

"She could work until she drops dead, and you're stuck with her. Humph." Jessi shook her head.

"Wait, what kind of 'extraordinary circumstances'?" Charmaine sat forward.

"If she causes any kind of damage to the estate. I don't remember the exact wording, but that's the way my lawyer summarized it." Mrs. Villiers said.

Jessi looked at Charmaine. "So, she might be snatching the goods around here. The last thing she wants is for us to find out."

"Yes, but she's worked here for years. Why cook up the story about ghosts being the cause now? I don't know." Charmaine said.

"Agreed. Besides, Yolanda is paid a generous salary. She may be many things, but she's not stupid. A few hundred dollars here and there won't equal the value of what she stands to lose, a pension for life in addition to social security and benefits." Mrs. Villiers looked at Charmaine. "Anything truly rare and valuable would be next to impossible for her to sell. She can't simply walk into a local pawn shop with Newcomb pottery or a Degas."

"Maybe one of her kids got in trouble. She could have found a market somehow. Desperate times push people to do stupid things. We need to check it out, even if it's a long shot," Charmaine said.

"I think you're wasting your time, but you're the professionals." Mrs. Villiers stood. "Yolanda is about to go home, so she shouldn't disturb you again. I'll be here for at least another two hours."

"We shouldn't be much longer," Charmaine said. "I'll check in with you before we leave."

"Fine." Mrs. Villiers nodded to them both and left.

"What a family, huh?" Charmaine turned to say more, but Jessi was gone. "Jessi?"

With no answer or sign of her sister, Charmaine heaved a sigh. She continued looking through the house. The formal dining room looked like the showplace of antiques it had been for over one hundred years. The long table held two crystal flower bowls that sparkled. Fresh white and red roses had been artfully arranged in them. Charmaine heard a droning voice describing features of the house. She moved to the ladies' parlor to avoid the tourists.

Nothing looked unusual, but then Charmaine couldn't see or talk to ghosts. Her job for this visit was to check more mundane details. Mrs. Villiers had emailed them a list of items in each room. Charmaine read through the inventory. A seventeenth century Japanese Amari Vase should have been on the small round table between two chairs.

"That thing is worth almost ten thousand dollars," Charmaine muttered.

She double checked the list and then made a slow circle of the room. A footstool, with a cushion embroidered by Mrs. Villiers' ancestor, was missing as well. Charmaine tapped her smartphone to make notes. A shout startled her and she dropped it.

"Everybody stay calm. Uh, nothing to worry about," Jessi yelled from somewhere in the house.

"What the hell now?" Charmaine started to run toward the commotion, then remembered her phone. She went back, retrieved it from the Persian carpet, and raced to find out toward the growing sounds of a fresh commotion.

"I didn't sign up for a ghost tour," a short white woman with garish red hair said. She cowered against a man. "Harry, you made me come. Just had to see New Orleans. I never liked your cousins anyway."

"Edna, for Pete's sake. Don't make an even bigger fool of yourself." Harry tried to get her to loosen her hold on the front of his shirt without success.

"Nothing happened, ma'am. Just a..." Jessi struggled to come up with a description, but Edna jumped back in.

"I saw a woman dressed in a long black dress. It's the woman in the portrait we saw in the living room. I know what I saw," Edna blurted out.

"The formal parlor. It's where the Villiers family entertained their guests for almost two hundred years," the tour guide, a young brunette woman said. She flashed a tentative smile. The group of ten tourists didn't smile back. Some murmured low to companions.

"You might have seen a... reenactor. That's right." Jessi waved a forefinger. "The... the owners hired an actress to give you a more authentic experience. Dressed in period costume."

"How wonderful," a woman with a British accent breathed. She glanced around the room, taking it all in.

Edna marched over to the tour guide. "Is that true Ashley?"

The guide glanced at Jessi and then back to Edna. "I- I mean um. Magnolia Grove goes to great lengths to recreate the atmosphere of the times."

"See? I told you not to make such a big deal. Geez." Harry scowled at his wife as he brushed the wrinkles from his shirt. A loud thump stopped his ridicule.

Charmaine exchanged a glance with Jessi. They both looked through one of the windows. A curtain of darkness had fallen in the hour since they'd arrived. A series of follow-up bangs set the tour group into a frightened huddle around the guide.

The young woman's wide-eyed gaze focused on Jessi, silently pleading for help. Mrs. Villiers rushed in from somewhere else in the mansion just as things went downhill. A loud hissing whisper bounced off the walls, eerily cutting through the anxious babble from the tourists. Everyone froze.

"Listen folks. We're testing out the sound effects for the Halloween festivities and..." Charmaine searched for words to continue her improvised explanations. As she struggled, the walls seemed to shake.

The hissing picked up volume until a high pitched screech made them all cover their ears. When it died away, the group of tourists scrambled for the nearest exit. Some headed for the arched door leading to the grand foyer and the front door. Others dashed for another doorway leading to the formal parlor. A series of screams and shouts indicated this must have been a bad idea. Then they stormed back through the dining room and through the archway. Pounding footsteps went through the foyer, across the wide front porch and down the outside steps.

"Oh my God, what is happening?" Mrs. Villiers had both palms pressed to her cheeks, pressing her pale face into an even more horrified mask.

Charmaine glanced toward the parlor but didn't make a move to investigate. She faced Jessi and gulped. "We gotta do something."

"How bad could it be? I don't see a trail of blood." Jessi pointed to the wool carpet beneath their feet.

"Uh…"

Charmaine's train of thought got cut off when Jessi pulled her by one arm. Jessi shouted at Mrs. Villiers to stay put. Since the elderly woman stood rooted to the floor in abject terror, her advice would no doubt be followed. Seconds later, they rushed into the parlor, but the sight before them made both skid to a halt. Two of the circa 1860s oil lamps floated in the air. Jessi whirled in a circle then stood in a listening pose.

"What?" Charmaine shouted to be heard over the racket.

"She's laughing. This ain't funny." Jessi shook a fist over her head.

"You see me laughing?" Charmaine yelled. She was almost knocked over by a terrified tourist.

Jessi ducked a crystal paperweight aimed at her head. She recovered in seconds. She planted both fists on her hips and marched to the middle of the large room. "Listen up, Georgina Turnbull Villiers.

This bullshit gonna stop. I'm so not in the mood for your ass." Jessi shouted.

"Calling out an angry ghost might not be our best option." Charmaine turned at the sound of loud voices and banging doors. "Oh, crap."

Mrs. Villiers, twin red spots on her cheeks, entered the room. Her neat hairstyle had come undone, with silver strands sticking up at wild angles. She swayed as though standing on a boat in rough water. "The catering staff is leaving. We'd planned wine and appetizers."

She stopped before saying more. Her gaze trained on the still floating lamps. She followed their movement, hypnotized. The flames in them wavered as if a breeze was blowing. Then Mrs. Villiers turned white and her eyes rolled back. Charmaine ran to her in time to break the woman's fall as she fainted. Grateful for Mrs. Villiers' petite frame, Charmaine still staggered under the weight.

"Um, Jessi. A hand over here?" Charmaine looked for her sister. Jessi paid no attention. She was busy trading insults with the ghost.

"Look, you dough-faced slave owning doxie! Go back to your special corner of hell." Jessi strode over to one of the levitating lamps, snatched it out of the air, and set it down. Jessie ducked in the nick of time. A large vase shattered against the wall behind her.

Charmaine dropped the semi-conscious septuagenarian into a nearby wing chair. She dodged a tea table, jumped high, and caught a flying porcelain figurine. She landed with a loud huff as she tucked the seventeenth-century treasure against her body.

"Aw hell no. The gloves are off bitch." Jessi pulled a gadget from her cross-body handbag.

"What- what's happening?" Mrs. Villiers spoke in a strangled voice. She blinked hard as though trying to get her bearings.

"Better take her outta here, sis. I got work to do," Jessi yelled over her shoulder.

Charmaine let out a groan but pulled Mrs. Villiers to her feet. "Let's go to the kitchen. I think we'll be out of her way in there."

"My guests, the tour... disaster..."

Mrs. Villiers jabbered on in broken sentences. Thank goodness she'd recovered enough to put one foot in front of the other. Slight of stature as she was, Charmaine couldn't have carried her dead weight. She would have had to drag the woman along the floor at best, not a good way to treat a well-paying client. Charmaine managed to pour lemonade down Mrs. Villiers while stuttering reas-surances neither of them believed.

Ten minutes later, Jessi marched into the kitch-en with a look of triumph. "Spirits with funky ass attitudes mess with me at their own peril."

4.
Past Crimes

The next day, Wednesday, Charmaine and Jessi continued to recuperate in her eat-in kitchen. Diamond had joined them to hear the complete details of their adventure at Magnolia Grove. With the morning off from her job and Indyah in her new day school, Diamond declared there was no way she would wait another day for the scoop. Then Scotty arrived as well.

"Funny how you two always seem to get here just as the coffee is done brewing," Charmaine joked and accepted his brotherly peck on her forehead.

Scotty gave Diamond a brief hug and a salute to Jessi. "You're a creature of regular habits. Breakfast is between seven forty-five and eight am. You never eat without a cup of good old Louisiana dark roast. How's my god-daughter?" Scotty said to Diamond.

"She had a case of the sniffles and a little cough. So glad I could let her stay with my great-aunt a few days. Can't take her to school or daycare sick. They'd call me right back to get her." Diamond chewed on a cinnamon roll. She sat on one of two barstools at the small extended counter.

"Hey, my grand-mama had a great remedy for babies with the croup. I can hook you up. She swears by it. Used on my daddy and all her nine kids." Scotty helped himself by pouring coffee into his favorite mug.

"Yeah, and all of them ended up throwed-off, except your daddy," Jessi retorted without looking away from her laptop.

She sat on the cushioned ledge of the bay window, her favorite spot. She fought Diamond to get to it first whenever they visited together. Jessi scrolled through documents and stopped to tap notes every few seconds. She'd check the dial on her gadget, then tapped more keys.

"Yeah, and daddy had a few quirks himself," Scotty returned with a good-natured chuckle. "Second thought, forget Nanny Bee's concoctions."

"How is the old devil by the way?" Charmaine sat at the table with Scotty.

"Sharp and mean as ever. So, what up with the new case?" Scotty savored his first sip from the mug then stretched out his long legs.

"Yeah, must be big if you asked us over." Diamond licked icing from her fingers as she spun to face the others from her perch.

"Me and Jessi get caught up in the supernatural sometimes. You two give us cleared-eyed, non-psychic perspectives. Plus, you're smart," Charmaine said.

"Wow. That makes me feel so... I don't know." Diamond jumped off the stool to hug Charmaine. "You think I'm smart enough to help."

"Of course. Stop listening to your sisters calling you stupid. Look where they are," Charmaine replied. She didn't add that Diamond's troubled family had enough shortcomings of their own. They had no right to insult anyone else. Least of all Diamond.

"I love y'all so much." Diamond let go of Charmaine. She grabbed a paper napkin to sniff into it.

"Our squad. No matter what went down at home, we had each other," Scotty added with a smile.

"Aw, y'all gonna make me cry with all this sweetness," Jessi didn't look up.

"Her way of saying she loves you, too." Charmaine winked at Diamond.

"Humph." Jessi pretended to ignore them.

"What in the hell happened?" Scotty settled against the chair back to listen.

"Everything was routine. I looked for wires or maybe a router that's controlling speakers. Any clue that the ghostly happenings are being created. Jessi was checking for signs of spirits." Charmaine paused to sip coffee.

"I thought spirits only come out at night. You know, like on television and the movies. 'The barrier between the natural and supernatural weakens with the setting sun'," Diamond intoned, her voice deepened with melodrama.

"When Spirits Walk, dun-dun-dun-dummmm!" Jessi put in, mimicking typical horror movie music at the end. She and Diamond cracked up like two thirteen-year-old girls.

"I remember that show. Corny. Now Tales From The Crypt, there was some scary ass shit," Scotty replied.

"Tales was good, but When Spirits Walk was the chips and dessert. Plus, it was locally produced. Wonder what happened to the host, Manic Marvin? He'd introduced these creepy old black and white movies," Jessi said.

"Yeah, my favorites were the zombies." Diamond stood and imitated the zombie stiff-legged walk.

"Y'all don't know what's up." Scotty waved a hand at them.

"Watching ol' Maniac Marvin and old movies actually helped me. I totally believed in ghosts when everyone called me crazy." Jessi grew thoughtful for a few seconds, then her expression brightened. "Anyway, don't be hatin' on Marvin. He was my first TV crush."

Diamond laughed loud again and sat. "I remember."

"You kidding me? He had stringy dishwater blonde hair, a hump on his back, and hair comin' out his ears." Scotty shook his head.

"I figured Maniac Marvin would accept me, crazy voices and all," Jessi quipped. "Besides, he was cute to me. I liked to get my freak on even back in the day."

Charmaine finished the last piece of her cinnamon roll and cleared her throat. "Excuse me. The case?"

"Yes. Proceed Det. Joliet." Diamond made a flourished wave of her hands and dipped her head in a bow.

"All of a sudden, stuff starts crashing. He, she, or it meant business." Charmaine looked around at them. Then she shuddered and downed more coffee.

"And in the daytime. Wow." Diamond blinked hard.

"By then it had gotten dark. We got there just after four in the afternoon. We started in the attic, which is huge. Then we worked our way down and..."

Jessi broke in. "Nah, you started up there. I kind of jumped around based on my readings."

You came up the stairs behind me and was bumping around. I told you to be careful not to break anything we might have to pay for, remember?" Charmaine frowned.

"I started to follow you. But I stopped on the second-floor landing. Then I went back to the first floor. Place is massive, three floors, plus the attic," Jessi explained to the others.

"I saw your shadow. You were making so much noise I... Then you mumbled something back when I told you to be careful and..." Charmaine's voice trailed off. "Oh, crap."

"Nope, wasn't me. I never went into the attic." Jessi stared at Charmaine as they both let the facts sink in.

Scotty sat straight as he looked at Charmaine. "Whoa, whoa, whoa. You tellin' me you didn't notice a ghost that close?"

"I'm a telepath, but only with live humans. How would I know if one of Jessi's phantom buddies was shadowing me?" Charmaine frowned in irritation.

"I studied puns in my English class. A phantom shadowed Charmaine. Ooo... I gotta use that. Pretty cool." Diamond took out her cell phone and tapped the screen.

"I wasn't trying to be clever, Dee," Charmaine snapped. "So, that crazy woman ghost stalked me. You should have felt her, Jessi. The heffa could have cracked open my head with a poker or something."

"Hey, don't blame me. I was doing my job. Since when do I have to babysit you in the field?" Jessi protested.

"Since forever because I can't see spirits, that's when," Charmaine shot back. "That other crazy ghost was throwing stuff all around at people. If it wasn't for my softball catching skills that vase would have knocked you out."

Scotty cut into their quarrel. "Stop. There's more than one spooky thing moving around the place at a time. Is that significant?"

"Better have my back. All I'm sayin'." Charmaine mumbled into her mug. Her frown deepened when she realized it was empty. She went to the pot on the counter for more.

Jessi blinked in thought for a few seconds, then snapped her fingers. "My EMF-ATDD Meter did indicate multiple readings."

"Does it come with a secret decoder ring?" Scotty cracked a grin. His face rearranged into a serious expression when Jessi shot him a cold look. "Um, sorry."

"As I was about to say..." Jessi got back to business. "My meter did indicate there might be more than one energy fluctuating at the time. I thought maybe I'd messed with it too much. It's so sensitive."

"What's an EM do-hickey?" Diamond asked.

"An Electromagnetic Field and Ambient Temperature Deviation Detector," Jessi explained, eyes sparkling. "None of this superstition, God nonsense for me. I can measure the fluctuations caused by our spirit, or non-corporeal counterparts. That's what Steve calls them."

"You measure ghosts?" Scotty raised an eyebrow.

"I'm talkin' science man. Ghosts are energy, matter that can be tracked and measured. I worked with Logan to make my ghost hunting gadgets go beyond what other people use. The stuff on the market is too, ordinary."

"Nothing about what y'all do is ordinary," Scotty said.

"Thank you," Jessi shot back with a sly grin. Then she looked at Charmaine. "Our modifications are still in beta, so I didn't assume the fluctuations were definitive. Obviously, I was wrong."

"You have multiple 'entities' moving around in the daytime. Sounds like they're getting stronger, which can't be a good sign," Diamond said.

"This stuff happened around dusk, so not exactly full daylight. And this is a large and very old house. In over two hundred years, a lot of folks died in there," Jessi replied.

"Yeah, and funerals were held in homes, too. Which means the body stayed at the house for days." Charmaine added.

"And don't forget the slaves. Most died, too young, from overwork, illness, and mistreatment. Or worse, being killed as punishment." Scotty's words made them all go quiet for several seconds.

"No, we should never, ever forget them," Jessi replied in a muted voice.

Diamond paraphrased part of a Catholic prayer for the dead. "May they rest in paradise, where there is no sorrow, no weeping or pain, but fullness of peace and joy."

"Amen," Charmaine said and glanced at her sister. "Are you thinking what I'm thinking?"

Jessi nodded. "Plenty of trauma, which causes spirits to get attached to a location. They're trapped if they died suddenly. They get turned around and don't move on. Or if they died by violence. Or if they have unfinished business, or..."

"Damn. How many reasons do ghosts have for hanging around?" Scotty said.

"Those are the top theories. No one has proven why spirits mingle with the living. Maybe they're carrying out some unknowable plan of the Almighty," Charmaine said.

"Here we go with the God stuff." Jessi dismissed Charmaine's religion theory with a flip of her fingers. "I plan to be the one who figures it out. I've been surveying spirits for the last year or so. Well, the ones that will talk. They're either stubborn or too scrambled in the head to answer questions coherently. Drives me crazy."

"Ending up dead could leave a body feeling less than chatty," Diamond quipped. "See what I just did? I created a play on words and—"

"Magnolia Grove has two ghosts prowling the place," Charmaine said.

"That we know of," Jessi put in, eyes sparkling with excitement. "There could be even more."

"Wow, a wonder nobody's been hurt." Diamond blinked, eyes wide.

"As a matter of fact, one of their overnight guest says hands closed around her throat. But that could have been a bad dream, or a cold coming on," Charmaine rush on when Scotty and Diamond started talking at the same time.

"Girl, y'all better stay away from that place," Diamond blurted out. "Nuh-uh, I wouldn't go back there."

"We've seen worse, Diamond. You're such a wimp." Jessi said with a snort.

"Like my granddaddy use to say, it's the live folks you got to worry about. None of this voodoo-hoodoo ghosts. Look, I'm not sayin' you and Jessi are nuts. Y'all know me better. Let's be real, 99.9% of most crimes have a very normal explanation. Greed, jealousy, revenge," Scotty said.

"Tell that to our last clients who ended up sliced and diced by the monster in their fine Garden District home," Charmaine replied.

"Science will prove there are different forms of matter and energy, which will explain the paranormal. That and everyday criminals." Jessi joined them at the kitchen table.

"Let's have this philosophical discussion another time, thank you very much," Charmaine cut in before Scotty could make a counterpoint. "Meanwhile, we haven't figured out where the antiques are going, or who is making them go. Spirits don't pawn stuff, or have any use for money."

"The ghosts could be pissed off folks took their stuff. Or that tourists are tromping around while they're trying to get their eternal rest. They're moving their property to keep some light-fingered crook from stealing things." Diamond helped herself to a third cinnamon roll.

"Spirits stashing away items? Nah." Charmaine shook her head.

"You just said a ghost was able to move objects. It had lamps and vases flying around. Maybe she decided to take what's hers." Scotty argued. Then he sighed. "Can't believe I just said that."

Diamond nodded. "Yeah, what's-her-face—"

"Georgina Turnbull Villiers," Jessi said. "Georgina Ann to her friends. She married a Villiers back in 1802. She died shortly after giving birth to their third child in 1804. Her portrait is in the house. She told me a little bit before I zapped her. Well, she screamed it at me. My head felt like it was going to explode. Diamond is right about one thing. She is one pissed off spirit."

"Glad I didn't hear her yelling." Charmaine frowned.

"Then the damn tourists were screaming like a bag of trapped cats and stampeding for the doors. Luckily I cornered Georgina using my EMF disrupter." Jessi grinned at the puzzled expressions from their friends.

Charmaine held up a palm like a traffic cop to stop questions from the others. "Another of her gadgets. Don't ask or we'll be listening to her for hours. Jessi, exactly what did this Georgina say?"

"Something about she cursed the day she married a Villiers. And her dear child wasn't the cause of her early demise." Jessi went to her backpack. "But y'all gotta see my own customized tools of the trade. Logan and—"

"Later. Georgina claims she was murdered? Hmmm." Charmaine frowned.

"Yeah, so?" Jessi rooted around in her backpack as she talked. "Murdered entities are the worse when it comes to being in a bad mood all the time."

"I would be," Scotty joked.

"Me, too." Diamond made a sour face. "I'd haunt the shit out of folks until I got some payback."

"Which is what they do many times," Charmaine said. "The family history of our client seems to have more than a few shady deaths. What if more than one murder occurred?"

"Sure as hell more than one unnatural death. I'm guessing Mrs. Villiers didn't tell us all the bloody details. The mortality rate for our enslaved ancestors was high." Jessi put down the EMF disrupter she held. The others became solemn again.

"Or she doesn't know more. Slave masters weren't eager to describe beatings, starvation, overwork, rape, and lynching in their family journals," Charmaine said. She shivered visibly as a chill of horror went through her.

"Yeah, they like plain old lying to cover up the real stories of how they tortured other human beings," Jessi added.

"Which means we need to go to the source." Charmaine downed the remaining coffee in her mug and stood.

"Yeah, Jessi's side piece would love to help out. The old guy who's a history professor." Diamond wore a mischievous grin.

Scotty performed a dramatic turn to face Jessi. "I gotta hear more about him. A big upgrade from the usual gangstas, huh?"

Diamond piped up before Jessi could speak. "Arthur W. Marigny is a distinguished professor of history at Tulane University. He's considered an expert on colonial Louisiana. He's got a lot of academic clout."

"You make it sound like I'm jumping some old guy that can barely walk. He's only fifty-eight. Artie is in great physical shape." Jessi squinted at Diamond.

"Ooo-wee. Tell us more about how in shape he is." Diamond giggled.

"Nope, I don't want to know." Scotty waved both hands in the air. "In fact, I'm trying to erase the picture that popped in my head. Jessi and some wrinkled up old dude. Lawd!"

"We got more important things to talk about than Jessi's sex life," Charmaine went on, cutting Scotty and Diamond's lewd banter.

"No, we don't," Diamond joked.

"My friendships are none of your damn business. All I'll say is he gets the job done. But being a former pro, I know how to keep my mouth shut." Jessi wore a wicked grin as she turned back to her gadgets.

"Whatever. I still like mine young." Diamond snapped her fingers.

"Young ones be broke all the time. Girl, I ain't got time for that," Jessi retorted.

"Bobby ain't broke, and he's barely in his thirties," Diamond said, referring to the boss at her part-time job at Tulane.

Charmaine heaved a sigh of frustration. "Damn, y'all bad as a bunch of teenagers talking trash in the cafeteria. I'm not talking about historical research. We need to talk to slave ghosts."

The last sentence brought the others up short. Three pairs of eyes went wide as they gaped at Charmaine. She smiled with satisfaction at the effect of her words. "Now that I have your attention..."

****

The next day dawned into a bright and crisp October morning. Jessi rode with Charmaine to the main offices of the Villiers family business. The company was, in fact, run by several branches. Charmaine had a list of all the family names in her android tablet. Five relatives worked in the business in various executive positions. Jessi enjoyed a large paper cup of hot chocolate. Charmaine had only eaten one scrambled egg. Her stomach was in knots at the prospect of interviewing Evelyn Villiers Harmon. She was easily the offspring with the most to hide, and the one Charmaine found most intimidating.

"I don't know why you're worried. Mrs. Vee put Evelyn in her place the first day we met," Jessi commented as if she were the telepath and could read Charmaine's thoughts. "You oughta be worried about Nicky boy. He's up to something. Why else would he be blocking you from getting a read on him?"

"You think Nicholas Villiers knows how to block a telepath? But he's a skeptic." Charmaine frowned at the New Orleans uptown traffic. She wheeled around a slow moving produce truck.

"Doesn't mean he didn't take just-in-case precautions. The Villiers family has as much crap with them as they have money, maybe more. But none of 'em look stupid to me." Jessi continued to scroll through the morning news on her cell phone and sip from her cup.

"Geez, look at these drivers. I'm gonna sell this damn car and ride the bus." Charmaine honked at the driver in a red Corvette. The young blonde woman ignored her.

"You been threatening to ride the bus or trolley for at least three years. We both know you lyin'. Anyway, Evelyn is more upfront than all of them.

She let us know from jump she doesn't believe in spirits or think much of her sister and brother."

"Laura opened up when we had lunch," Charmaine offered.

"And you trust her?" Jessi glanced at Charmaine.

"Hell no. I mean who jumps into backstabbing their own family so quick?" Charmaine tapped her fingers on the steering wheel as they waited at a red light

"Pretty much everybody we know, and most of the clients we've had so far," Jessi said with a dry laugh.

Charmaine hissed out a puff of air. "No lies detected. Can't argue with you."

"The good news is you get to interview two fine men. First Kadeem, next up is the fine white boy with bucks. This case is paying off in more ways than one, huh?" Jessi looked at Charmaine, a sly smile pulling her lips into a curve.

"Full stop on the smartass comments. I'm focused on gathering the information we need to wrap up this crazy case." Charmaine kept her eyes on the street. Still, her mind jumped ahead to what she would wear when she met with Nicholas Villiers.

"Uh-huh. You better be, 'cause sexy Nick could be just as devious as the rest of his people," Jessi replied.

They entered the building's parking garage. An attendant instructed them to get a token to validate, or they would have to pay. Charmaine circled up to the fourth level before she found an empty space. Five minutes after parking, they were on their way up to the twenty-fifth floor. Two women were in the elevator with them.

"The four people on your list are expecting you," Charmaine said low.

"Bet she was happy about that," Jessi replied.

One of the women got off on the fifteenth floor. The woman left had long hair pulled into a neat ponytail. Dressed in a charcoal gray suit, the skirt showed off her smooth brown legs. She darted side glances at Charmaine and Jessi. As they passed the seventeenth floor, she cleared her throat.

"Are you going to VSI?"

"Why do you want to know?" Jessi replied, cutting off Charmaine's more polite response.

"I'm Renesha Thames. I work there." The young woman extended a hand. She smiled when Charmaine took it.

"Nice to meet you," Charmaine said. "My sister Jessi. We're..."

"Not going to discuss our business on an elevator," Jessi broke in. She raised both eyebrows at the slim young woman. "So, now we know the employees love to gossip."

Renesha's eyes went wide. "Oh, no. It's not like that. You're supposed to speak to my boss. She told me. I'll be pulling any files you might want."

"But you've obviously been told what we look like and given info from somebody else," Jessi persisted.

"Well, ah. A few of us know about problems in accounting. Okay, problem is not the right word. I heard it was in the real estate division... I, uh." Renesha clutched the file folders she held against her body. "Please don't tell Mrs. Harmon I said anything. The Villiers family is real strict about employees discussing business. Like paranoid." Then she winced. "Wrong word. I didn't mean..."

The elevator gave a slight bump as they arrived at the executive level floor. Charmaine spoke up. "You have an office?"

"No, a cubicle, and it's not private at all." Renesha looked around as though not happy to be seen with them.

Charmaine put a hand on her arm. "Relax. We're not going to say anything. You must know someplace we can talk."

"If anyone sees us, we'll say we decided to interview you first since we bumped into you on the elevator," Jessi said.

"Right." Renesha seemed a bit more relieved but still anxious. She continued to look around as several people passed them.

"Look, girl. The faster we get outta this hallway, the better it will be all around." Jessi's voice got louder with each word.

Renesha jumped. "Follow me."

The young woman's high heels left dents in the carpet as she marched ahead of them. Moments later she led the way to a room stacked with printer paper and other supplies. Long and narrow, the far end had a second door. A rectangular table sat in the middle with chairs.

"We should be okay in here." Renesha blinked hard as she glanced at their surroundings.

"Let's sit," Charmaine said with a smile. "Listen, Mrs. Marguerite Villiers gave us full permission to talk to anyone we decided might aid our investigation."

"I don't know anything about what's happened at Magnolia Grove Plantation," Renesha rushed out before Charmaine could go on.

"Yeah, but you heard about it. Who's talking?" Jessi said. Her sharp tone made Renesha start again, eyes wide and mouth open.

Charmaine used a gentle approach. She gestured for Renesha to have a seat. Once all three were settled, she began. "We understood that management of the historical property is separate from VSI. So, we have to wonder how you know."

"We handle hiring for them, too. There are three historical properties. I guess you know that already."

"Yeah, but give us the details anyway," Jessi said.

"There's a mansion in the Garden District and a building on Magazine Street. The Magazine Street property is an antique shop and art gallery. They rent it out. The owner is a cousin. He pays market value rent though." Renesha looked at the door when she heard a sound.

"No one will be surprised you're talking to us," Charmaine assured her with a smile.

"Dang, the Villiers family has money on top of money, huh?" Jessi got up and walked along one wall. Renesha's gaze tracked her movements.

"So, you know about the thefts from Magnolia Grove," Charmaine said to distract Renesha. She didn't know what Jessi was doing but figured Renesha didn't need to know either.

"Mrs. Junot is nervous they'll blame her. She's the head of HR. I mean, if valuable items have gone missing and all," Renesha said.

"Y'all do background checks on potential new hires, huh?" Charmaine took her tablet computer from her cross-body bag. She opened a notepad app. "See? I have it here."

Renesha turned from watching Jessi to look where Charmaine pointed. "Hmm, yeah. We run checks with the State Police. Drug tests, too. But Mrs. Junot hired a couple of her relatives."

"Maybe she didn't follow all the rules when checking them out?" Charmaine offered.

Renesha crossed her arms. "She let her cousin's daughter resign after about a month. I know she was grooming that girl to take my job. When reams of paper and then a portable printer for a laptop went missing, Leslie disappeared. I'm not saying she did it, but..."

"What's Leslie's last name?"

"Wilson, lives in Metairie. Mrs. Junot's nephew still works in engineering and maintenance. They take care of all of the buildings. The company has a couple of warehouses." Renesha had relaxed into the interview. "Yeah, nothing changes. I have to be perfect in every way, follow every rule. But they can walk in all shady like and get away with anything."

Charmaine nodded in sympathy. "I assume the nephew isn't an engineer."

"He has a degree, I give him that. Ethan completed a course at Delgado in HVAC and business technology management," Renesha replied. "More than I can say for Leslie."

"Oh?" Charmaine leaned an elbow on the table.

"Leslie has a drug problem. Mrs. Junot pretty much helped raise all three of her cousin's kids." Renesha went into full insider mode. She took a couple of chocolate covered mints out of her pocket and offered Charmaine one. "Have one, courtesy VSI. They keep them for business customers."

"Thanks. Do you know if Leslie has an arrest record?" Charmaine unwrapped the candy and popped it into her mouth.

"Technically, no. She went into one of those drug diversion programs. Expunged. I only know because we got to talking one day. Mrs. J. skated on that one. Not that I'll ever talk. I'm not anywhere near high enough on the org chart to be seen or heard by the big bosses." Renesha sighed. "I have an HR management certification, a degree, and six years of experience. I could run our office in my sleep."

Charmaine savored the mix of melted chocolate and mint coating her tongue. Even the candy at the

Villiers' corporation was high end. "But Mrs. Junot is a family member?"

"No, but her mother worked for old Mr. Villiers. But if old Mrs. Villiers found about Leslie?" Renesha drew a finger across her throat.

Jessi walked back to the table. "Um, you're late for your appointment with Mrs. Harmon."

"Shit." Charmaine jumped to her feet. "You—"

"Yeah, I'll finish here and move on. I've got time before my first interview." Jessi turned to Renesha. "I won't bite. This time."

Renesha gasped and leaned away from her. "I, I don't know much else."

"The files?"

"Behave," Charmaine snapped at Jessi as she hurried out.

"I'm telling you all I know, promise," Renesha stammered.

"I meant, oh never mind."

Charmaine only had time to give Jessi the evil eye as a warning. Then she hot-footed down two halls and skidded to a stop at the wide glass doors that led to the executive suites. Before she opened them, a deep voice stopped her.

"Good morning." Tanner Gladstone stood at the end of the hall. He crooked a finger at her to follow him.

"I'm late already and..."

"No worries. I told Evelyn you were with me, getting a rundown of our organizational structure. Her video conference ran longer than expected anyway." Tanner opened a door that led to a roomy, bright office. "Of course, she'll act like you inconvenienced her."

"Meeting with you wasn't on my agenda." Charmaine glanced around. His office looked good. Apparently, Evelyn's dislike of him didn't carry weight. Corner office, nice décor.

"It is now." Tanner smiled at her and swept a hand out for her to take a seat.

Charmaine settled into a leather chair. She looked up at him since he remained standing. "You obviously planned this detour for a good reason."

"I'm going to help you with very sound advice," Tanner said.

"Please do."

"Don't milk the ghosts and goblins thing for all it's worth. Do your little stage act and go on your merry way." Tanner tilted his head to one side. "I think we understand each other."

Charmaine calculated the risk and rewards of slapping the arrogance off his face. Jail. NOPD and the Orleans Parish DA would be delighted. She tamped down her irritation with the man.

"What's your real job? Wait, I'm getting something." Charmaine put her fingertips to both sides of her temple. She closed her eyes for a few seconds and then looked at him again. "You help keep their dirty secrets buried so deep no one can sniff them out."

Tanner's smile slipped as his jaw tightened. "You have no idea."

"But I do. Being psychic is part of my little stage act. Remember? The question is, whose side are you on. Maybe Nick's." Charmaine noted the way his nostrils flared at the mention of the Villiers male heir. She decided to mine the vein. "I wouldn't have guessed Nick was trying to depose Evelyn and her hubby. He seems laid back, more into being a trust fund kid than a business man."

"What you think you know is irrelevant. I—"

"Evelyn doesn't want you around. Laura... she doesn't trust anyone completely. Mrs. Villiers thinks you're totally loyal, but I'm getting a different feel." Charmaine felt a rush of heat from Tanner. She was literally getting warmer as she got close to the truth.

"I see you've been rehearsing. I give it two out of four stars," Tanner snapped.

"But back to Nick. I'm looking forward to exploring his view of the situation. Maybe I need to get closer to him if he's got you running his errands inside the company."

"One hint that you're trying to hurt Nick or any of the family, and I'll take action. You're not exactly in good standing with the local police. You know what I mean." Tanner walked to the door and pulled it open to signal she could leave. "I'm sure Mrs. Harmon is ready to see you now."

Charmaine took her time getting up from the chair. She brushed non-existent lint from her slacks, adjusted her cross-body handbag and walked past him. "Bye, bye for now. One last thing. As threats go, that was pretty lame."

She marched down the hall away from him without looking back. She arrived at the glass doors leading to the executive offices once more. A tall, lithe blonde man sat at a desk. He answered a phone and handed papers to a woman. His hazel-eyed gaze swept over Charmaine in seconds, appraising her. She tugged at the knit blue sweater blazer she wore over black leggings. When he glanced down, Charmaine looked at her boots. The man ended the phone call.

"Are you Mrs. Harmon's nine o'clock?" The man, Harlan Murphy according to the name plate on his desk, glanced at his watch and back at Charmaine.

"Yes. Um, sorry I'm late. I, I mean we, my sister and I, started interviewing an employee as part of our inquiry. Then Tanner Gladstone..." Charmaine heard herself babbling under the man's scrutiny. Before she could continue making a fool of herself, he raised a palm.

"Mrs. Harmon has a ten thirty meeting, so you'll have a little less than twenty minutes of her time." Garland stood. He waved away a woman who approached him holding out a sheet of paper. He walked off without looking to see if Charmaine followed.

"Twenty minutes should be plenty of time I—" Charmaine broke off and marched after him. She smiled at the woman, who gave her a look of sympathy. Seconds later they arrived at double doors at the end of the hallway. He knocked once and opened the door. He stood aside as Charmaine entered.

"Ms. Joliet understands that she has fifteen minutes." He ignored the squint Charmaine aimed his way.

Evelyn nodded, gaze still on a wide monitor. "Thank you, Harlan."

Charmaine walked across the plush wool rug. She stood for a few moments behind one of three brown leather chairs facing Evelyn's desk. She studied the screen Evelyn seemed so absorbed by. Columns of figures and texts, but Charmaine couldn't read the contents. When she took a step closer, Evelyn tapped the keyboard until a photo of flowers popped up.

Shifting her gaze to Evelyn's face, Charmaine smiled. "I apologize for being a little late."

"Let's understand each other, Ms. Joliet. You work for my mother over my objection. Stories about restless souls from the past roaming Magnolia Grove are a marketing ploy. Nothing more. What we're dealing with is either missing records or employee theft. Period." Evelyn let out a long breath as if tolerating Charmaine took effort.

"Then you should be pleased your mother hired us to figure out which it is. My agency will report on what we find. I'm not going to juice up the facts if that's what you're worried about." Charmaine took a seat without asking.

Evelyn sat straight as she studied Charmaine for a few seconds. The size of the office, her desk, and the expensive blood red power business suit screamed she was in control. Then she removed reading glasses that matched the color of her suit.

"Your website talks about tracking down information in this world and the next, or something like that. Your phone number spells out the word spirits. So far everything I've seen suggests you're more entertainers than real professional investigators."

Charmaine was officially fed up. She lashed out, sending a mental probe to read the woman's thoughts. In fact, Charmaine didn't "hear" the thoughts of others. The impressions she received were like visual images of words and sounds. She'd given up trying to explain it to others. What she got from Evelyn Villiers Harmons was a mishmash of emotions, anxieties, and resentments. Evelyn blinked at the impact, a look of confusion clouding her brown eyes for a few seconds. She rubbed her forehead.

"Mrs. Harmon, you obviously understand marketing. While my sister and I have psychic abilities," Charmaine paused when Evelyn gave a huff of cynicism. "Our 'colorful' marketing hook isn't hype. Mrs. Villiers chose us because we can handle the investigation in a way no one else can."

"Let me guess. Ridding people of angry spirits makes the cost of your 'services' go up. Once you find out a menacing phantom inhabits a dwelling, your hourly rate increases by a decimal point." Evelyn raised an expertly arched brow.

"We don't make up ghosts to scam people with padded fees," Charmaine said, her voice even. "I'm not here to sell you on whether or not we're the real deal. So let's skip the tap dance about my credibility."

Evelyn's expression tightened. "Yes, you're a licensed therapist. You've been in trouble with the law, but nothing nearly as serious as your sister."

"Did Kadeem Hardy tell you that? Hell, he could find out about us with a basic internet search." Charmaine smiled at the surprise that made Evelyn's mouth twitch. She took out her tablet. "But yeah, you got it right. Let's begin."

"I don't have—"

"To answer my questions? Your mother says you do," Charmaine cut in. "And last time I checked, mama still runs things around here. Since we're on the subject of who's in charge... you want to take over the company. Correct?"

"You're not as smart as you think, Ms. Joliet," Evelyn snapped.

"You're convinced that Mrs. Villiers should retire to Florida or somewhere far away. Probably thought your late daddy should have left you in control from jump. But that's not how the will read. Fortunately for you, your brother isn't thirsty to run things. He likes to party. Now your sister and brother-in-law are a different story." Charmaine swiped the screen as if scrolling through background material as she spoke.

"Don't waste your magic tricks on me. Coffee break rumors and guesswork," Evelyn hissed. Her mouth turned down, turning her face into a sour mask.

"Your assistant won't find out anything, so don't divert his time from the Marshall contract or getting copies of the warehouse inventories."

Evelyn gasped as she fell against the rich leather of her executive chair. "How did you?"

Charmaine looked at her with a slight smile. "Magic."

Evelyn inhaled, exhaled and recovered her composure. She sat forward again. "Whatever else you might be, I have to give you points for flair."

"Gee thanks. So maybe we can save time. If you set up the spooky happenings at Magnolia Grove, cut it out. Scaring people as part of a plan to satisfy your ambitions isn't nice. Not to mention trying to make a case that your mother is mentally unstable." Charmaine expected Evelyn to call security and have her thrown out. Yet she got another read in a flash. Amusement. She studied Evelyn's expression transform from anger to mirth. "Ah, you think I should be looking at Laura, Nicholas, or possibly both."

"You've done your homework, found someone who talks too much and used public records very well. I'm too busy doing the real work of keeping VSI profitable. Laura and Nick have way more imagination than I do. I deal in facts, figures and the bottom line, like my father."

"I haven't ruled out any possibility."

Evelyn snorted in contempt. "Well good for you. My mother is eccentric enough. She doesn't need any help from me."

"What does that mean?" Charmaine tilted her head to one side. Anticipation spiked through her. They were about to stop sparring and get to the good stuff.

Instead, Evelyn glanced at the digital display one her computer screen and stood. "You're the psychic private investigator. Go find out. I have a meeting."

Her assistant swung the door open right with precision timing. "City representatives and the Marshall Corporation team have arrived," he announced with a pointed glance at Charmaine.

Evelyn walked around the desk and past Charmaine without looking her. She took a slim file folder from him as she strode out of the office. "Good luck with your detecting, Ms. Joliet."

Two minutes later Charmaine stood at the elevator waiting for Jessi. They exchanged texts. Jessi was about to wrap up. Charmaine studied the tasteful prints on the wall. When Kadeem rounded a corner, Charmaine doubted his appearance was a coincidence.

"Morning, Ms. Joliet." Kadeem strolled closed to Charmaine and brushed his fingers along the sleeve of her jacket. Then he leaned down and whispered. "Let's get together this evening."

"You got something for me?" Charmaine whispered back. She ran her tongue over her bottom lip while looking at him.

"You damn right I do." Kadeem stepped back when voices came closer. A man and woman came out of a door. He watched the couple until they disappeared down another hall. "We can't talk here. Too many eyes and ears. Later."

"Talk?" Charmaine gave him a head to toe gaze.

"I promise we'll end the evening with plenty of action." Kadeem winked at her. He left, his long-legged stride giving him a swagger. The tailored navy blue suit added to his sexy.

"You hooked another cute employee, or is that Kadeem?" Jessi spoke over Charmaine's shoulder.

"I'm not randomly out here picking up dudes." Charmaine stared after Kadeem for a few seconds longer before she faced Jessi. "And yes, that's Kadeem."

"Hmm, slim guys move like snakes when they're doing you. A real turn on. I remember this one client I had that could—"

"Skip the scandalous trip down memory lane about your former profession." Charmaine broke in. A group of three women came toward them. She hit the elevator down button.

Jessi grinned back at her. "Whatever. I see you survived meeting with mean ass Evelyn."

"She doesn't trust her brother and sister any more than they trust her. Lovely family," Charmaine muttered. A bell tingled to announce the elevator had arrived. "Let's go."

They weren't alone during the ride down, so Charmaine and Jessi didn't talk. Jessi had the token that would allow them to avoid the parking fee. Minutes later, Charmaine guided her Chevy Cruze into heavy Central Business District traffic.

"What did you find out? I'm guessing not much," Jessi said.

"She spent most of the time letting me know she thinks we're trash. I'll say one thing though. They might not like each other much, but when it comes to keeping secrets? They're in total agreement. Tanner Gladstone cornered me for an unscheduled side conversation. He feels we're a threat. Not sure why."

"Hmm, be interesting to figure it out," Jessi replied.

"Wonder if Nicholas Villiers knows Tanner's got a serious crush on him." Charmaine grinned when Jessi let out a whoop.

"I sure as hell did not see that coming. Nicholas Villiers was eyeing you up like for real. So, that means he's bi? Your date with him could turn into a serious par-tay." Jessi cackled.

"I don't have a 'date' with the guy. And I've got enough to explain to the big guy upstairs as it is. Freaking two guys is not on the menu," Charmaine wisecracked. "Anyway, I'm not sure Nicholas feels the same about Tanner."

"Tanner is a frustrated lover. Shit, these folks are complicated."

"Kadeem wants to meet tonight. I'll get more from him. Then I'll interview Nicholas." Charmaine frowned, but not at the gray truck that cut her off.

"Try to get some actual work done. Okay?" Jessi teased.

"Oh shut up," Charmaine tossed back. Then they both dissolved into school girl giggles.

5.

He's Too Good To Be True

That evening, Charmaine broke her own rule, never go to a target's house. She'd met Kadeem at Lenora's Grill for a bite to eat. Soon she was tasting him in his renovated townhouse on N. Johnson. Kadeem proved resistant to her mind reading skills so far. Charmaine thought being on his home ground, where he was most comfortable, would help her learn more. Also, if she was totally honest, it was a short drive, and he had his own gift. Making her hot in record time. The plan had been for them to cruise over to Pelican Bay for their famous daiquiris. After a lot of sexual teasing over a barely eaten meal, they agreed the drinks could wait.

"Whew! I love the way you combine business with pleasure, girl." Kadeem lay on his back. Perspiration rolled down his chest.

Charmaine lifted her hips and rolled off him to one side. She lifted her thick hair from her neck and fanned her face with one hand, making a note to get it cut short again. "You should switch out these satin sheets to cotton. They're cooler and dry faster. You sweat. A lot."

"I thought you'd like sliding against this silky material while you enjoyed this smoothness." Kadeem pointed to his body. He blew out more air.

"Oh, so you were sure I'd come to your place, huh?" Charmaine gave a feline stretch. His reaction was predictable as he gazed at her full breasts.

"Nah, it ain't like that, baby. I'm just optimistic. We clicked last time so..." Kadeem arranged the pillows, then lay propped up in the bed.

"Uh-huh." Charmaine padded across the hard-wood floor to her handbag. She took it to the bathroom.

"I got a fresh bar of soap in the closet," Kadeem called from the bed. He didn't move. "I'd get it for you, but I'm tore up right now."

"No problem. I got my own."

Charmaine used the liquid soap in a travel-sized bottle in her purse to take a quick shower. She found a fluffy clean towel in a bathroom cupboard. Kadeem walked in while she dried herself.

After watching for a few seconds, he got in the glass walk-in shower. "You come prepared, huh? Your own condoms, soap and everything. You got toothpaste and a brush in that bag, too?"

"I don't stay overnight," Charmaine replied.

"Hell, you gone make me fall in love." Kadeem laughed loud as he turned on the water. "Don't bother searching my place while I'm in here. You won't find anything."

"What makes you..." Charmaine broke off and laughed along with him. "Thanks for saving me the trouble."

She left the bathroom, put on her panties and dressed in one of his shirts. The light blue cotton stopped just above her knees. Charmaine gave her lips a light coating of watermelon lip stain. She raked her finger through her hair. Neat, but still tousled would suit her purposes. When Kadeem emerged from the bath wearing a cotton robe, Charmaine was in his kitchen.

"You wanna go out for drinks now?" Kadeem sat on one of three stools at his kitchen island.

"I'd say we got everything we need right here." Charmaine smiled at him. She held up two bars of chocolate. Then she put those down and pointed to a carton of milk. "I know a recipe for French hot chocolate. You have all the ingredients."

"Love the stuff. Brown sugar is in the canister right over there." Kadeem pointed. He watched her for a few minutes. "We really do click ya know. We like the same food. The same kind of sex, hard and soft at the same time. Now I find out you make one of my favorite drinks just the way I like it. All to keep me warm on a chilly night."

"It's still pretty warm outside, Kadeem. This is Louisiana after all." Charmaine kept the heat low beneath the pot of milk.

"You know what I mean." Kadeem continued to study her.

"Don't go all soft and gooey on me. We got business to discuss," Charmaine tossed back over her shoulder, but kept stirring.

"My girl," Kadeem murmured, followed by an appreciative laugh.

Charmaine added two large sections of chocolate to the pot. She whisked it as it melted. A minute later, she poured the steaming liquid treat into cups Kadeem had retrieved. They went to his living room and sat on the sofa.

"I'm nobody's 'girl'. Remember it." Charmaine lifted her cup to him and drank. The rich flavor flowed across her tongue.

Kadeem's eyebrow went up as he lifted his cup in a toast and sipped. He sighed. "Being my girl would be so terrible? C'mon. We made much noise up in here."

"Sexing you doesn't mean you rule me. Neither does fixing you a cup of hot chocolate," Charmaine replied.

"Nah, you got me wrong. I didn't mean it that way." Kadeem clapped his free hand on Charmaine's bare thigh. "We got something special. Admit it."

Charmaine picked up his hand with two fingers, lifted it and pushed it away. "So corny. Let's talk about your deal offer, player."

"You need to let down that hard wall and let a brother in." Kadeem held up a palm. "Okay, okay. Business."

"Thank you."

"I know you've been thinking about me," Kadeem said with a smile.

"Please." Charmaine grunted and rolled her eyes.

"You're smart, so I know you'll make the right decision." Kadeem gazed into her eyes.

Charmaine allowed her expression to soften. She stared into eyes that matched the dark chocolate she'd melted in milk. Felt a click in her mind, and Kadeem opened up to her. She put a hand on his thigh, leaned in, and sighed when he brushed a thumb across her bottom lip. His thoughts flowed into her, including a comparison between sex with her and Laura Villiers Mandeville. Charmaine managed not to hide her delighted surprise at that nugget. Laura liked dark chocolate even more than Kadeem.

"Will I?" Charmaine let out a slow breath. *Fool thinks I'm under his erotic spell.*

"I'll even sweeten the deal, a ten percent cut of anything we make." Kadeem let his robe fall open just enough.

Charmaine looked down, pleased to see he was responding to her closeness. She massaged the growing lump until he sucked in a deep breath and let it out. "Tell me more."

****

Friday morning found Charmaine in her home office early. She logged into her account at the clinic to catch up on case notes. Jessi came in and dropped into one of the office chairs, a cup of coffee in hand. One leg dangled over the chair's arm.

"You're up early," Jessi said and yawned.

"I don't know why you pay rent. You come in here any time you want, make yourself at home before sunrise." Charmaine continued to type up a summary of her therapy session. Her client clung to the delusion that her landlord was sending chemicals through the wall outlets. At least she'd convinced her to stay on her meds for a month.

"Nah, I spent the night here. You didn't notice because you came in so late." Jessi raised an eyebrow over the rim of the coffee mug when Charmaine glanced at her.

"I know you're not trying to check my lifestyle," Charmaine drawled, then turned back to her notes.

"I'm all for any method that gets us information for a well-paying case, sugar. Freak Kadeem much as you want." Jessi giggled at her own joke.

"Whatever. Why did you spend the night at my place? And you better had cleaned up my guest room and bath is all I know." Charmaine gave Jessi a mean side-eye to emphasize she was serious.

"It's all good, and we'll get to my sleepover later. What did you find out?"

"Kadeem says we can blackmail Laura and Nicholas. They've been quietly moving money in the company. Even Laura's husband doesn't know about it. Kadeem wouldn't tell me how he found out. My best guess is sleeping with somebody in the finance department. Oh, and he's also sleeping with Laura." Charmaine nodded when Jessi's mouth fell open.

"I like his moves," Jessi said.

"Jessi..."

"I'm not saying we gone take him up on his deal, but I can admire his technique. Look at the way the dude is working his plan and planning his work. He gets a job, probably because of his aunt. Manages to get hired in security no less, and finds his way into lovely Laura's bed. Big ups to my man Kadeem." Jessi lifted her mug in salute.

"She prefers getting it in the back of her Mercedes SUV. Brings air freshener and wipes to clean it up," Charmaine said with a short laugh.

"Yeah, we wouldn't want the kiddies smelling sex on the way to soccer practice, now would we?" Jessi grinned, then grew serious again. "What else?"

"He can't do much searching on his own, too risky. Kadeem wants us to dig up the rest of the dirt. I told him we have a hacktivist on call for when we really need to go deep. Do I need to add he's not telling it all?" Charmaine finished the last sentence of one case and closed the file. She turned to Jessi.

"Hell no. I wouldn't expect anything else from a street graduate." Jessi swung her leg down to the floor. "What did you read in his devious little mind?"

"His Aunt Yolanda is mixed up in the missing antiques, but I didn't get a clear... picture." Charmaine frowned as she recalled the jumble that scrolled through her mental vision.

"No mystery there. She steals the stuff, hands it off to him, and he fences it." Jessi shrugged. "Easy as can be."

"Except Mrs. Villiers is right. You can't just walk into any old pawnshop with priceless heirlooms. They don't know what to do with that stuff. I can't see Kadeem or Yolanda having connections to high-end fences."

Jessi leaned back, a frown of concentration on her smooth brown face. Charmaine went on to the next case file. She was way behind on updating her notes. Thankfully her immediate supervisor was a lazy woman more interested in her cheating husband. Once Charmaine caught up, she'd generously offer to help her catch the guy and his girlfriend. First, she had to update the files, or the business office would bust them both. The clinic couldn't bill for services without her billing codes. For the next five minutes, she typed while Jessi thought and sipped.

"Mrs. Villiers hasn't reported the thefts to the police," Jessi said. "Why?"

"She doesn't want bad publicity scaring off her guests." Charmaine stopped typing in the middle of a sentence and turned to Jessi again.

"Right. You just figured out bad publicity doesn't fly as a reason. With her influence, the police wouldn't put her on blast. In fact, nobody would know or care enough to look for a crime report. Stolen goods? That's everyday crime in GNO," Jessi said, referring to the Greater New Orleans area that included several contiguous parishes.

"They've got two huge attics full of pricey goods. All she'd have to do is replace what's missing. So, maybe Mrs. Villiers knows who's taking the stuff, or suspects. She'd protect Yolanda to keep her from spilling family secrets."

"Yeah, but then why bring us in to investigate? She could just ignore the occasional missing doo-dad and keep it moving. Yolanda gets paid off on a regular basis with her little bonuses, and the family skeletons stay in the closet. Everybody's happy." Jessi sat forward, elbows on both knees.

"Something scared her. Maybe the guest being attacked upped the stakes too much. We're supposed to be the fixers who handle the problem discreetly. No flashing police lights or possible media coverage." Charmaine squinted as if that would help her see clearer through the tangle of motives.

"Or she also suspects her kids are up to no good. Mrs. Villiers obviously knows they're fighting over the goods like dogs over a big bone," Jessi offered.

"Bone hell. We're talking a big pile of Kobe steaks with a side of foie gras." Charmaine swallowed. "Damn, I didn't eat breakfast."

Jessi jumped to her feet and ran off. "Glad you said something."

When she returned with coffee, bacon, hot biscuits, honey, and butter, Charmaine grinned. "Bless you!"

"I don't just stay without paying some kinda way. In spite of you claiming I don't," Jessi wisecracked. She put the tray to one side on top of Charmaine's desk. She sat down while Charmaine drizzled honey over one of the two biscuits.

Jessi chewed on one end of a slice of bacon. "Something upset the balance enough that Mrs. Villiers brought in strangers, meaning us."

"Paying off Yolanda with an enhanced salary way beyond her actual value is one thing. Taking family heirlooms? That might be enough to tip Mrs. Villiers over the edge. But she could have just confronted her." Charmaine stared at her biscuit, theories rolling around in her head. "No, all three of her children agree she's superstitious."

"Humph, or she's one hell of an actress. She looked scared enough to shit in her hundred dollar panties." Jessi waved her bacon in the air and then chomped on the end of it.

"Nah, mama was real that day. I could tell." Charmaine devoured buttery goodness for a few minutes as both sat in thought.

"We need to find out all the dirty, juicy details of what Evelyn, Laura, and Nick are up to. Was your meeting with Kadeem worth it?" Jessi wiggled her eyebrows.

"I can't believe how quick you time warp back to middle school," Charmaine muttered around a mouthful of biscuit.

"You're trying so hard to be a good church girl that I can't help it." Jessi laughed at the evil eye Charmaine gave her.

"Well, I'm failing bad." Charmaine looked at the food and lost her appetite. She pushed the plate away. Even the coffee tasted bitter on her tongue.

Jessi's grin faded. She grabbed a napkin from the tray and wiped her hands. "According to the Bible, God gave us sex, right? So, he can't be opposed to us enjoying ourselves."

"Under certain conditions."

"Artie says the Bible as we know was put together like a puzzle. Add in all the translations from ancient Hebrew, Aramaic, Greek? I don't think it's clear cut. People like simple, so grabbing onto a set of black and white rules makes 'em feel better. Life is way more complicated than do this, don't do that. Forever, Amen." Jessi rose and poured herself a cup of coffee.

"You've been doing deep philosophical thinking and discussing. I've sparked an examination of religion, huh? Converting you will help me out big time on judgment day," Charmaine quipped.

"Don't count on me running up to the altar any time soon, girl. Guys like Sykes are self-appointed self-righteous tyrants. Most church folks are hypocrites. Some of me and Diamond's best customers were preachers, deacons, and a few church ladies." Jessi's gruff laughter dripped contempt.

"No details. Please." Charmaine clapped both hands over her ears. She closed her eyes as well. Then she opened one. "Don't tell me Bishop Sykes was one."

Jessi cackled, then grew louder when both Charmaine's eyes popped open wide. "Calm your religious nerves. Never met the good reverend. Look, all I'm saying is you can live a life of principles, compassion, and ethics without being religious."

"Bishop Sykes says secular humanism will lead our world into fire and brimstone damnation." Charmaine raised an eyebrow.

"Humph, Bishop Sykes can kiss my secular humanist—"

"Jessi!" Charmaine broke in to head off her blasphemy.

"Assertions," Jessi finished with a smirk. "Artie taught me that one."

"I'm not so sure Dr. Marigny is a good influence on your young, impressionable mind," Charmaine joked. She and Jessi cracked up. "Uh, all this heavy talk of religion and morality is too much so early in the morning. How did we get on that subject anyway?"

"Kadeem as an asset of information on the case." Jessi let loose one last cackle.

"More important, he's a player in the Villiers' Who-Wants-To-Be-A-Millionaire game. Chip off the old block. His aunt goes for the gold, and so does he. Except Yolanda thinks Kadeem is out of his league," Charmaine said.

"Mrs. Villiers wants us to solve the ghost problem and keep her family's secrets. Laura wants you to expose Evelyn's secrets, but keep hers. Wonder what Nicky boy wants?" Jessi picked up her laptop. She opened it and read for a few seconds.

"I intend to find out tonight, and no jokes," Charmaine added when Jessi wound up to toss out a wisecrack.

"You took all the best assignments this go-round. Next case, I'll get to have the fun meetings," Jessi said with a squint.

"Agreed. Now get out of here and come back with some dirt on the family. I'm doing all the heavy lifting." Charmaine smirked when Jessi frowned back.

"Hey, taming pissed off spirits count. And that's another thing, I got a gut twinge that the Villiers family past has something to do with what's happening now."

"How?" Charmaine savored the last drop of rich coffee and went back to her clinical notes.

"I don't know. Shit, look at the time." Jessi stuffed her laptop into her bag and swung it over her shoulder. "Dr. Blaylock don't play. Her class starts at nine, and she expects us to be in our seats at eight-fifty five sharp and ready to roll. I need a decent grade in her class. See you later."

"Remember what pays the bills. Get on your snooping job," Charmaine yelled over a shoulder as she tapped keys.

"Yeah, you gonna be workin' it tonight I bet," Jessi called back. The thump of the front door shutting cut off the sound of her laughter.

"Remind me to whip her butt later," Charmaine said to the ceramic figure of a Black ballerina on her desk.

****

Upperline Restaurant was full, not surprising on a Friday evening. Charmaine dressed in black velvet jeans and a deep red sweater to keep off the October chill. As she approached the pretty blonde hostess, Nicholas Villiers appeared like a magician. He put a hand under Charmaine's elbow and turned to the woman in the same smooth motion.

"My guest has arrived, Lizette. We'll take our table now." Nicholas smiled at Charmaine. "Thanks for indulging me. I have so many meetings at the office, I needed to end the week some place less... like a chore."

"I hope my interview with you won't be too awful. We could have put it off until Monday or Tuesday when you're not so busy."

Charmaine let him guide her like a pro between the tables of well-heeled diners. In truth, she was delighted to finally see the inside of Upperline. Her budget would never allow her to eat there. Thank goodness Jessi hadn't thought to ask where they'd be meeting. Here she was, having a meal at one of the city's top restaurants with a fine trust fund kid. Nice way to gather facts for their investigation. Jessi would have never stopped harping on it. Charmaine savored the perfect time to drop the nugget. Nicholas' melodic baritone cut into gloating at her baby sister's expense.

"Not at all. I looked forward to seeing you from the moment of your invitation. You may be working for my mother, but we can enjoy ourselves in the meantime." Nicholas pulled out a chair for Charmaine. He sat once she got settled with help from a waiter.

"Here is our wine menu, sir. Madam." The waiter attempted to hand them cards, but Nicholas waved them away.

"Bring us the Caymus Napa Valley Cabernet Sauvignon 2013, Doug. You don't mind me ordering for you? I promise you won't be disappointed." Nicholas looked at Charmaine.

Charmaine held his gaze as she brushed her hair back over both shoulders. "Warning, I'll hold you to all promises."

"I believe in delivering way more to assure complete satisfaction," Nicholas replied.

The waiter looked back and forth as though he was at a tennis match. Then he tucked the wine menus under one arm. "One of our finest red wines. I'll be back shortly."

He relaxed his elegant lanky frame against the back of the chair. Dressed in a black dress shirt open at the collar, tucked into gray wool suit slacks, he looked, smelled, and smiled like money. Even in the impressive surroundings, the man had people stealing glances at them. Or rather at him. His social set would no doubt spend the weekend abuzz with speculation.

"So... Mr. Villiers." Charmaine cocked her head to one side as she waited for him to answer her unspoken question.

"Nick. Please." He started to go on but stopped when the waiter approached.

Doug came, poured their wine, and left. Charmaine let the smooth taste flow over her tongue. Against her will, she closed her eyes and sighed. When she opened them, Nicholas looked back with the ghost of a smile. Her gaze followed the lines of his face and the curve of his thin lips. No one feature stood out, but all together they added up to a delectable package.

"I recommend the New Orleans Dinner for two." Nicholas waved to the waiter, who hurried over to do his bidding.

Charmaine glanced at the menu. Seven items of their most popular gourmet dishes, including roasted duckling with a choice of sauce. "Sounds good to me."

Once Doug left again, Nick sipped wine and gazed at Charmaine over the glass. Then he set it down. "You've talked to both of my sisters?"

"You know the answer, Nick. In fact, I'm sure you know every comma and period of our conversations." Charmaine let the atmosphere of privilege wash over her. She needed to keep her head in this game.

"Laura, yes. Not Evelyn. I tried, but she has always resisted my charm. Witches are like that." Nick's expression hardened, his mouth turned down.

Charmaine got a glimpse of his not-so-charming nature. She smiled inside. Bingo. "Yeah, Laura made it clear there's no great love between y'all. Bet she started in on you back in the day."

"A story as old as time and not all that unique. My mother had a hard time getting pregnant. Evelyn was the miracle baby and was treated as such. But then the rest of us came along. She's been annoyed ever since." Nick squinted and looked away.

His body language told Charmaine that there was way more to the story, but she wouldn't press. He'd be open if he felt in control. "Laura says Evelyn and her husband have plans to rule the empire, so to speak."

"The brilliant and plodding Robert J. Harmon. He gets things done. Mother is practical, along with the board. He's competent at what he does. But she'd never allow them to make him CEO." Nick brushed his expensive slacks, confident of his place as heir apparent.

"But with enough support he might get the job. I've seen the reports in business publications. Double-digit profit increases, expansion in foreign markets. Impressive results since he was made vice president and COO shortly before your father died. With those kind of results, even Mrs. Villiers might be happy to let him plod along." Charmaine sipped her wine to cover a smile at the reaction.

Nick turned a razor-sharp gaze on Charmaine, eyes narrowed. "What else do you know about us?"

"That you folks wrote the book on keeping a lid on family affairs. Most of what I know is from public records. Nobody is willing to talk. Too scared of the legendary Villiers wrath." Charmaine mixed in the truth enough to reassure him.

"Bull. Laura is dumb enough to sleep with Kadeem. Yes, Charmaine. I know about her side piece. Has he contacted you to work his own back door deal? So damn predictable these..." Nick waved a hand.

"These ghetto Black folks like me?" Charmaine supplied when his words trailed off.

"Nothing like you. I don't have much use for white trash either. Go on, call me a snob. Call it ghetto, trailer park trash, whatever you want. This mentality to live low, to connive and use others." Nick studied Charmaine for a reaction. "I feel like we can be open, honest with each other."

"Backstabbing, theft and worse goes among the rich. I can name a long list of millionaires who ended up in prison. Didn't we just mention your sisters? Something about them trying to burn each other?" Charmaine worked to keep the knife-edged scorn from her voice and expression. He got the message anyway.

"Ouch. I can't argue with you, not when you use our own words to prove your case," Nick said with a dashing smile. "Don't worry, I'm not insulted."

"I wasn't worried," Charmaine replied and enjoyed more of the fine wine. Might as well drink up before he had Doug toss her out.

Instead of getting angry, Nick laughed out loud, a melodious sound that turned female heads. "What a great change. Most of my dates are unoriginal."

"I don't consider this a 'date'. I came to interview you for our investigation." Charmaine flashed a brief smile that dripped ice water.

"Ah yes. The restless spirits that haunt the halls of Magnolia Estates." Nick laughed again.

The waiter whisked in with a tray bearing various dishes. A female wait staff came with him. In moments, they set out the soup and appetizers. Doug put the finishing touches on setup, nodded his approval to the waitress and turned to them. "Enjoy."

"Their turtle soup is fantastic." Nick winked at Charmaine, no hint that she'd delivered a side of put down along with their meal.

For the next few minutes, Nick led the way in casual talk. Charmaine, content to enjoy the excellent meal, allowed him to go on. Dinner met her expectations for how the rich lived when eating out. The food was superb. Every one of the seven sampler-sized dishes delighted Charmaine's taste buds. She made a mental note to start saving up her nickels for a repeat visit. Might take her a few months, but Upperline would be worth it.

Doug swooped back in with perfect timing to remove empty plates. "How did you like everything?"

"I'd go back there and kiss the cook, but I don't want to get arrested." Charmaine grinned at Doug, who grinned back.

"Excellent. Did you save room for dessert?" Doug looked from Charmaine to Nick.

"Lord no. I'm more than full." Charmaine puffed out her cheeks, which made Doug laugh.

"Prepare two orders to-go of honey-pecan bread pudding with toffee sauce. We'll have coffee though."

"Sure thing, Mr. Villiers." Doug dashed off to obey without another word.

Nick turned to Charmaine. "Have it later, a special treat from me to you. You have to try it. I schedule extra sessions with my personal trainer just so I can gobble it up at least once a week."

"You're lucky, well rich, enough to have one. I'll have to run an extra five miles around the 'hood to work it off," Charmaine quipped.

"You might have grown up in 'the hood', but you're not a product of it. You and your sister have survived hell, but you have two degrees and Jessi is working on one. Unlike Evelyn and, to some degree Laura, I don't think your psychic skills are a scam," Nick said.

"You're a true believer! Welcome to the fold, my son," Charmaine joked. Her body hummed when Nick let loose another magical laugh. Or was it because of the rich food chased by fine wine?

"Not so much, but I'm open to explore new experiences. Maybe what you call paranormal is nothing more than enhanced intuition. Some people have a gift for reading others, even situations." Nick sat one elbow on the table. He gazed at Charmaine, into her eyes and then at her mouth.

"I do have intuition, and right now it's saying you want something from me like your sister," Charmaine added when his violet blue eyes lit up with lust.

He eased against the dining chair again. "Laura has her own agenda. She wants her husband appointed CEO and to pave the way for her son."

"He's fourteen," Charmaine said with a laugh.

"My sister may look like a lightweight, but she's a planner. She and Evelyn have more in common than either realize," Nick murmured. Then he shook off a thoughtful pause to glance at Charmaine again. "My nephew is a genius, and not just because his parents think so. Ryan could finish high school by age sixteen, have an MBA by the time most kids are seniors in college."

"And your mother would approve?"

"She might, but mother is also a traditionalist. I'm the eldest male, and I have a son. So..." Nick waved a hand. "You're the psychic. You tell me."

"If you don't screw up too bad, and your son shows some level of competence, Mrs. Villiers will follow tradition. Does she have that kind of power?" Charmaine didn't have to pretend interest in the inner workings of the old money families.

"Not alone, but my aunts and uncles back her. We're still a family-controlled corporation."

"So, now you're going to tell me how I fit into your scheme, and how it relates to my investigation. I can't wait. More wine, please." Charmaine winked at him.

Nick grinned, signaled to Doug and ordered. The waiter complied in seconds. Once he left, Nick allowed Charmaine another sip. "My needs are simple. Evelyn and Laura have their own ambitions.

I need enough information to keep both in check, but I'm not looking for an all-out family war. You're checking up on all of us anyway."

"Of course," Charmaine agreed, fascinated with his line of reasoning.

"My goal is to keep the balance. I'll allow Robert to remain COO since he's good for everyone's bottom line. Ryan would make a fine COO as well when the time comes. In ten or twelve years I think. Laura gets what she wants, which is to keep Evelyn from getting what she wants at all cost. The family fortune won't just be secure, but will grow." Nick reached beneath the table with his left hand and rubbed Charmaine's thigh. "Everybody gets enough to keep them quiet, if not happy."

Charmaine moved her leg until it rested against one of his. "What about the investigation?"

Nick looked at her for a long moment. He blinked a few times as though trying to regain his equilibrium. "Um, get rid of the ghosts and Mother will be happy. She'll even forget about a few missing knick-knacks."

"Antiques worth thousands are hardly 'knick-knacks'. I think you underestimate your mama." Charmaine slid her hand up his thigh. The heat from his skin came through the silk and wool blend slacks. When Nick squirmed, she claimed victory.

His mind opened up. The familiar clammy feel of larcenous intent washed over her senses. Nick had his own agenda, including putting Mrs. Villiers out to pasture. He wanted control of the family wealth. The waiter came back with the check and Charmaine's dessert, breaking the spell. She removed her hand. Nick grunted as if she'd slapped him; and in a way, she had. Charmaine wore a sweet smile as he rushed through paying the bill. Moments later she followed his metallic blue BMW sedan to his uptown townhouse. The development was one of two dozen valuable company owned properties. Nick lived in a spacious unit inside the gated complex. Not that Charmaine had time to admire the luxe design or décor. For the next four hours, she continued her research. The interview moved from lush carpeting on his living room floor, to the expensive sofa and finally to his master suite upstairs. Charmaine so enjoyed this part of being a private detective. Nick shouted approval of her method of information gathering more than a few times.

6.
Twisted Turns

Charmaine needed to rest and recover because investigating was hard work, especially when it came to Nick Villiers. They'd had a second "meeting" Saturday night. Interviewing Nick had taken a lot out of her. She decided to stay home from church Sunday. Not so much from guilt. Okay, she had to be honest. Taking literal pleasure in her work on this case had her feeling less than worthy. No doubt the pastor would aim a well-timed sermon on lust at her. At least, Charmaine feared so. Why take the chance? She chose to sleep late, have a private conversation with God, and make a visit to City Park. The October day had warmed up into the low seventies.

Dressed in a soft knit exercise suit with matching athletic shoes, Charmaine had a run. When she rounded a corner, Jessi and Diamond came into view. Diamond pushed little Indyah in a stroller.

The toddler wore a pink and purple mini-jogging suit with a princess on her cute pink shoes.

"You're consistent," Diamond called out. "Jessi said you'd be here instead of church. Your meeting with Nicholas Villiers must have been something else."

"Yeah, sis. I skipped Sunday school a lot, but even I know hiding out in a garden doesn't work. Eve tried it." Jessi raised an arched eyebrow at her. She was dressed in faux leather chocolate brown leggings and comfortable flat suede calf-high boots. Her oversized sweater still managed to hug her curves.

Diamond wore a more subdued outfit of jeans and a jacket, to fit her young mother mode. "Leave her alone, Jess. Like we can talk."

"Hey, I'm tryin' to save her from hypocrisy. Doesn't your God hate lukewarm Christians?" Jessi turned to Charmaine again.

"Why y'all stalking me today? Yanking me out of my serene moment." Charmaine ran in place for several minutes while they watched. Then she hopped onto the grass and performed cool down stretches.

Jessi grinned, making it plain she wouldn't be deterred from teasing Charmaine. "Keeping in shape for more interviews. Great idea."

"Okay, Jessi. I'm over letting you push my buttons. In fact, I've ditched them all, so don't bother looking for new ones." Charmaine flashed a nasty smile at her sister.

"Fun while it lasted." Jessi affected a fake expression of disappointment. "Guess I'll have to find another way of getting on your nerves."

"Girl." Charmaine rolled her eyes. She finished up her stretches.

"We came looking for you to talk about the Villiers case," Diamond said. She struggled to get Indyah settled. The toddler made it clear she wanted out of the stroller with loud yelps. With a sigh, Diamond gave in. She unhooked the belt around the baby's tummy. Indyah gleefully scrambled free. "We have results from our own research."

"And that's a reason to disturb my day off?" Charmaine replied. She gave them both a frown of irritation.

"I have an eight o'clock class tomorrow and then work until almost six. I won't have time to talk." Diamond kept an eye on Indyah, who marched around on the grass.

"Same for me; Monday I have three back-to-back classes, then a lab for my anthropology class. We're looking at artifacts excavated from Marksville and Bayou Jasmine. We both have full days ahead until

Wednesday. Figured we might want to share info while Nick's interview is still fresh in your mind." Jessi stood, legs apart and both hands in her sweater pockets.

"Yeah, fresh," Diamond echoed. Her eyes sparkled with interest.

"In other words, you want dirty details," Charmaine retorted. She ignored them and followed Indyah.

The toddler led them across the lovely gardens toward one of the park's play areas. The adults sat on a bench with a view of the slides and swings. Indyah went straight for her favorite first. She scrambled through pint-sized bright colored tunnels with a group of squealing kids.

"Gorgeous day." Charmaine squinted up at the cloudless blue sky. Sunshine painted the scene a cheerful yellow tinge. "Do we have to talk about backstabbing rich folks and murder?"

"Yeah, we kinda do. Mrs. Villiers will probably get impatient soon. She's not the only one. I'm getting sick of those people." Jessi stretched out her legs. "Let's clean out her ghost vermin and keep it moving."

"We need answers about the missing family loot, too. She may not call the police, but she at least wants to know. I figure so she can go after them herself," Charmaine said.

"What do you think she'd do?" Diamond watched Indyah as she talked.

"Her family would be easy. She can threaten to cut them out of the business, tighten the flow of money into their bank accounts. Dealing with Yolanda is more complicated. She's got the goods on family secrets, and less to lose," Charmaine replied.

"Look, I don't care what she does. I'm not messing with these people forever because you have two new play things." Jessi waved a hand to chase away a moth fluttering around her head. "Damn bugs. Let's get to business so I can leave. The game starts at two. I don't have all my snacks lined up."

"We're having a football party. The Saints gonna beat Tampa Bay like Luke Cage beat up gangstas." Diamond slapped a fist into her open palm.

"You wish. Y'all never gonna give up on them getting to another Super Bowl, huh?" Charmaine laughed.

"True Who Dats forever," Diamond yelled. She giggled as a group of guys close by answered with hoops.

"Whatever," Charmaine said. Though not a sports fan, she wanted the New Orleans Saints to win. She just wasn't interested enough to try to understand football, or watch. "What is this vital information that led you to disturb my day of rest?"

Gaze still on Indyah, Diamond nodded. "Okay, so Bobby says Nick has two ex-wives and three kids. Two girls with the first wife, and a son with the second one. First wife didn't produce a boy, so his mama and daddy weren't too thrilled. They just didn't get along. Anyway, two affairs later, divorce. Second lasts about three years before she'd had enough. Then I hit the jackpot. Bobby dated wife number two for almost a year."

"This is where it gets good," Jessi put in.

"Anyway, she basically stalked Nicholas for a few months after they separated. Bitter girl. She says her former father-in-law offered her lots of rewards to sex him up. She thinks the first wife agreed to it, but mostly to get back at Nick." Diamond wrinkled up her nose. "Ewww."

"Amen," Jessi said with a scowl.

"Okay, it's confirmed. They're effed up. No shock." Charmaine shrugged.

"There were whispers that the father didn't die of completely natural causes back in 1998. Some say he was helped along. Two superstitious ex-staff say a ghost scared him to death. So far, that's all Bobby told me. He had to rush off to a conference in Amsterdam, so you'll have to wait another two weeks if you have follow-up questions." Diamond waved to Indyah, who was too absorbed in playing to notice.

"The death certificate says he died of natural causes. I can't see a doctor covering up murder, not even for a big bucks family," Charmaine replied with a frown.

"Yeah, anyway, Bobby says that Nick took his father's death especially hard, which was surprising. They fought a lot," Diamond said.

"Poor guy. Losing a parent is hard," Charmaine murmured.

Let's not skip over the fact that he's a suspect in both the thefts and maybe his daddy's murder." Jessi gave Charmaine a side-eye glance.

"He's not a killer, Jess. Sure, he's the typical privileged rich white boy. But he's more into partying than coming up with schemes. And before you mention him and Laura, she's the one with big plans. Nick wants everyone to get their fair share." Charmaine warmed at the memory of his long fingers stroking her inner thigh.

"I thought you said she was all into that Kadeem dude," Diamond whispered as an aside to Jessi.

"I hear you," Charmaine retorted. "I don't get the feeling Kadeem is a killer either, but climbing out of the ghetto can make a people ruthless."

"Um, you do know rich people have murdered for money, too, right?" Jessi sighed. "See, that's why I prefer working the game. No getting all in the feels just 'cause some guy strokes you right. Even when I'm dating, I keep my head straight. As Artie says, every human interaction involves some kind of exchange. Sometimes it's a fair exchange, sometimes not. I like to be in control to make sure I get the fair kind."

"So we come out on top," Diamond added. She giggled as she and Jessi shared a fist bump.

"I'm not getting in 'my feels' about Nick Villiers as you put it. I did get into his mind. He's less of a schemer than Kadeem." Charmaine thought back to the slender brown sugar of a man. "But even Kadeem didn't come off as brutal."

"Not while y'all were burning up his sheets, of course not. Hey, wait a minute. You can't be thinking of keeping them both." Jessi grabbed Charmaine by the shoulder. "Oh hell no, Diamond. She wants them both."

"My sister from another mother. All hail the queen." Diamond executed a dramatic bow to Charmaine.

"Girl, what is Scotty gonna say?" Jessi blurted out.

Charmaine turned to her sister with a scowl. "Excuse me? Scotty is not my daddy. I don't require his approval."

Jessi raised both eyebrows at her. "Uh-huh."

"You go to him to get advice on your lifestyle choices? No." Charmaine answered her own question while Jessi's reply was still forming. "Besides, I thought you wanted him to be my man before."

"I was just trying to help y'all make up your minds. Like, be special friends who bang once in a while. Y'all too wound tight." Jessi sighed when Charmaine glared at her. "Look, all I'm saying is don't get sentimental. I know you want the true love thing."

"Girl, please. I'm not trying to live a romance novel life. Nick hasn't messed up my critical thinking when it comes to this case," Charmaine said and regretted her choice of words.

"Uh-oh, she likes him, Jess. Trouble." Diamond exchanged a glance with Jessi.

Charmaine looked from her to Jessi and back. "Don't try it."

"Try what?" Jessi blinked at her.

"Analyzing me based on our childhood. Besides, a string of therapist did a better job. I like connecting with men during sex. Sue me for having emotions, and not using my body for commercial purposes." Charmaine stood and walked away. She stared at the children playing for a few moments. "And no, I'm not longing to have a baby either."

Jessi rose to stand next to her. "Now that we've fixed your life, you won't have to call on Iyanla."

Charmaine looked at Jessi for a few moments, then burst out laughing. "Thank God. I can't be having a meltdown on television."

"Or telling all my business, too. I'd apply an ass-whipping you'd never get over," Jessi joked and laughed with her. "What's next?"

"We should—" Charmaine stopped when Diamond gasped and cut in.

"Shit." Diamond jumped to her feet.

Charmaine and Jessi followed her insistent head jerking in the direction she wanted them to look. Detective Harrison of the New Orleans Police Department stood on part of the paved path for a few moments. Dressed casually in a brown long-sleeved shirt, jacket, and jeans, he could have been simply out for a pleasant walk. He scanned the park from behind sunglasses, then his gaze settled on them.

"I hope Harrison is here for the fresh air." Charmaine frowned.

Her hope faded fast when a female uniformed officer joined him seconds later. The woman had almond brown skin with hair dyed to match pulled back into a neat bun. She wore her duty belt low to accommodate a growing spare tire.

"Go over there with Indyah, Dee. Y'all casually walk the hell on outta here," Jessi said low, though at that distance Harrison couldn't have heard her.

"Yeah. Trouble." Diamond's breathing sped up.

"You're psychic now, Diamond? Cops don't automatically equal a problem," Charmaine replied, forcing a note of optimism into her voice.

"Black folks don't need super powers to know the police equals bad shit 'bout to go down." Diamond walked away, her strides increasing in speed the farther away she got.

"Give me one example of the police showing up to give happy news," Jessi muttered. She took out her phone, turned her back, and tapped the screen fast.

"Texting for a lawyer is a bit premature, little sis." Charmaine watched the officers. "Wonder what they're waiting for?"

"A warrant maybe." Jessi didn't look up from her phone. "My girl Cam gave me this police scanner app. She created it."

"See our names?" Charmaine didn't get any kind of broadcast from the two officers, but that wasn't definitive. Her telepathy didn't turn on at the push of a button like a radio.

"Nope, but the cops aren't generally so stupid. Would be a big help if more of them were." Jessi slipped the phone back into her pocket. Then she turned to face the now approaching officers of the law. "Get ready."

"Stay ready." Charmaine smiled at them and waved as if she hadn't a care in the world. "Nice to see you, Det. Harrison."

"Okay, Ms. Joliet. You start off lying to me. Not good," Det. Harrison called back, his tone good-natured. He stopped a few feet away from them. "Hi Jessi."

"Hey." Jessi have a curt nod of acknowledgment to the officer with him.

"I see you're enjoying this lovely day with a friend. I won't tell Mrs. Harrison," Charmaine stage-whispered. The female cop gave a short hissing laugh empty of humor, but said nothing.

"Official business, ladies," Harrison said. "Y'all working for a Mrs. Marguerite Villiers, unreported thefts of antiques. Should be a police matter."

"I don't believe it's a crime though. A private citizen can choose to not call the police when their own property goes missing," Charmaine replied.

"Yeah, she decided to call us in to get real results," Jessi added with a smirk. "See me? I tell the truth. I thought they'd fired your ass, Officer Armstead."

Charmaine's skin prickled at the look of animosity the two women exchanged. She was missing a serious backstory between them. Harrison glanced at the officer, his thick dark eyebrows pulled together over the sunglasses.

"Let's keep things civil." Harrison spoke as much to his colleague as to Jessi.

"No worries." Officer Armstead smiled as she squinted into the sunshine. "Where'd your little pal Diamond run off to? Maybe I could talk to her while y'all chat."

Jessi made an exaggerated show of looking around. "Who? All I see are perfect strangers."

Det. Harrison held up a palm when Armstead opened her mouth to reply. "We came here to talk to them. It's good."

"Yeah, okay. You're familiar with these two. Got it." Armstead looked off across the park.

Harrison gave Armstead a warning scowl, but it was wasted. The officer seemed anything but intimidated. His jaw muscles jumped. Charmaine and Jessi looked at each other but made no comment. Their silent agreement was to exploit the seeming tension between them.

"So now y'all agree on how to proceed, we can go on with our lives. Tell us why you're here." Charmaine crossed her arms to appear defensive. She was willing to let them think they'd unsettled her already.

"Thought you could read minds." Armstead barked a short laugh.

"You know what—" Jessi stabbed a forefinger at the cop as she took a step forward.

Harrison moved to block her. "Back up."

Jessi craned her neck to glare at Armstead past his bulky frame. "Uh-huh."

Harrison turned to the officer. "Come to think of it, let me handle this part. You go check in to see if there have been any other developments."

"Yeah." Armstead gave Jessi a look that signaled they still had business before she strode off.

"You need a shorter leash on her," Jessi muttered. She continued on with more colorful suggestions with what Officer Armstead could go do to herself and where she could go.

Charmaine waved at Jessi to be quiet. "And the reason you tracked us down is..."

"You were with Nicholas Villiers this weekend. What time did you leave his place Saturday?" Det. Harrison said.

His question got Jessi to stop mid-rant. "See, you need to do your homework. She met with the guy Friday."

"What's happened to him?" Charmaine felt a chill because she already read it wasn't good.

"I need to know what time you left him and his state of mind, like if he seemed worried or upset." Harrison took out a paper notepad, pen poised above it.

"He was just fine. Wha—"

"Why did you meet with him?" Harrison glanced up at Charmaine.

"First you tell us why you're asking. Then we decide if we're answering." Jessi shot Charmaine a warning look.

"We're working for his mother," Charmaine blurted out. "Is Nick okay?"

"You saw him two nights in a row. At his place. That's some dedication," Harrison drawled.

"Now we're at the part where Charmaine and me walk away. We don't have to discuss our case with you unless it's connected to a serious crime." Jessi pulled Charmaine by the arm. "C'mon. A mocha latte would go down real good right about now."

"Nicholas Villiers, aka Nick to you, was found dead last night. Murder serious enough for ya?" Harrison shot back.

"No, there's some mistake." Charmaine stumbled as she pulled away from Jessi. "I was with him last night until ten o'clock, or eleven."

"Exactly, which is why I'm here. We found your business card and a brochure in his home office. You're on the security video which shows you entering his townhouse both nights. The footage that shows when you left Saturday is missing. You got an explanation?" Harrison took off his sunglasses to stare at Charmaine.

"I don't understand." Charmaine rubbed her forehead.

"You went in Friday, all friendly and touchy-feely. Left Saturday at one in the morning. Got back to his house Saturday afternoon at four-thirty. The security camera strangely stopped working at ten o'clock that night. We know because the fancy system has a separate clock that shows when video stops. The alarm didn't signal Crown Protection there was a problem." Harrison drilled each point home while watching Charmaine's every move.

"He... I went home. Nick called to tell me I'd left my work cell phone. Must have fallen out of my jacket or purse." Charmaine felt as though the ground had shifted beneath her feet. "I need to sit down."

"Take it easy." Jessi glared at Harrison and then led Charmaine to the nearest park bench. Harrison followed them.

"You have two cell phones, huh?" Harrison tucked his sunglasses into one pocket and the notepad with pen in another.

"One for work, the other for personal use. The work number is for our private investigation agency, and my colleagues at the clinic where I work part-time."

"Charmaine, stop answering his questions. You can chat with a lawyer from now on," Jessi said.

"Yeah, you two get into enough trouble that you have one on speed dial," Harrison said, his tone dry. He glanced over his shoulder. "Look, we don't have any reason to arrest you as a suspect."

"Damn right you don't." Jessi placed a protected hand on Charmaine's shoulder. "You've upset my sister enough. Go away."

"I'm not the enemy here, okay? You're connected to the victim. Plus, you may have been the last person to see him alive, other than the killer that is. One way or the other, you're gonna be questioned. Y'all haven't made friends with certain members of the NOPD." Harrison jerked a thumb in the direction Armstead had gone. "One example."

"She's an asshole," Jessi replied by way of explanation.

"An asshole with a badge, a gun, and a baton who will happily cuff you in connection to this case. My boss—"

"Another asshole," Jessi said.

"Your mouth and shitty attitude will make things worse," Harrison hissed. "Murphy would love to take the path of least resistance. As would Sanchez in the DA's office."

"He's right. Now's not the time to be trippin'. Harrison has helped us before," Charmaine said, cutting off Jessi's heated protest.

"Which has also been noticed by more than a few. I'm not sticking my neck out any more for you two. Y'all always land smack in the middle of freaky cases where somebody ends up bloody." Harrison combed long fingers through his short-cut afro. "But you've also helped me a couple of times."

"Damn right," Jessi replied.

"A debt that has been paid a few times when I kept your smartass outta lock up." Harrison pointed at her. "So don't get funny with me."

Charmaine huffed out a cleansing breath and then looked up at him. "What do you want to know?"

"What the hell, Charmaine?" Jessi shook her by one shoulder.

"He's trying to talk to us before Murphy and the rest show up. Then he'll have to watch himself." Charmaine looked at her.

After a few moments, Jessi nodded reluctant agreement. Though she still wore a sullen frown. "Better not be a trap is all I'm sayin'."

"We don't have much time. His mother has been notified, and they should be arranging for her or another family member to identify the body once he's moved. Word is already out you're involved some kinda way. Murphy or his second in command could show up any second." Harrison looked around again as if expecting to see his grim-faced commander.

"Okay."

Charmaine shuddered at his reference to Nick as "the body". Mere hours ago she'd been wrapped around a warm, breathing passionate man. She hated to think of him sprawled out cold, cops stepping around him like he was an object.

"You were on a case for his mother, you said." Harrison gestured for her to go on.

"She wants us to get rid of ghosts scaring the tourists at their bed and breakfast. And some of their antiques have gone missing." Charmaine breathed deeply to steady her nerves. She struggled not to get a mental picture of Nick with a bullet hole in him.

"You met with him outside of what we could consider normal business hours, at his house, twice." Harrison cocked his head to one side.

"We don't work normal business hours. Goblins don't show up promptly at nine each morning, and knock off at five in the afternoon," Jessi quipped. "Get to your point."

Harrison transferred his sharp gaze to her. "Hey, best believe Murphy will ask why you were at the son's house when the case is centered at Magnolia Grove. Not to mention he's not your client."

"Nick... Nicholas Villiers and I had dinner. We spent time together, not all of it talking about his mother's case." Charmaine felt foolish sounding so prissy.

"Which isn't against the law. I'd also like to point out it doesn't violate any licensing regs either," Jessi added.

"No, but some will say it gives her motive," Harrison replied. He turned to Charmaine.

"Shit." Charmaine bit her lower lip.

"Which is what will hit the fan when Murphy finds out. How much you wanna bet the victim's rich relatives will use muscle to get the case solved?" Harrison pointed to Charmaine. "And puts you in the bullseye."

Jessi spun to face him. "Nah, son. We won't lay down for a setup."

"Then you better get ready. Have no doubt the train has already left the station," Harrison snarled. "You got bigger problems than me, girl."

"We gonna figure out who killed him. Believe it," Jessi replied.

Harrison, a deep frown twisting his face, opened his mouth to reply. Instead, his cell phone insisted he answer it. He raised a forefinger at them to signal their conversation wasn't over and hissed, "Stay put."

Charmaine and Jessi watched him walk away as he talked into the phone. His voice started out low, rumbling like a storm of misfortune headed their way. Jessi paced a few seconds before she spoke.

"This is not good." Jessi shook her head hard enough to make her braids bounce.

"I'm sure Nick would agree," Charmaine replied with a deep sigh.

"Please don't tell me you got hooked on White Chocolate," Jessi retorted.

"It's just... I liked him, and now he's... gone." Charmaine waved her hands, despair pressing in on her. "I hate it when people I know become a statistic."

Jessi's expression softened. "Yeah."

"What the fu..." Harrison's voice carried over the voice of kids having fun nearby. Then he lowered his voice again. Moments later he marched back to them.

Charmaine stood beside Jessi as they waited for him. "Something else has happened. A complication of some kind."

"Don't try that mind freak crap on me. I'm not in the damn mood," Harrison snarled. "What the hell you two playin' at? And no smartass answers or I'll lock you up right now."

"For real though, we got no clue what you're talking about." Jessi glanced at Charmaine.

"I'm not... I can't..." Charmaine stammered as her voice seemed to fail her. She got the mayhem in his head, a riot of anger mixed with questions. Her emotional state about Nick made getting a clear "read" next to impossible.

Harrison huffed at the sisters as if they were at fault for all his troubles. "The dead guy is not Nicholas Villiers."

****

Monday morning continued the ball of confusion that began on Sunday. Never a good start to a week. Charmaine sat across from Mrs. Villiers. She'd had Yolanda drive her 2017 Lexus sedan to Charmaine's house. The fabulous rich brown luxury car looked odd next to Charmaine's blue Chevy Cruze. The color was called Autumn Shimmer to be precise. Charmaine knew because she spent time online staring at the Lexus options with great longing.

The housekeeper glanced around Charmaine's home office with a critical eye. Yolanda looked like she might run her finger over a bookshelf looking for dust any minute. Instead, she tucked her purse under one arm and stood next to the door. Charmaine offered coffee and left to get it when Mrs. Villiers accepted. Fortunately, she had a fresh pot. Not that she needed to hurry because she suspected they'd search her office. Not really. Charmaine moved fast anyway. Better safe rather than sorry.

"Here we go."

Charmaine rolled her grandmother's favorite serving cart, circa the 1950s, into the office. A carafe held dark roast coffee. Though she half expected Yolanda to insist on serving, the older woman took a seat in the chair next to her employer. Charmaine filled three cups. She studied the two women. Mrs. Villiers poured cream and six teaspoons of sugar into her cup. Yolanda took hers black. Once she settled in her office chair behind the desk and took a sip, Charmaine put her cup down.

"Some weekend, huh?" Charmaine looked at Yolanda, then at Mrs. Villiers.

"Nicholas had nothing to do with that... person they found in his townhouse. My goodness. My son lives in one of the most exclusive neighborhoods in Orleans Parish." Mrs. Villiers blinking at Charmaine, as if a fancy address was evidence of innocence. "Clearly the man tried to break in and somehow was hurt."

"Mrs. Villiers..." Charmaine's words trailed off. She shook her head, at a loss for how to reply to her outlandish theory.

"Nick keeps a gun. I say the guy tried a home invasion and got a bullet," Yolanda, wiser to the ways of the street, took over. "The guy has a bad rap sheet. The only reason they didn't tell Mrs. Vee about his juvie record is 'cause it's sealed."

"Okay," Charmaine replied. "So, the police identified the victim?"

She didn't say anything more for a few seconds. Yolanda gazed back at her, a stony expression on her brown face. Mrs. Villiers slurped more coffee. Anxiety apparently made the socialite's elegant manners vanish.

"No, but who else could it be? You got something on your mind, just say it," Yolanda snapped.

"I'll ask the obvious question. If that's what happened, a burglary or home invasion gone wrong, why didn't he call the police? Where is Nick?" Charmaine gazed from one to the other of them.

"When the hell does a burglary or home invasion go right? Makes no sense to say 'gone wrong'," Yolanda barked instead.

"It sure as shit went wrong for the dead dude." Charmaine bit off more sharp language when Mrs. Villiers gasped. "Pardon the strong language, ma'am. But I mean, let's get real."

"We need you and your sister to find out what happened. You know about these things, drug dealers and gangs." Mrs. Villiers glanced at Yolanda and back to Charmaine.

"Wait. Hold up a minute. I don't know what you think you know about Jessi and me, but we're not hood criminals." Charmaine stood to emphasize her annoyance. "So, don't be coming to my house like we're going to be your ghetto version of Charlie's Angels."

"No, no. I didn't mean to imply," Mrs. Villiers stammered. Coffee sloshed onto her designer slacks as her hand shook. She didn't notice. Instead, she continued to babble.

Yolanda cut off her boss's protests. "You wanted real, so here we go. Your sister has been arrested for drugs and prostitution. You both got involved in not one, not two, but a string of different murders."

"Those were cases we investigated and—"

The name Keisha Front ring a bell? Yeah, I see it does. She says you and baby girl know about a guy that disappeared long ago. Y'all was just teenagers." Yolanda held her cup of coffee, still in a calm pose. She looked like she was engaging in simple chit-chat between ladies.

Charmaine fidgeted with items on her desk. She cast a quick side glance at Mrs. Villiers, and then back at Yolanda. "Kadeem been doing his homework for you, I see."

"Now we understand each other, you can take a seat again." Yolanda drained the last of the coffee, head back as her throat worked. She took the time to grab a napkin from the serving cart and dab her lips. A bit of raisin colored lipstick stained the paper she dropped back onto the tray.

"What does our past have to do with the hot spot Nick is in?" Charmaine sat on the edge of the chair.

"Just getting you straight about catching an attitude with us. We both know you're familiar with the streets, so don't play innocent. Mrs. Vee has hired a lawyer for Nicholas." Yolanda stopped and looked to her employer.

"Yes, um, he's the best attorney in Louisiana. Of course, my son will cooperate with the police." Mrs. Villiers nodded and smiled. "Naturally you'll be paid well."

"Your high-powered lawyer probably has his own investigator. Why would he..." Charmaine frowned the question at Mrs. Villiers.

Mrs. Villiers seemed to have recovered her nerves. She put the still half full cup of coffee on the edge of Charmaine's desk. "Nick and I insisted. Also, it seems your reputation for getting at the truth is well known in certain circles. I promise you, this is a good development for your business."

"Right, we're pulled into a murder case. The DA, NOPD, and now your fancy lawyer, are all tickled pink to have us involved. I'm tingling with excitement myself at this point." Charmaine crossed her arms tightly and glared at them.

"It is what it is, girl. Doesn't matter what you feel, y'all in this thing. No way out of it," Yolanda replied in a mild tone.

Charmaine was about to deliver a venom-laced reply, but the sound of tinkling bells stopped her. She glanced at the cell phone near her elbow. Yolanda and Mrs. Villiers both craned their necks to take a look-see. Charmaine picked it up and read, angled so they couldn't. Jessi's short text read "911".

"I have to take a call. Excuse me." Charmaine left the room, shutting the door behind her firmly. Once she was in her living room, she tapped in Jessi's number. "What's up?"

"Word on these streets is this shit is way deep. Can you talk?" Jessi said.

"Nah, they're still in my office. They want me to go see Nick," Charmaine said. "I got that much from Mrs. Villiers. Yolanda doesn't agree, but I'm not sure why. Something smells rotten about this whole thing."

"What was your first clue, sis? The pack of lies or the dead body?" Jessi said. "Hey, don't go with them alone."

"I get the feeling they'll want to leave straight from here and go to wherever Nick is." Charmaine glanced in the direction of her office.

"Screw that idea. I'm gonna skip my two classes today. Get the address and set it up for around one thirty." Jessi ended the call without waiting for Charmaine to reply.

"Damn it."

Charmaine scowled at the phone but didn't call her back. Mrs. Villiers and Yolanda looked suspiciously nonchalant when Charmaine entered her office again. They appeared not to have moved. She scanned her office. Not that there was anything for them to find. Her file cabinet was locked, and her computer password protected. She doubted the two women had hacker skills.

"Was that important?" Mrs. Villiers spoke up first.

"Another matter. I'm not agreeing to anything until I talk to Nick," Charmaine said to let them think she was playing right into their hands.

Mrs. Villiers shot Yolanda a quick side-eye. Traces of a smug smile tugged at her thin lips. "Of course. We can go now."

"No, I can't. Give me the address. I'll meet with him at two o'clock." Charmaine opened the map app on her phone.

"You won't share his location with the police?" Mrs. Villiers frowned at her.

"Hell no, she won't. Her and Jessi been in too much trouble," Yolanda replied.

"Wrong. I won't tell the police because you're my client. You're not asking me to break the law, and Nick isn't a suspect. Yet. If, and that's a big question mark... If I decide to add this to your bill, I'll want his side of the story first." Charmaine lifted her eyebrows at them. "Well?"

Mrs. Villiers pursed her lips as she glared at Charmaine for a few seconds. "63 Lakeview Dr."

Charmaine entered the address. She looked up sharply at the two older women. "Slidell. Are you freakin' kidding me?"

"Eden Isle to be precise," Mrs. Villiers replied and lifted her chin a few millimeters.

"The police will think his next stop is out of the country at this rate." Charmaine looked at Yolanda.

"Like you said, he's not a suspect. He can go anywhere he wants," Yolanda shot back.

"Hmm." Charmaine noted the fierceness in her tone. Nicholas Villiers, the last surviving male heir, had a lot of folks on his side. "Jessi and I will be there at two."

"Wait a minute." Yolanda frowned.

"You hired us as a team. Look, you paid me to get rid of ghosts and figure out where your antiques were ending up. We're fully prepared to deliver on the first job. But I'm not walking into an unknown by myself. Take it or leave it." Charmaine looked at them with an impassive face. "No refunds, by the way."

"Ain't nobody trying to set you up," Yolanda snapped before Mrs. Villiers could speak.

"Good. Now that we've established the ground rules, let me know if we should show or not." Charmaine waved her cell phone. "I can delete the address to your exclusive Eden Isle hideout and forget we ever talked."

Mrs. Villiers stood and hooked her designer handbag in the crook of her elbow. "His lawyer will be with him. He'll have the particulars."

"Are you sure this lawyer can—"

"He'll be wherever I need him to be," Mrs. Villiers replied. She gave Yolanda a sharp jerk of her head to indicate she was ready to leave.

"Be on time," Yolanda said. Charmaine gave a gruff snort as her only response. Yolanda scowled, and then followed her employer out.

Charmaine followed them down the hall to her front door. She watched as Mrs. Villiers climbed into the passenger side of the Lexus. As the car backed out, Charmaine closed the door and leaned her back against it. She didn't see the cheerful foyer or the table with her Christmas cactus in a flower pot on top. Instead, she saw the faces of the players in her own little drama.

"The smell around you folks is getting worse by the minute."

7.

Killer Good Looks?

Hours later, Jessi steered her 2014 black Jeep Renegade along Interstate 10 toward their destination in St. Tammany Parish. Traffic wasn't so bad, but an accident on the bridge section slowed them down. Charmaine tried not to stare at the expanse of Lake Ponchartrain beneath them. She'd mostly conquered her phobia about bridges, but... Which was why Jessi drove them to Eden Isle. Since they were early, by at least one hour, Charmaine didn't care. She munched on home pecan candy courtesy of Scotty. He could not only knock out killer cocktails, but he could cook. Charmaine relished the smooth treat as it melted on her tongue.

"Scotty's candy is the best in the land. Sure you don't want some?" Charmaine sighed when Jessi smacked her lips to signal annoyance. She wrapped up the unfinished pecan candy and stuck it in her purse.

"Dead guy in his house, face so messed up they can't identify him yet. What's taking so long? If it was a burglary or home invasion gone wrong, the criminal would have a record." Jessi shook her head. "I don't like it. Feels like we're being played."

mplicate my life." Harrison stabbed a forefi trap."

"Me neither, and that bothers me even more. We know you have an alibi. What I can't figure out is what kind of motive they'll claim you have. But still..." Jessi frowned, but not at the solid line of vehicles slowing them down. "They're up to some-thing."

"Yeah, well the best way to get a clue is to get up close and personal with them," Charmaine re-plied.

"I guess. I went back to Magnolia Grove for a chat with Georgina, with her mean ass self." Jessi changed lanes to avoid a second minor accident ahead of them.

Charmaine felt a brief spike of anxiety as the Jeep slowed. She ignored thoughts of cars plunging through the concrete barrier and concentrated on bad-tempered spirits instead. "And she says they're all no good and should get the eff outta her house, right?"

"Had one hell of a time getting her off that dead horse, pun intended." Jessi gave a dry laugh at her own black humor. "Anyway, she says there's something funny going on with this generation."

"As opposed to the murdering, slave-owning, land stealing previous generations. Gotcha," Charmaine retorted.

"Hey, Georgina has her faults, but so far she's been pretty upfront with me. Too bad spirits don't know everything. There are limits to what they can see, hear, and of course, do. The Third Eye Association says they're not supposed to affect living world events. But they break that rule all the time." Jessi referred to the organization of people with paranormal abilities. They maintained a large body of research, including scientific data.

"Ghost rules and regulations. Where are those written down exactly?" Charmaine shook her head.

"Very funny. Certain boundaries seem to be clear based on what we've observed." Jessi picked up her bottle of soda from the cup holder and took a swig.

"I'll tell you where to find the book ya need. The Bible. They're all evil, though maybe they don't know they're being used. I'm not clear on it all. Bishop Sykes says—"

"Hold it a damn minute. Don't quote nothing that fake preacher says to me," Jessi snapped.

"He's just saying what's in the Bible, Jessi," Charmaine protested. She twisted to face her sister, ticking fingers off on her hand. "In Matthew they're called unclean spirits. They return to the house and bring seven more with them."

"Do not turn to mediums or necromancers, do not seek them out, and so make yourselves unclean by them: I am the Lord your God. Leviticus 19:31. I guess Bishop Sykes wants to pour anointed oil all over us and drive out our demons." Jessi glanced at Charmaine and then ahead again. After a few moments of heavy silence, Jessi laughed. "Umph, I didn't have to consult a necromancer to figure it out."

"He's not so bad," Charmaine mumbled.

"Has he laid hands on you yet to drive out the demons? Because you're seeing into people's thoughts. Oh, and give me a heads up if your church members come to stomp the evil out of me."

"Don't be so dramatic. People fear what they don't understand." Charmaine looked out at the water, for once not anxious about riding over the lake.

"God made everyone and everything. Correct?" Jessi pushed on.

"Of course."

"So, God gave us paranormal abilities and made us unclean, if we follow the dogma to its logical conclusion. Why? Like most religious stuff, it doesn't make sense."

Charmaine blew out a huff. "Okay, fine. I don't know all the whys and wherefores."

"No shit," Jessi retorted.

They rode without speaking, a heavy silence between them. Jessi turned on the radio after a few minutes to fill the void. Thumping R&B music didn't lighten the mood. Charmaine felt a familiar sense of despair, like her very existence was so... wrong. They'd been called crazy by some and possessed by others. The fact that she and Jessi weren't even more messed up was a miracle. If Charmaine's paranormal ability forever separated her from a loving God, then why try being good or even nice to other people? She'd never been offered a choice to be psychic. Jessi was right about one thing. Since God created everything, then he created them. He had a reason for it.

They reached the exit just as sunshine broke through the overcast sky. The exclusive waterfront community spread out before them. Charmaine had checked the real estate listing. Anyone wanting to live in Eden Isle had to have the bucks to pay up. No surprise the Villiers owned a home there.

"Turn here." Charmaine pointed ahead.

"Yeah."

Jessi glanced at Charmaine and back at the street. Seconds later they parked in the driveway of the spacious house. The neat front yards with wide driveways lined the street. A chilly breeze ruffled the leaves of two tall palm trees planted on the manicured lawn. Charmaine stared at the sur-roundings, feeling out of place. Another familiar feeling.

"Look, hold onto your beliefs. I shouldn't keep trashing you about the whole religion thing." Jessi shrugged.

"You're asking valid questions. I get it." Char-maine unbuckled her seatbelt but didn't move to get out of the Jeep. "And I don't have answers..."

"Neither does the righteous Bishop Sykes." Jessi bit off more when Charmaine winced. Then she gave Charmaine a playful poke on the shoulder. "Hey, that Jesus guy wasn't so bad. Gotta love a dude who hung out with hookers and saw the good in them. Hope for me, right?"

Charmaine laughed, a little at first. Then more as she thought about the absurdity of their ongoing debates. She doubted if church folks at Life Abundant Full Gospel Tabernacle discussed religion with as much fervor as two confirmed sinners.

"Yeah, lucky for both of us he had a soft spot for harlots."

"And thieves, street hustlers, and loan sharks. Hell, pretty much everybody in our circle will be in the Jesus squad when he comes back." Jessi giggled with delight when Charmaine gasped for air. "Speaking of which, let's go into this den of iniquity."

"You're too much." Charmaine got out of the Jeep and slammed the door shut.

Jessi followed her out. "Damn. I don't even feel like we need to lock the car."

"Looks... perfect." Charmaine glanced around. She didn't mean it as a compliment. "So this is where the wealthy escape the dirty, loud, crazy that is New Orleans."

"Hell, I miss the city already," Jessi muttered. She marched up to the door and pressed the bell button hard.

A short Latina dressed in a blue uniform dress and white sensible rubber-soled shoes answered the door. "May I help you?"

Jessi shot a side glance at Charmaine, then looked at the housekeeper. "Yes, we're here to see..."

"Thank you, Maria. These are the guests I told you about." Nick strode across the polished hardwood floors and swept up Charmaine in a tight hug. "Thank God you're here."

A tall man with a calm, commanding presence emerged next. "Elliot Forstall, Mr. Villiers attorney."

He seemed unsure what to do or say next. Jessi and he stood watching as Nick continued to hold onto Charmaine for dear life. He rambled on about how awful a time he'd had, that he was innocent, and she had to believe him. Charmaine responded by planting a series of kisses on his cheek.

"What the actual fuck?" Jessi whispered. She turned to the lawyer as if expecting him to explain what they were seeing.

For his part, Forstall continued to blink fast and hard at the emotional reunion. Then he cleared his throat loudly. "Let's go into the living area. We have coffee made."

"Yeah, and I hope it's the Irish kind. I'm gonna need something to help unscramble my brain." Jessi followed him. When Charmaine and Nick didn't move, she turned back. "We got stuff to talk about."

"Yes, of course." Nick let go of Charmaine but grabbed her by the hand.

Charmaine blushed when Jessi raised both her eyebrows at her. "Yeah, better hash out what's going on."

Maria rolled out a cart with coffee, soft drinks, and pastries on it. Charmaine and Jessi gaped at the stunning open floor plan. Floor to ceiling windows let in a view of the water. Stairs led upstairs. The second-floor landing looked out over the downstairs. A huge swimming pool took up part of the backyard. An outdoor kitchen sat in one corner of the patio. The housekeeper made sure everyone was served before she retreated.

"This place is a big wow," Jessi blurted, ignoring the cup Maria had placed on the table before her. She stood and went to the windows. Then she turned to face them again.

"We come here when we don't feel like going all the way to Florida. Of course, it's not the same as Palm Springs," Nick said, and he waved a hand dismissing the posh surroundings.

"Naturally," Jessi shot back and sucked her teeth. She sat down again in a chair facing the sofa. "So tell us, Nick. Who's the dead guy?"

"Right to the point as always," Nick said and squeezed Charmaine's hand. He inched closer to her on the tan sofa that could fit a good ten more people.

"Before we get to that, let's set some expectations. Okay?" Forstall went on before anyone could speak up. He picked up a file on the end table at his elbow. "First, Mrs. Villiers has agreed to add some addenda to your agreement, to include investigations that will aid in her son's defense."

Jessi grabbed the file from him and flipped it open. She glanced up moments later, eyes wide. "Is this number right?"

"Yes, Mrs. Villiers is prepared to adequately compensate you for an extensive, and somewhat complicated investigation. What started out as a simple case has turned into one that is more..." Forstall spread out his hands.

"Complicated. We definitely figured that one out, Mr. Forstall." Jessi looked up from the contract again. "By the way, are you by any chance related to Grayson and Alyssa Forstall in New Orleans?"

"Cousins," Forstall clipped. "I'm aware of your reputation."

Nick looked at him with a puzzled frown. "I don't understand. You've worked with Charmaine and Jessi before, Elliot?"

"We completed an investigation for Mr. and Mrs. Charles Forstall. They had... trouble in their Garden District home."

"I didn't hear anything about it." Nick looked at Charmaine.

"We took that trip to Belize around then," Forstall said and went back to shuffling his files.

"You two travel together." Jessi cocked her head to one side.

"Elliot and I have known each other since... what? Seventh grade at Isidore Newman." Nick glanced at the lawyer. "I trust him."

"Isidore Newman School, established in 1903. Where annual tuition is the price of a car. And not a cheap car either." Jessi let out a low whistle. "Got it. We're hanging with the big dogs. Very impressed. But before we sign anything, I wanna know the name of the dead guy, why he was at your house, and how he ended up dead."

"Without a signature, we have no written contract that you'll keep our communications in strict confidence," Forstall countered, and he pointed to the contract Jessi still held.

"And as an attorney, you also know that we're bound by law as a private investigative company to keep client information zipped up," Jessi countered.

"Mrs. Villiers, yes. This agreement adds Mr. Villiers to the contract, and by extension makes you part of his legal defense team. I know you can't withhold information about criminal activity. But of course, you know we're not asking you to." Forstall held out an ink pen to Jessi.

"Do we? I can't help but notice your client is hiding out here in lovely Eden Ilse while a corpse is littering his fancy condo." Jessi looked from him to Nick and back.

"And why do you need a defense lawyer if you didn't kill the guy?" Charmaine gazed at Nick. She searched his expression for tells, any sign of the truth.

"So many questions, so little time." Jessi tapped her wristwatch. "Tick-tock. The police will be here any minute I'm betting. We sign nothing without answers."

"We don't talk without a signature. So, if you're position won't change..." Forstall shrugged. "Fine. Meeting over. We'll each take our chances with the police."

Tension stretched between them as no one spoke. Nick seemed on the verge once but stopped when the lawyer shook his head. Nick pressed his lips together. Thirty seconds into the standoff, Charmaine stood and strode across to Forstall. She grabbed the form, slashed her name on the line in question, and shoved it across the coffee table.

"There."

"Shit, Charmaine. Why in the hell?" Jessi stomped in a circle a few times. Then stopped and glared at her.

"Signing gives us a layer of protection," Charmaine replied. Then Charmaine sat next to Nick again on the sofa, her leg touching his. "Thin, but better than nothing."

"A check to cover your expenses," Forstall added and handed Charmaine a slim legal-sized envelope.

Jessi tapped a fist against one thigh as she stared at Charmaine for a few seconds. "Fine, but we're going to have a serious talk later."

Nick sighed. "Listen, I know you don't—"

"Who's the dead guy and how did he get dead in your house?" Jessi hissed at him. She transferred her intense gaze from Charmaine to Nick.

Forstall jumped in to answer while Nick's mouth still hung open. "We don't know. The police aren't releasing any information for some reason. They've put details on lockdown."

"Don't talk stupid to us," Jessi retorted. "He lives there. Doesn't matter what the cops say or not for now. Who was at your house in the last twenty-four hours? Besides my sister of course."

"It could be Tanner," Nick blurted out before his lawyer could intervene. "C'mon, Elliot. We can't ask them to help and then tie their hands by keeping quiet."

"Or lying. Not that we won't find out anyway." Jessi gave Nick and the lawyer an icy smile that vanished into a frown in seconds.

"Tanner came by to visit, er, talk about business Saturday after you left. He's a night owl, and since I was still up when he called..." Nick added with a distracted frown. "His parents moved to Panama eight years ago. They'll be devastated. I should call them..."

"You can't do that when you're not sure it's him. Unless... you are sure." Charmaine took Nick by the hand and stared into his eyes. "You should tell us what happened now, Nick."

Nick nodded. "Tanner wants, wanted, a bigger role in the company. He claimed my father had promised to make him my confidential assistant or even a second chief operating officer. But that's crazy. Neither of my parents would ever promote a non-family member that high."

"Because of tradition," Charmaine prompted when Nick fell silent for several seconds.

"Right. Either by blood or marriage, all of the big jobs stay in the family. Practical reasons, you see. Even with in-laws, their financial and family interests become tightly bound with ours. So, loyalty isn't simply based on sentimental reasons."

"Because feelings change," Jessi said. "Cold and calculated. I like it."

Charmaine squeezed his hand. "Go on."

"Tanner said Laura and her husband at first said they'd support his getting the job. But lately, they seemed to have cooled on the idea. We have a big meeting coming up, and he wanted to be on the agenda. I told him I'd get back to him."

"Playing him off, instead of telling him straight out what the real deal was gonna be," Jessi said. "He got pissed, y'all fought, and bye-bye Tanner."

"Tanner can go from zero to sixty in seconds, a real volatile type. That's another strike against him. Mother likes, liked, Tanner. But even she didn't think he could handle that kind of authority. It was late, I was tired and... I'd had a lot to drink." Nick rubbed his forehead.

"You gotta be kidding. Don't even try that 'I don't remember anything' bullshit on us." Jessi waved her arms around. "Are you hearing this? The guy seriously thinks we'll buy the old amnesia line."

"Dial it down a few notches, Ms. Joliet," Forstall said, still in calm defense attorney mode.

Charmaine ignored them both. Instead, she focused on Nick. "You used drugs. Weed? Cocaine?"

"I might have smoked with Tanner, and we had a few lorries... more whiskey. I don't know. Tanner started yelling about what we owed him. Then he tried to hug me and—"

"Lorries. You popped opioid pills. Did you know about this?" Jessi looked at Charmaine.

"Hear him out," Charmaine replied. "Go on, Nick."

"I..."

"They argued. Mr. Gladstone let himself out, and my client went to bed. Another employee, Mr. Kadeem Hardy was supposed to talk to him, reason with him. Maybe they met later. We don't know." Forstall turned to Jessi. "All we know is that Mr. Villiers didn't kill anyone."

"Damn, that was quick. You have a defense and somebody else to take the fall already. You earning that coin, son," Jessi retorted.

Charmaine stood and walked over to Jessi. She wore a frown when she faced the two men again. "That doesn't explain why and how he got back into your house though."

"Yeah, there's a whole lot missing. Why would Kadeem be at your place on a Saturday night? For that matter, doesn't make sense that Tanner would show up either. Unless he was stalking you, and Kadeem was following him around." Jessi glanced at Charmaine.

"Of course I knew how Tanner had a thing for me, but I didn't feel the same. I don't know why Kadeem was there," Nick said.

"Wait a minute. Are you saying now you remember Kadeem showing up?" Charmaine raised both eyebrows at him.

"We partied together, so yeah. It wouldn't have been unusual for him to drop by. The doorbell did ring." Nick's voice trailed off and he rubbed his forehead harder. "I just don't know."

"Because you were high out of your mind. Too, too convenient." Jessi turned to Forstall. "All of this will be settled when the security video is examined."

"Except the video stopped working," Forstall replied. Then he pressed his lips together.

"You said the police haven't released any details. How do you know about the security camera going offline?" Charmaine said.

"Yeah. Good question." Jessi crossed her arms.

"The building manager called Nick. The police had him access the surveillance equipment. The computer and monitors are in a secured area," Forstall replied without missing a beat.

"Right." Jessi drew the word out as she studied him.

"Anyway, we don't know for sure who they found. Maybe it was Kadeem. You said Tanner was unstable," Charmaine said.

"He could become physical, too." Nick stood and walked over to Charmaine. "I should have been more understanding with him. Got him help. He'd been in therapy when we were kids."

"Instead you helped him with booze and drugs. Nice." Jessi rolled her eyes.

"I've made mistakes, but..."

"My client has a prescription for the pills, and drinking is legal. Possession for the amount of marijuana he had is a misdemeanor," Forstall put in.

"All neat and tidy. Smooth. Real smooth." Jessi looked at Charmaine.

"You seem to have lined up all your legal ducks. Why do you need us?" Charmaine looked from Nick, who seemed confused at best, to the lawyer.

"The burning question on the tip of my tongue," Jessi added.

"You have a stake in assisting us sort through what really happened. The police came to you for answers. Or did I get the wrong information?" Forstall gazed from Jessi to Charmaine and back again.

"In other words, you didn't want us pulled in. But Mrs. Villiers trusts us because we're ghost chasers." Jessi's lip curled with distaste as she looked at him.

"And I wanted you." Nick stood and crossed to Charmaine. He grabbed both her hands in his larger ones. "You know me, us. I wouldn't kill anyone. Definitely not Tanner. I considered him a friend."

Jessi looked at them for a few seconds. "Yeah, well that's all sweet and stuff, but we're going to follow the facts."

Charmaine pulled free of his hold. "What Jessi said. We're not going to lie or hold back if the police question us."

"And if they don't?" Nick asked.

"Humph. Trust me. The cops will be on our doorstep until they figure out who was killed and why. We've got history," Jessi shot back.

"We'll deal with NOPD, make it clear that you weren't with Mr. Villiers during the time in question. Now that you've signed." Forstall wore a faint smile.

Jessi let out a snort of disgust. "So, you were prepared to offer us up if we hadn't."

"No, we wouldn't have," Nick said and looked at the lawyer. "Putting targets on your back was never part of the plan. Believe me."

"Sure I do." Jessi snorted to punctuate her feeling on the subject

"We need to take care of a few things today, like contacting Det. Harrison. I'll be in touch," Forstall replied.

"You don't need us to hold Nick's hand then." Jessi glanced sideways at Charmaine. "Let's get out of here. My eyes are starting to water from the stink."

"Charmaine..." Nick started. Then he stopped when she gazed back at him without expression. "Do what you have to do."

"Oh, we will. Best believe we will," Jessi answered.

****

By eight o'clock that night, Charmaine's mind had untwisted somewhat. A Sazerac and the congenial vibe at Scotty's club helped. The place was typically closed on Mondays, but Scotty let in a few of his close friends. Mostly it was self-serve those days, while Scotty did paperwork.

Charmaine nursed her second drink while the soft buzz of muted conversations floated around her. Four of Scotty's old Army buddies hung out. One woman, a staff sergeant still on active duty, kept telling funny stories about the soldiers in her squad. Their laughter tried to chip through Charmaine's dark mood. Yet her inner cynic, born from street life and family chaos, returned to remind her not to get played. Nick had to be lying. So she sat mentally sketching out the who, what, why, and how of the Villiers family.

"Bad shit going down." Scotty dropped into the seat facing her on the other side of her booth.

"Um." Charmaine avoided returning his gaze.

"Saw it on the news. Didn't say much. You figure this Kadeem dude did it?"

When she didn't answer, Scotty tapped the rim of Charmaine's empty glass. When she nodded, he got up and took it to the bar. Moments later, he returned with another Sazerac. Scotty sat down, pushed the glass across the table, and waited.

"Would help if we could find him." Charmaine took a sip. The subtle taste of Anise tickled her tongue. She looked at Scotty.

"I already made a couple of calls. You know his family are low key gangsters?" Scotty sat against the bench back.

"Yeah. Wait, explain what you mean."

"So back in the sixties, his daddy and uncles decided to be their own crime syndicate. The shoot 'em bang-bang stuff wasn't profitable. So they've been in stuff like moving stolen goods since then. They were some of the first to get into identity theft in the seventies. Real pioneers." Scotty smiled.

"Wonderful. Something to bring up during Black History Month," Charmaine wisecracked and rolled her eyes. "So, missing antiques would be right up their alley?"

"They mostly steal electronics, designer clothes, and appliances. For a long time, they specialized in burglarizing construction sites. They hijack delivery trucks. Mostly nobody gets hurt. In the eighties, some of the younger members got into dealing. Broke up the family a bit. Kadeem's grandfather and uncles split on the opposing side. Yolanda married a drug dealer and sided with the drug trade branch of the family for years. He was shot up back in 1989. Then she hooked up with another dealer, had three kids for him to add to the two she already had."

Scotty waved to two of his friends. He excused himself to exchange goodbyes before they left. Another man came in after ringing the bell. He and Scotty shared a brother-man embrace. Once the newcomer got settled, Scotty returned with a mug of ginger ale.

"All interesting history, but..." Charmaine sat forward and lowered her voice. "Does it help us find Kadeem?"

"We need to figure out who he'd run to in times of trouble. Problem is, it's a big family. But they tend to skip town when things heat up. To Houston or Oakland, California. Got extended relatives both places." Scotty rubbed his jaw. "My sources say Cali. They get far away when it's bad."

Charmaine grunted and took a swig from her tumbler. "Murder is bad alright."

"Thing is, they tend to shy away from violence to settle disagreements or scores. Only as a last resort. Not because they're shy about popping off a few rounds, mind you, just not their style." Scotty gulped down half his mug of ginger ale.

"You drink that stuff like it's got a kick," Charmaine teased.

Scotty tapped a forefinger to his temple. "Gotta keep a clear head. Start sampling the goods, and next thing you know, you're out on the street begging for handouts instead of being in charge."

"Words of wisdom, but since I'm not the boss..." Charmaine drained the last of her Sazerac and grinned at him.

Scotty shook his head as he laughed at her. "Point I'm making is, the family that fought against getting into the drug game said as much. They turned out to be right. Long string of folks ended up getting hooked."

"I don't even have to guess. Things went downhill," Charmaine replied.

"Six snitched on their kin in exchange for plea deals. Stole from 'em, too. A couple ended up dead. Still unsolved. No more happy family cookouts," Scotty said in a dry tone.

"Tragic." Charmaine snorted.

"Yeah. Anyway, I had to sort through who was who to figure out where Kadeem would run. They generally stick to family, even with all the drama. But I figure he's with his cousin Lateef in Palo Alto. Get this, the guy works in the tech industry. Cleaned up after a few arrests as a juvenile," Scotty said.

"Maybe he's helping with the identity theft side of the family business?"

"If he does, he keeps it well hidden. He and Kadeem have been close. Maybe because Kadeem is semi-straight, a job with the Villiers Company and all." Scotty shrugged.

Charmaine pushed aside the empty glass and waved away Scotty's offer to refill it. "Yolanda is pilfering the Villiers family goods. Kadeem knows about, even helps. Tanner finds out. They fight. He's dead."

"So why isn't Nick on the phone giving them all up toot sweet?" Scotty counters.

"Hmm. Thanks for the monkey wrench." Charmaine frowned and reconsidered her refusal of another drink.

"I don't get where the ghosts come in. Maybe Yolanda gets Kadeem's help setting it up to throw the old lady off their trail. You said Mrs. Villiers is no fool, but she's superstitious." Scotty looked at Charmaine.

"Maybe Nick knew what they were up to, but didn't talk because... They've got something on him. Yolanda knows where all the family bodies are buried. She even bragged as much to us once."

"Must be something heavy. He's rich, got clout, and he's the apple of his mother's eye." Scotty shook his head as he rubbed his jaw.

Charmaine heaved a deep sigh. "Nick may have lied about him and Tanner. They might have been lovers for a minute, and he doesn't want mama to know. Or the rest of the world."

"Humph." Scotty wore a skeptical expression.

"Hey, you never know. Sometimes people have hang-ups about sex. Could be she'd forgive anything but her golden boy being gay."

"You really don't want Nick to be caught up in shady stuff, much less murder. Like the dude, huh?" Scotty stared at his mug of ginger ale instead of her.

Charmaine ignored Scotty's question. "He mostly thinks about partying, a little bit about business. A lot about where he'll go for dinner, or his next fancy vacation. He goes along with Laura's scheming to backstab their sister Evelyn, but leaves most of the work to her."

"You could be reading him wrong. You always say telepathy isn't an exact science. It's not like you get it right all the time, or even can know everything someone is thinking." Scotty lifted his mug and gazed at her over the rim as he drank.

"Hmm. Jessi would love to hear you mention science in the same sentence as paranormal phenomena. She's got you coming round to her side, eh?" Charmaine replied with a short chuckle.

"I'm saying, the guy could be lying and all up in some seriously shady shit. You wouldn't know because you like him." Scotty fixed her with a steady stare down.

"Except the ghosts are real, not made up," Charmaine replied, still ignoring his attempt to analyze her blind spot. "We've established they exist beyond any doubt. Starting with the two times they tried to beat our asses."

"Another thing we know is real, the family has plenty of funky secrets." Scotty was about to go on but stopped. He blinked in surprise over Charmaine's shoulder and then grinned. "Look what cat dragged in, as my great-granny used to say."

Jessi strolled over, taking off her gloves to keep out the chilly fall air. "Your great-granny would know better than to think anything or body dragged me anywhere."

"Name what you're having." Scotty stood.

"Trini rum punch," Jessi said.

"You joking, right? I'm not the mixologist in here tonight. Now if you're going to fix it yourself."

Jessi flipped the fingertips of her right hand in the air at Scotty's scowl. "Fine, beer." After he walked off, she picked up Charmaine's empty glass and sniffed. "I see he gave you what you wanted."

"Tell me you come bearing good news."

"Weird, disturbing. Can't deliver on good. Or maybe it is." Jessi stuffed the gloves into the pocket of her leather trench coat. Then she took it off.

Although she carefully draped the coat over the back of a chair, she didn't sit.

Charmaine felt electric needles of anxiety along both her arms. "Meaning?"

"Tanner Gladstone. I talked to him. Well, what's left of him."

8.
Ghost Of A Chance

"Let me get this straight in my head." Charmaine blinked at Jessi across the table. They still sat in Scotty's club, though he'd warned them not for long. He was ready to go home.

"Tanner's spirit, essence, ectoplasmic atomic molecules, or whatever it is, showed up when I went over to Nick's place. But he's gone now. And no, I don't know why." Jessi nodded and took a gulp from her beer mug. "Hey, this is good shit."

"From Peru. Only the best for you," Scotty called out across the bar. "Ten minutes and I'm throwing y'all outta here."

"He's giveth, and he taketh away," Jessi yelled back.

"Whatever." Scotty waved at her and headed to his office.

"They let you in the crime scene?" Charmaine said.

"Uh, hell no. Harrison would strangle me with a smile on his face if he knew. I gently lifted the police tape and put it back across the door. Went in and made sure not to disturb anything. These days they finish up pretty fast. Not sure why they've still got it marked off."

"So, Tanner just, poof, appeared?" Charmaine whispered even though the last of Scotty's pals had gone.

"Basically. They don't knock on the front door, Char. Anyway, he doesn't remember what happened. He's a bit confused. Thinks he met up with Kadeem at some point to talk about something important. Then he was at Nick's looking down at his own body." Jessi heaved a sigh. "I didn't get much sense out of him before he floated off into the great unknown."

"What was this important something?"

"He couldn't say."

"Where did he meet? Did Kadeem shoot him, and why?" Charmaine huffed out a groan. "You killin' me here."

"Try not to use phrases like that around the dearly departed," Jessi retorted. "Look, it's not uncommon for the dead to not remember details. Especially when they died violently. It's not a perfect science like you're always telling me. There's some degradation of the matter when the process takes place."

"What?" Charmaine blinked at her.

"My friend Logan, the physicist, actually, he's decided to specialize in biophysics, he says all life is matter in some form. He thinks death is a form of evolution. His theory—"

Charmaine shook her head. "Later, Jessi. Did Tanner say anything helpful?"

"Nick is involved, but all he cared about was finding him. Tanner really had a hard on for Nick. Did they ever have a thing going on?" Jessi raised an eyebrow at Charmaine.

"No, far as I can tell anyway. I think it was mostly one-sided. Nick cared about him as a guy friend sort of thing, I think." Charmaine chewed on her fingernail for a second, realized what she was doing and stopped.

Jessi cleared her throat. "You're sure?"

Charmaine noted her glass was empty with a frown. She drummed her fingertips on the table top. "Pretty much. I don't know."

"Ask him."

"I can't..." Charmaine started, then glanced up at her sister. Jessi cocked her head to one side.

"Girl, listen. The cops would love to cap our asses for a murder charge. These folks are lying like fancy Persian rugs. We got mixed up ghosts who can't give us all the details. Your mind reading is coming up empty. When in doubt, just fucking ask." Jessi pointed at her for emphasis.

"He could lie," Charmaine replied.

"And you'll get a clue on whether or not he is lying. One thing that's pretty reliable, body language. Combine that with intuition and mind reading... bam!" Jessi hit the table with her right fist.

"Right." Charmaine turned the empty tumbler round and round as if another drink would magically appear.

"Unless you don't want to know," Jessi murmured.

"Hey, I'm not some moon-eyed teenager with a crush on the popular boy. Just cause I kinda like the guy... Fine, we'll talk to him again." Charmaine sat straight.

"No, you go alone. I don't think he'll tell it all if I'm with you. Besides, I want a crack at the sisters. Then I'm going back to Magnolia Grove. This all started with the mansion." Jessi finished her beer and stood.

"Evelyn and Laura are old school when it comes to the whole class thing. Oh, they consider themselves liberal but—"

"Yeah, you tried the deference and diplomacy method. Time for some hard knocks." Jessi put on her coat.

"I wasn't acting like the help begging Missy Ann to answer my questions," Charmaine replied with heat.

Jessi gave her shoulder a pat. "Calm down."

"First you act like I'm so horny for Nick I can't focus. Then you say I'm overly impressed by these rich..." Charmaine ended muttering under her breath. She put the tumbler to her mouth, having forgotten it was empty. She put it down again with a thump.

Jessi blew out air and sat across from her again. "Look, people blurt out information when they're angry. And we both know how good I am at pissing people off. Not to mention it will be fun taking a crack at Evelyn and Laura."

"Yeah."

Scotty appeared, keys in hand. He jingled them to make a point. "Hey, you two. Out."

"Yeah, yeah. Thanks for the beer." Jessi grinned at him.

"Next time you're paying," Scotty tossed back.

Jessi's grin vanished. "Some friend you are."

Charmaine ignored their subsequent debate about bar tabs, free drinks, and friendship. Scotty's deep rumble and Jessi's spirited clap backs faded. Charmaine concentrated on wiping condensation from the table top. Then she took her tumbler and Jessi's mug to the sink behind the bar. Her mind turned over Nick's alibi, his story, and all that Jessi had said.

"Hey, don't fix another drink while you're there. Y'all takin' advantage of a brother. I swear," Scotty yelled.

"Leave my sister alone. She's got stuff on her mind," Jessi said and poked him with her elbow.

"I'm not all worked up about Nick," Charmaine protested.

"Bad idea falling for a client, especially one that might be a killer," Scotty said.

"I'll remember your advice." Charmaine gave him a sour look.

Scotty held up both palms as he followed them out. "Just sayin'."

Jessi and Charmaine stood on the paved parking lot as he set the alarm and locked the front door. They both looked around the night as though considering where to go and what to do next. Then they faced each other at the same time.

"Night ladies. Stay out of trouble. If you can't be good, be careful. Oh, and remember to call if you need a character witness." Scotty let out a gruff laugh at the old joke. He'd racked up quite a police record before and after his Army discharge. He stopped in the motion of climbing into his Range Rover and stared at them. "Oh hell. I know that look."

"Magnolia Grove," Jessi said.

"Good a time as any. I'll drive. Leave your car at my house." Charmaine buttoned the front of her heavy sweater.

"I don't want to know," Scotty shouted.

"We weren't planning to tell you anyway," Charmaine yelled back and got into her car.

****

It was eleven o'clock by the time they arrived at the plantation complex. Not on purpose. There was nothing significant about the midnight hour, no matter what legends said. According to Jessi, spirits appeared based on who they'd been in life. Where and how they'd died also played a factor. Though they did tend to favor night time, the later the better. Mostly because the energy of the living subsided as most went to sleep. At least those were Jessi's scientific explanations. She'd gone on about atoms colliding and threshold displacement or something. In truth, Charmaine's mind tended to wander, and her eyes got glassy after the first ten seconds of Jessi's lectures. All to convince Charmaine that religion was crap and science had the answers. Bottom line, the old blues song was right. The night time was the right time. The later, the better. The added advantage of everyone being gone was a big plus. Almost everyone. Gravel crunched under Charmaine's tires as she steered off the paved driveway and around to the north side of the big house.

"We need a plausible explanation in case the security patrol shows up." Jessi pointed along the darkened path. "Park over under those trees. Your car will be harder to spot."

"Won't help much. I'm not crazy about spending a night in jail for burglary. Maybe we should..." Charmaine looked out into the inky night. Oak and magnolia trees loomed like giants ready to snatch them up. She shivered.

"Oh, put on your big thong panties," Jessi shot back. "Besides, we can call Mrs. Villiers. Tell her we're on the case, sneaking up on the ghosts."

"What the hell are you doing?" Charmaine looked at her sister.

"Gearing up for a fight." Jessi adjusted a strap and stuffed more items in her pockets.

"You're wearing a shoulder holster, and..." Charmaine snatched an object from Jessi's hand too fast to be blocked. "Pepper spray? Right, make the spirits sneeze themselves into a fit."

"Hey!" Jessi grabbed at it and glared at Charmaine. "Look, we're wasting time. No, I'm not carrying a gun. This is my new sidearm. Logan and Thi helped me make a pistol version of my matter zapper."

"A souped-up stun gun. You and those baby Dr. Frankensteins are a menace, I swear. Detective Harrison will just love catching us armed and breaking in." Charmaine heaved a sigh.

"Look at him with those big brown eyes and he'll melt all over you. Now c'mon." Jessi grabbed the keychain sized canister. "Besides, it's not pepper. Everyone knows that has no effect on ghosts."

"Of course they do," Charmaine replied. She looked around again. "Feels like we're being watched by somebody or something."

"This baby has sage, salt, and a few other secret ingredients. I tested them on Lucas. Works like a charm." Jessi giggled. "Pun intended. Get it? I—"

"You're ghost boyfriend agreed to be your lab rat. Perfect. What a life."

"Lucas isn't my boyfriend for the one millionth time. I can't help it if he's attached himself to me. Thank God he can't leave his haunt territory in the Garden District." Jessi continued checking her camera and electromagnetic field meter. "Okay, let's go."

Jessi jumped from the passenger's seat and was off into the night. Charmaine sputtered out a few ineffectual whispers for her to come back. Then realizing she didn't want to sit alone in the dark, Charmaine followed her. The sound of Jessi's size seven hiking boots crunching ahead guided her in the dark. Charmaine muttered a curse word and then turned on her small flashlight. Five minutes of walking brought her to the first of four tall Victorian styled lamp poles. These lit up the wide front path to the wide veranda that wrapped around the front of the grand home. More lights bathed both the first and second stories of the house.

"Wow. Impressive." Charmaine took in the beautiful sight. Two huge wreaths hung on the dark green double doors.

"Yeah. Rape, pillaging, and slavery pay well," Jessi retorted. She let her flashlight sweep down the dark side of the house. "Let's go. I have a key to the side door."

"How did you..."

Jessi glanced around their surroundings. "You don't want the answer."

Charmaine grabbed her by the arm and pulled Jessi back. "The alarm system is on."

"Let's check. If Yolanda and her relatives are stealing, she might have left it off." Jessi marched down the side path without waiting for Charmaine.

"Oh good. I want to bump into Yolanda's thug nephews in a dark alley," Charmaine grumbled. But having no choice, she followed Jessi. When she caught up to her, Charmaine whispered close to Jessi's ear, "Besides, we were just going to stay outside and let the ghost come to us. Whats-her-name."

"Georgina. Look, the last guests checked out yesterday. They won't have the next group come until Friday afternoon. This is our best chance to look around without them knowing." Jessi let out a tiny whoop of joy. She pointed to the line of green lights blinking on one of three wall control panels. "Told ya."

"What if they're in the house?" Charmaine whispered.

"Then we'll have a standoff. They sure can't dial 911 to report us." Jessi gave a jerk of her thumb.

"Wait a minute." Charmaine yanked her back again. "We need a better plan. Make sure we see them before they see us. If not, then..."

"My matter zapper will work on the living, too. Dual purpose, baby." Jessi grinned as though she looked forward to a fight. "I tried it."

"Jesus. Who in the world let you... never mind." Charmaine peered around. The fact that nothing moved in the dark didn't reassure her.

"Look, Yolanda works late, makes sure she's the last one out. She leaves the alarm off. Her shady peeps come fairly early, steal what they want, and slide out. They ain't gonna be hanging around." Jessi shook free of Charmaine's hold and took a step.

"Wait!" Charmaine grabbed for her again but missed.

"Stop it." Jessi let out an angry puff of air. She unlocked the door with the key. "My street sources told me how they prefer to operate. They also said that her daughter and nephews are scared to be here, especially late at night."

"Wonder why Georgina and the other spirit doesn't scare them away? She hates people messing with her belongings. Jess!" Charmaine flinched at the sound of a bell chiming.

"Doesn't send a signal to the company or set off the main alarm. Just to alert anyone inside that a door was opened." Jessi aimed her flashlight at the floor. She jerked her head as a command for Charmaine to follow her.

"Yolanda's daughter is right. Nothing charming about Magnolia Grove at night," Charmaine said low.

"Don't insult the place or Georgina will be even more pissed," Jessi said with a chuckle. She shook Charmaine off a second time. "I'm just kidding. Me and old Georgie girl have become pals. Sort of."

"Who dares to tramp around in my home?" A hollow voice rang out.

Charmaine jumped and stumbled against a side table. "Geez, she talks loud for a ghost."

Jessi froze and spun to face her. She turned her flashlight on Charmaine. "You heard her?"

"Yeah. Sure as hell ain't Casper the Friendly Ghost. Stop blinding me with that damn light, and let your buddy know it's you," Charmaine grumbled, a hand covering her eyes.

"Char, you heard her. A dead person." Jessi still stood with the light in her face.

"Right. Now get that thing out of my face. I..." Charmaine lowered her hand.

"You're not supposed to hear dead people, only the thoughts of live ones. This is amazing. The scientific implications—"

A flying meat cleaver whizzed by Jessi's head and sliced into rose-pattern wallpaper behind her. Charmaine squealed as an antique oil lamp came flying next. She ducked behind a chair of the sun room they'd entered. Jessi faced the direction the objects had come from.

"Hey, cut that out, Georgina," Jessi shouted.

"Well, if it isn't the cheeky darky spiritualists come calling the middle of the night. I suppose you shall try and convince me you're not thieves," Georgina replied. A line of daguerreotypes in frames on the mantel rattled ominously but didn't take flight.

"People don't say 'darky' anymore." Charmaine scowled into the dim interior of the house. Soft light from night lights made the furniture look like shadows, but gave some visibility.

"I don't give a fig for what they call politically correct language of these times. Do I?" Georgina chuckled. "And you have failed to explain this intrusion."

Charmaine could imagine her pointing an accusing ghostly forefinger at her nose. "Well, we... have a few questions for you."

"Can you see her? Over there, in the doorway leading into the music room," Jessi whispered.

"No, don't see her. Just the voice coming from... everywhere seems like," Charmaine whispered back.

"Oh, stop those nonsense efforts to be quiet. We heard you coming miles away," Georgina said. "Well, maybe not miles."

"Right." Jessi switched off her flashlight and sighed.

Charmaine shuddered from the sensation of biting ice rubbed on her back. The after effects of hearing a ghost left a chill. "My nerves are rubbed raw."

"Let us go to the ladies' parlor, dears. A sip of brandy will do you good. Oh, yes. Marguerite keeps a bottle handy. Come." Georgina's voice floated away.

"Good idea," Jessi breathed.

"We're about to have drinks. With a woman who's been dead for almost two hundred years. We're out of our minds," Charmaine muttered.

"Two hundred two years and six months. But who's counting?" Georgina called back. Then her hollow musical laughter bounced off the walls.

"She's a helluva hostess though." Jessi strolled after the ghost like they were at a house party. She closed the heavy damask drapes in the parlor and turned on a lamp. Jessi pointed at them when Charmaine entered. "They won't see it. Heavy, like blackout curtains."

"Oh good," Charmaine quipped.

"You'll have to do the honors. My ability to lift objects is limited. Actually, it's strange that I'm able to move anything. I suppose the strength of my anger helps."

Charmaine poured two fingers of brandy in goblets and handed one to Jessi. "Well, I'd be permanently pissed off if my husband had murdered me."

"Yes. Worse still, he had quite a few brushes, as they call it in coarser circles." Georgina sniffed.

"So he liked painting. So what?" Charmaine went to a chair and jumped when Jessi yelped.

"Not there. Georgina is sitting in that one," Jessi said.

Charmaine stared at the paisley fabric but saw nothing. "How am I supposed to know?"

"Follow my voice, dear," Georgina replied.

"Excuse me for not knowing ghost social rules."

"Well if there are rules, no one told me. One minute I'm in my own bed. Still in one of the rooms upstairs by the way." Georgina pointed to the ceiling. "Next thing I'm standing down here in the parlor next to the fireplace."

"You said something about your husband doing some painting," Jessi said and plopped down on another stuffed chair.

"Pardon?" Georgina frowned at her.

"His brushes." Jessi shrugged.

"Tsk, tsk. Brushes is a less refined term for... amorous congress." Georgina cleared her throat.

"He had lots of smokin' hot sex. She's blushing. Are you actually blushing?" Jessi laughed and slapped her thigh.

"You mean he had mistresses." Charmaine strained in hopes she could see a ghost look embarrassed.

"Ahem, yes. Of all stripes and colors. I suspect he fathered more than one darky bastard," Georgina said, her voice bitter.

"Hey!" Charmaine scowled at what to her was an empty chair.

"Cool down, it's how they talked back then," Jessi said with a dismissive wave of one hand. "Maybe that's why he killed you, to cover up his dirty deeds."

"Sadly, the practice of cavorting with mulatto mistresses was all too common among otherwise respectable gentlemen." Georgina heaved a long hissing sigh. "We wives suffered a great deal."

"Not as much as the poor slave women and servants. They didn't have much choice but to submit. Their lives depended on it," Jessi replied.

"They suffered? Humph! Some of my husband's friends bought them houses, paid for the education of their bastard children," Georgina shot back.

"We say illegitimate or wrong side of the blanket even." Charmaine didn't feel as forgiving as Jessi.

"Sure, dress up the entire filthy practice to make it more palatable. That is what is wrong with the times you live in. Any form of immoral depravity is excused with pretty language. Well, not I. In my day, there were strict consequences. Of course, we women had little power. We wielded what influence we could to protect our honor and our children's legacies." Georgina lifted her chin, back straight.

"Still, your husbands provided for their mistresses financially. And the children shouldn't suffer for their poor choices," Charmaine argued.

"And I'll remind you again. Women of color were faced with a huge imbalance of power. Refuse and lose everything, even your life. When a white man stood over you, unbuttoning his breeches..." Jessi let out a sharp breath and gulped brandy.

"We wives had to submit as well. Our duty. My grandmother and mother advised me to grit my teeth and suffer it. My wedding night was a horror. Alexandre William Villiers rutted atop me like a beast. He bellowed that I was his property to do with as he chose, my father and brothers be damned." Georgina blinked away ghost tears.

"Her father was a wealthy and powerful man in West Feliciana Parish," Jessi said aside to Charmaine. "Artie looked him up for me."

"Of course, I could raise no complaint. Father would have agreed with him, as did society and the law. In a sense, a wife was as much property as a slave. James only valued me for producing his children." Georgina's sorrow turned into rage. "Animal."

"You died after the fourth child," Jessi spoke softly.

"Fifth. A girl, Charlotte." Georgina rose. She seemed to glide over to an oil portrait in an ornate nineteenth-century frame.

Charmaine paid attention and followed the sound. "Hmm, pretty girl. She, um, looks like you."

Georgina laughed. "You can't tell. But yes, she does look like me."

"So, white men had the power over their wives. Then your husband didn't need to kill you to hide his affairs." Jessi looked at Charmaine.

"He wanted to clear the way for another white wife maybe?" Charmaine shrugged back. "We know the men is this family were ruthless."

"Oh, dears. You have no idea how true a statement that is," Georgina said with force." Jessamine Treme was Alexandre's plaçage. His youthful wild oats, or so his father called her. Alexandre did not put her aside after our marriage. He didn't think I'd find out about her, but I did."

"Right, she had his babies. Hey Jessie, like me." Jessi grinned but grew serious again when Georgina glared at her humor. "Sorry, go ahead with the story."

Georgina's face contorted into pure bitterness. "They had one child, a boy. He tried to hide the truth, but I found out."

Jessi gave Georgina a skeptical frown. "Which was?"

"Alexandre paid for his education. Nothing but the best for his bastard: private tutors, violin lessons and more. I paid one of my slaves to follow him. He'd set her up in a pretty little cottage. They tried putting a layer of respectability over such loathsome behavior. When I found out he planned

to send the boy to France for more education..."
Georgina's hands balled into fists.

Charmaine sat forward. "Girl, this is better than
a Tyler Perry soap opera."

"Alexandre intended to leave his bastard some
of our property," Georgina went on.

"He couldn't have done that legally." Jessi looked
at Charmaine. "Could he?"

"You tell me. From what I remember, illegitimate children couldn't inherit. Not even if they
were put in a will." Charmaine shrugged and enjoyed a sip of expensive brandy.

"Men did as they pleased in my day. They found
ways, believe me. So, I took matters into my own
hands," Georgina said. "I would not have him place
that darky above my son."

"What?" Charmaine blinked at her.

Jessi studied Georgina for a few seconds. "You
paid someone to kill a child. Talk about a cold-
blooded bitch."

"He was a man of almost eighteen," Georgina
shot back. "This child, more than the others, would
have brought shame on my family. I would never
suffer a child of mine to share his rightful legacy
with a—"

"Let me stop you right there." Jessi stood, hand
on her pocket.

Charmaine recognized that dangerous gleam in her sister's eyes. "Jess, take a breath. Getting pissed about stuff that happened two centuries ago won't help anybody, least of all us. We can't start a fight up in here and attract attention."

omebody cranked up the A/C or there's a cold she's a child killer. Just one shot and we solve two problems. No more scaring the tourists, and we deliver a little rough justice for the kid's sake." Jessi took a step to Georgina.

"How foolish you are. I am beyond any of your useless attempts to punish me." Georgina wore a smile of contempt as Jessi stood over her.

"We came here for answers. If you zap her, we lose a source of information." Charmaine grabbed at Jessi's arm to stop her.

Jessi danced out of reach, her modified stun device in hand. "I can find others. This house has more spirits than St. Louis Cemetery."

"Your sister is wiser than you. I know more of the family history than any of the others. I've been here the longest, watching each generation. I know where the bones are buried. Literally." Georgina spoke in a mild tone.

"Right, so what happened to Marguerite's husband?" Charmaine talked fast, unsure if she'd be able to stop Jessi in time.

"He did not die from completely natural causes. He reminded me too much of my late husband." Georgina let out a hiss of disgust. "He deserved what he got."

"Damn, he was your great-great-great... your descendant," Jessi sputtered. "You really are one bit of poisoned smoke."

Charmaine jumped between them, or at least where she thought might block her sister's view of the ghost. Not being able to see Georgina didn't help. "Shut up, Jessi. Who killed him?"

"Humph. You see? You two need me. But I won't tell. He was no better than his forebear, my debauched husband. May they both burn in hell." Georgina laughed.

"Maybe I'll let Jessi give you a few taps from her Taser gun. Oh, don't laugh too hard. She's fixed it so the charge messes with spirits, like you." Charmaine pointed where she thought Georgina sat.

"She's moved from the chair," Jessi mumbled and jerked a thumb about six feet to their right.

"I don't believe you," Georgina spat.

"Yes, you do," Charmaine replied, aiming her comment in the new direction. "Or you wouldn't be shaking in your boots across the room now."

"Boots indeed. You obviously have no idea what a lady wears. I wouldn't even have allowed you to be a house slave. Only the fields and gardens for you!"

"She's itching for a beat down, Char." Jessi hissed again like an angry cat ready to pounce.

"I say... you're trapped here," Charmaine replied to Georgina, a restraining hand waved at Jessi not to act in haste.

"Poppycock," Georgina grumbled.

"You're not hanging around Magnolia Grove because you like it here. Life was unhappy for you in this house. A husband whose real passion was saved for a mistress. I'll bet your friends knew and pitied you. His family didn't like you much either." Charmaine slung out the words like darts aimed at Georgina's pride.

"How dare you..."

"But we understand rejection, isolation. Having the children didn't completely make up for it. We know how lonely you felt. Don't we Jessi?" Charmaine switched to a sympathetic tone.

"Do you think me a fool, girl? You have no idea what a white woman of my breeding feels. You wish me to share the most intimate details of our line. And for what?" Georgina's voice echoed, an eerie sound in the empty mansion.

"Umm, justice? To protect your family name maybe." Charmaine grasped what few straws she could think of in a pinch.

"Is that supposed to be a joke?" Georgina huffed.

"Girl, please. She kills children. Dirty baby killer." Jessi hit the trigger on her Taser gun. The buzz caused Charmaine and Georgina to jump.

Georgina flitted to another far corner. "What is that- that thing?"

"Ah, saw you flinch. You felt the charge even at a distance. Just think what happens when I get close to you." Jessi gave her best mad scientist chuckle.

"I have not killed any children! Darkies are not even human, no more than cattle," Georgina argued.

Charmaine heaved a deep sigh. "Not your best defense."

"He was a grown man. In my day, young men his age fought in wars, owned property..."

"You mean white guys." Jessi grimaced with distaste. "You people disgust me."

"Back to the murder," Charmaine broke in to head off more conflict before they got answers.

"Which one?" Georgina said, not an ounce of levity in her question.

"Which one, she says. This family... damn. And got the nerve to look down her nose at us!" Jessi let out a groan of disgust.

"Will you two— wait, I heard a noise." Charmaine cocked her head to one side and listened.

"I don't hear anything. Unless it's another triflin' ghost kin to this one." Jessi gave Georgina a scowl of scorn.

"No, I'm telling y'all. Somebody is moving around in here." Charmaine strode to a window and looked outside. "I think I see something. Could be a car or SUV. Bushes are blocking my view."

Jessi joined her. She twitched back a portion of the heavy drapes on the other side of the window. "It's pitch black outside. Everything looks like a clump of something." She was about to go on when a solid thump stopped her.

"Oh dear. Silly me. I forgot to mention that servant's larcenous relations planned to come back tonight. Two of them are quite frightful." Georgina chortled and sat down. Suddenly she held a piece of needlepoint. She starting stitching, humming a tune.

"What in the hell... I thought they only came early. Kadeem never mentioned—"

"Of course, he wouldn't," Georgina cut in. "You thought your fellow miscreant always played fair with you? How amusing."

"She's full of shit. I'll go check it out." Jessi held the Taser close to her side as she headed for the door.

Charmaine stepped closer to what seemed an empty chair. She squinted at the ghost she could only hear, not see. "How many are there?"

"Hard to say, dear. Sometimes as many as three hulking scoundrels show up. Most times it's two. But those two are a mean pair. You know, I heard one of them mention having gone to jail for beating a woman." Georgina clucked her tongue in dismay.

"I'd love to choke you. Jessi, wait. We should go together," Charmaine said as she spun around to face her sister.

"Which would be a big help, if you'd come locked and loaded. I've told you more than once, weapon up," Jessi whispered back with a frown.

"I'm not carrying a gun around," Charmaine shot back. Another heavy thump indicated Georgina hadn't lied about the size of the intruders.

"Right, Miss Social Worker. Ya gonna counsel them not to shoot our asses?" Jessi continued toward the door as she talked.

"She has an excellent point, dear," Georgina said, followed by another snicker.

"Shut up you sack of poisonous gas." Charmaine swung at where she thought Georgina's head might be.

"Tut-tut. Such rudeness. Save your energy for the fight ahead." More ghostly laughter.

A male voice came, muted as though trying to keep his voice down. "What's that, bruh?"

Charmaine crept close to Jessi, who stood at the door with it cracked open. Twin spots of light blinked back and forth. Two flashlights. Then came soft rustling of fabric. Footsteps muffled by the antique reproduction rugs moved away.

"Man, I told you that ghost shit is for tourists. Mama plays it up to keep them from wandering over here at night. But we don't gotta worry. Last guests left a few days ago. Now let's get the swag and move it." A second male voice, deeper and older, seemed to be moving away from the library. A sound stopped him. The flashlight beam swung back in their direction. "You think Larry came in?"

"Nah, he knows to stay in the damn car. Almost got us jacked up on the last job," the first man replied. "Bruh, I'm tellin' ya. Somethin' ain't right about this old house."

"Some good stuff in here. Dre, get that bowl," Georgina said, her voice disguised to pitch low. Then came the sound of something falling.

"The hell she up to?" Jessi mouthed.

A female answered in a voice gruff with irritation. "Don't tell me what to do."

"I didn't say nothin'." A fourth voice, another male, came back low.

The older man gave an angry grunt. "Them lyin' muthas. Dre and 'nem in here tryin' to get their own haul."

"Aw hell no. Let's teach them a lesson," the second man answered. Being double-crossed seemed to have made him forget to be scared.

The quiet rustle of fabric signaled the first two burglars approached before them. The other two voices moved closer from the dining room, which placed them on the opposite side of the parlor. Charmaine and Jessi stood trapped between two groups of determined, ill-tempered criminals.

"Here," Charmaine whispered.

She pulled Jessi with her into the folds of the draperies. Thick and plentiful, the dark color and bulk would hide them both. The windows were deep so that they could move into the recess. Even if the thieves turned on the lamps, Charmaine and

Jessi wouldn't stick out. Charmaine shuddered, then fidgeted with her hands.

"Keep still," Jessi breathed close to Charmaine's right ear.

Charmaine, her nerves shot, started to speak. Jessi clamped a hand over Charmaine's mouth. She could feel Jessi frowning at her with a death stare. With effort, Charmaine tried to get her terrified, jittery movements under control. Ghosts and goblins might startle her, but they had no physical power against the living. Jessi's sources had told them Yolanda's kinfolks tended to shoot and then ask questions. Charmaine reconsidered her view on carrying a weapon.

"Somebody in here," the female said.

"Naw. I told you, Larry and them got in early," her companion replied. A click followed his words.

"What the hell you doing, tryin' ta get us caught?" the woman growled.

"The security guy is in his car sound asleep. Aunt Yolanda thinks ahead. She spiked his hot chocolate with a coupla sleeping pills. Just enough to give him a good long nap," the man replied. He sounded confident. "Them thick curtains hides the light. We solid. Hell, might even take time to get a drink of this fine liquor."

Jessi risked a quick peek from one side of the drapes. Charmaine held her breath. She couldn't chance moving or speaking to stop her bold sister. Then she let it out when Jessi eased back in position. They both tensed as a cold wave of air stirred the draperies. Georgina's ghostly voice came from behind them.

"The plot thickens."

Charmaine suppressed the automatic urge to scream shut up. Jessi tensed, her body signaling a desire to strike out at the spiteful spirit as well. Instead, they took the smart route and remained still. They listened as the two sides squared off.

"Your ass ain't gonna drink nothin' but my fist. Get da fuck outta here." The deep voice came from the other end of the room.

"Da hell? Troy, Curtis, y'all supposed to be..." The woman said.

"Who we got here? Uh-huh, Sheniqua and Dre. We didn't wrap up early like you thought. Drop what you holdin' and get out," the older man snapped.

"This is our set up," older man's partner added. "Y'all know the damn rules.

"Place is full of loot, enough for all," Dre replied. "Look, Troy, we—"

"This ain't a damn negotiation. Move, or else," Troy said.

"Listen up, Curtis. We shared before," Sheniqua spoke up. "Troy know it, too."

"Nah, don't even try it with me. Troy just told y'all. Ya need to get on outta here. Now."

"You gonna shoot us? Madea will beat your ass silly if we mess up this game. We make a lot of noise, it's gonna attract attention. That security guy is sleep not dead," Sheniqua replied with heat.

"Play with me if you want, Sheniqua," Troy rumbled.

Charmaine felt sweat roll down beneath her sweater. Her back started to itch. In seconds, it became unbearable. Maybe the stress of their predicament made it worse, but then her allergies kicked in. Dust on the window ledge and in the folds of the drapery didn't help. Not only did the itch spread to her shoulder blades, Charmaine fought the urge to sneeze.

Jessi pressed an elbow into Charmaine's left side and mouthed, "Don't. You. Dare."

"Somethin' movin' in here. Look, let's get the crap on the list Aunt Yolanda gave us and go," Curtis said.

"Stop actin' like a lil' bitch," Big T snapped at him. "Dre, Sheniqua, I'ma tell y'all one last time. Bounce outta here. This ain't your job."

"Yeah, well Kadeem says there's plenty to go around, and the old lady won't report it all. Insurance will pay them off," Sheniqua replied.

"Kadeem ain't in charge of shit," Troy broke in.

"You ain't either, Troy," Dre said.

"Put that gun down." Sheniqua's shriek implied confidence her cousin would shoot.

"You remember what happened the last time one of y'all fucked with my business?" Troy's rumbled pronouncement rumbled like the approach of a dangerous thunderstorm.

Charmaine almost lost the fight not to let loose a sneeze. A small squeak came out. She squeezed her eyes shut as if that would help. A noise outside made Jessi start. The draperies moved with her.

"I told y'all somethin' in here with us. Those curtains moved, T. I swear," Curtis said.

Troy turned to Sheniqua and Dre. "Who y'all brought with you?"

Sheniqua snorted. "Look at them. Jumpin' at every shadow like two scared babies. Now we gonna get what we came for and leave."

"Girl, you done pushed me one inch too far," Troy replied.

"Hey, man, quit waving that gun at me or I'll make you suck it like you did in prison." Dre's voice moved closer, a sign that he'd advanced on his cousin.

"What the hell did you say to me?" Troy shouted.

"Big bad T got turned into somebody's punk ass girlfriend inside," Dre said and gave an ugly laugh.

"Troy, Dre, c'mon. Y'all be cool now," Curtis cut in.

"You gonna die mutha— "

After a crash, the thin line of light from the lamp Dre had turned on went out. More sounds of a struggle and angry grunts. Sheniqua let out a string of profanity. The man named Curtis squealed something had touched him. Seconds later the ruckus got even more chaotic. Georgina let loose a shrill moan that echoed.

"I told y'all," Curtis shouted.

"You gone learn today," Troy yelled.

"Grab his gun, Dre. Grab the damn gun," Sheniqua said, then started cussing again.

The deafening blast from a pistol made Charmaine stumble. She grabbed for anything to stop her fall. A drawstring ended up in her fist, and she yanked as she went down. Seconds later the draperies pulled back. She and Jessi stood exposed, frozen before the scene of a violent family feud. At first the combatants didn't notice. Then Sheniqua let out a screech and pointed at them. Troy and Curtis continued to crash around the room, turning over furniture. Another shot went off. Moments later, one of the men shouted in pain.

"It burns. I'm bleeding. I'm bleeding!"

Charmaine couldn't tell which one screamed in panic. She pushed away from the glass window pane at her back. "Apply pressure or he could bleed out and die," she blurted out.

Jessi yanked her away. "Now ain't the time to play nurse."

"You will all die tonight in this house. All of you filthy thieves. Your throats will be torn out, your entrails devoured."

Georgina boomed as though through a loudspeaker. Her maniacal laughter followed. Only Charmaine and Jessi could make out what she said. The others only heard loud swishing. The room became cold and the walls appeared to vibrate with a buzzing noise.

"Da fuck?" Troy stood and fired off rounds in several directions.

Curtis pulled a thirty-eight special, a look of wild terror on his flat brown face. He followed his cousin's lead as he shot a small statue on a mantle.

"You see it, T? Did you get it? Shit, man. I'm getting' outta here!"

Jessi succeeded in dragging Charmaine to the floor as the sound of sirens keened in the distance. They half rolled, half crawled along the floor keeping close to one wall. Shouts from the four burglars continued, mixed with more gleeful gruesome threats from Georgina. Moments later, another voice joined in from outside.

A voice amplified by a bullhorn cut through the noise. "This is Deputy Rathborne with the Jefferson Parish Sheriff's Department. Come out of the house, hands up. Let's end this with nobody gettin' hurt."

Yolanda's larcenous kinfolk froze. They blinked at each other, weighing their options. Jessi's grip on Charmaine's arm tightened. She needn't have worried. Law enforcement arriving made Sheniqua forget about them it seemed. The woman licked her lips as her gaze darted toward an exit that might take her out the back. The men began a spirited debate on what to do to fix their predicament. The next voice spoke with authority as if anticipating their next move.

"This is Trooper Mike Ellis with the Louisiana State Police. Folks, there's no way out. Don't make a bad situation worse."

"They get SWAT out here, we screwed." The man named Curtis, his voice shaking, followed his assessment with a curse word.

"You finally realized we got bigger problems than some fuckin' ghost that don't exist," Troy retorted. He ignored angry words from Sheniqua and Dre as he moved to the door. "Look, I'm comin' out."

"Shit, damn it." Dre croaked as he hugged a chair as a shield.

"He's right," Sheniqua replied. She slipped a small automatic pistol from somewhere in her clothes. Then she followed Troy's path. Moments later the others, all muttering profanity, gave up as well.

"First time I'm glad to hear from the cops," Charmaine breathed out.

"Oh yeah? Now we gotta explain what we're doing in here," Jessi whispered back.

Georgina giggled. "Don't worry, dears. I'm sure you'll come up with a creative story."

"Bitch," Charmaine and Jessi said at the same time.

9.

"What Had Happened Was…"

"So, let me get this straight, and help me out if I don't get it exactly right." Deputy Rathborne's thick black eyebrows, dotted with gray wiry hairs, bunched together as he frowned.

Det. Harrison stood against one wall in a corner, arms cross. His jaw muscles worked overtime as he glowered. Charmaine squirmed in the chair of the interview room. Just like her current position with the authorities, there was no way to get comfortable on the hard metal seat. Likewise, the chilled temperature seemed designed to freeze the truth out of suspects. The offices of the Jefferson Parish Sheriff's Department Fourth District no doubt wasn't meant to be warm and cozy. Definitely not for those apprehended.

"You're an employee at Magnolia Grove Estate," Deputy Rathborne continued after glancing in a folder before closing it.

"I work for Mrs. Marguerite Villiers. Det. Harrison knows," Charmaine said. She flinched when Harrison's scowl deepened, something she hadn't thought possible.

"You honestly believe I'm going to be a character witness for you?" Harrison growled.

"I'm not lying. Call Mrs. Villiers."

"Oh, we will. But first, tell us which of your duties puts you in her house after midnight with a crew of known felons," Deputy Rathborne said.

"All of whom had sacks of stolen valuables in their possession," Det. Harrison added. A slight smirk gave away how delighted he was to pile it on.

"It's not how it looks," Charmaine replied, her voice shrill from the tension grabbing her throat muscles.

"Oh yeah? Well, it's looking real bad right about now." Det. Harrison snorted.

Charmaine opened her mouth wide to protest her innocence in the face of two skeptical lawman frowns. A knock on the interview room door interrupted her effort at an award-winning performance. Another deputy, this one in plain clothes, stuck his head in. He glanced at Charmaine briefly before he spoke to Deputy Rathborne.

"Sarge, call for you." The man gave a jerk of his head to indicate he needed to take it.

"We'll be back soon." Rathborne shot Charmaine a look that said she was still in trouble.

"Shit." Charmaine turned to Harrison. "You know damn well we didn't break in Magnolia Grove. Marguerite Villiers hired us."

"Uh-huh. How you ended up at her mansion in the middle of the night is the million dollar question." Det. Harrison's raised eyebrow even looked like a question mark.

"We investigate paranormal phenomena. Working late into the night is part of the job description," Charmaine said.

Then she launched into a detailed description of how ghost hunters worked. She threw in a bunch of scientific names for devices Jessi used. Thank the heavens Charmaine paid enough attention to her rambling on about this or that gizmo. She was able to pepper her discourse with impressive-sounding technical details. Charmaine felt quite impressed with herself until the NOPD detective made a rude noise, something between a snort and an imitation of a fart.

Harrison tilted his head to one side. "Bull... Shit."

"That wasn't very nice," Charmaine shot back. His amused expression rubbed her already exposed nerves raw.

Harrison's expression became serious again. "Look, under most circumstances, you girls are fun to watch. But you keep turning up with dead bodies."

"First off, we're women. So, stuff the patriarchal patronization. Thank you very much." Charmaine sat straight.

"Here we go with the 'feminist warrior' crap," Harrison muttered.

"Second, we don't turn up with dead bodies. You talk like we carry them around in the back of my SUV, sprinkling them all over New Orleans," Charmaine continued.

"Nah, not only New Orleans. You branched out to the suburbs. The city limits got too tight for you, I suppose."

"See, that right there is your problem, detective. The police can't think outside a narrow little box. You need a simple explanation. Dead body, Charmaine Joliet is within ten miles of it. Conclusion, she's got something to do with said person ending up a dead body."

Charmaine wound up to blast him even harder, despite his series of more rude grunts. She stopped when the door swung open. Deputy Rathborne came in with Jessi right behind him.

"The owner called, along with her attorney. They both confirm that these two psychic investigators had full permission to examine the premises as they saw fit." Deputy Rathborne paused to give them the full effect of his contempt. The other deputy with him rolled his eyes in agreement.

"Wonder why Mrs. Villiers saw fit to have a lawyer on the call?" Det. Harrison stood and gazed at Deputy Rathborne.

"Yeah." Rathborne gazed back at him.

"Let me guess, the lawyer's name is Elliot Forstall." Det. Harrison looked at Charmaine sideways, then back at the deputy.

"Yep. How'd you know?" Deputy Rathborne looked from him to Charmaine and back.

"I'm investigating a murder and her son is involved," Harrison said.

"Involved as in..." Rathborne tilted his head to one side with interest.

"The corpse was found in his house, worked for the family's business, and was a friend of her son's. Or something." Det. Harrison transferred his intense gaze to Jessi and then Charmaine.

"Look, as enjoyable as your hospitality has been for the past few hours." Jessi stretched, rolled her shoulders, and then fluffed her thick braids. "My sister and me could use some hot coffee, a hardy breakfast and a nap."

"Smart-ass," the other deputy mumbled low, but loud enough to be heard which was what he intended. Tall with red hair and a ruddy complexion, he gave Jessi a stony look.

"Enough," Harrison replied with a quick look at the man.

"I'm sure you guys would love to charge us with something, or at the very least shoot us," Jessi said.

"We're here to enforce the law and protect the public," the redheaded deputy blurted.

Jessi faced him. "As recent high-profile deaths of black women in police custody prove—"

"Hey, don't fling that activist BS around. Nobody is impressed. I clean up behind you people killing each other every damn day of the week," the deputy broke in.

"Stand down, Donaldson," Deputy Rathborne said, his voice calm. His deputy obeyed, but his eyes burned with outrage.

Det. Harrison wore a taught expression as he faced the deputy. "Us people?"

"I didn't mean you," the deputy replied.

"Yeah, right," Det. Harrison turned his attention to Deputy Rathborne. "Bottom line, you can't charge either of them. Mrs. Villiers basically said they had permission to be on the premises."

Deputy Rathborne heaved an exasperated sigh. "About sums it up."

"I'll take these two back to their vehicle so they can get home." Harrison looked at Jessi. "Enough with the social justice talk."

Jessi held up both hands, palm out. Charmaine let out a puff of air with relief that her mouthy sister got his message. Minutes later, they were at the redheaded deputy's desk collecting their personal effects. In less than an hour, they were headed down River Road back to Magnolia Grove. The horizon showed edges of brightness as dawn approached. By that time, it was close to six o'clock in the morning.

"So, what did they find out from Yolanda's relatives? I'm thinking we pretty much solved the missing antiques part of our case." Jessi spoke from the back of Harrison's unmarked cruiser, a white Chevy Malibu. "Hey, your car smells pretty nice. Most of the time cop cars stink like crazy."

"And you would know, based on your frequent rides in the back of police cars. Probably cuffed," Harrison retorted.

"Hey, be polite. We helped you catch some criminals last night," Jessi replied.

"Unbelievable. You two are..." Harrison shook his head as he steered into a curve.

Charmaine glared at him. "Look, detective, we've had a stressful night. What started out as a routine on-site assessment of nocturnal activity— "

"Oh c'mon. Enough of the ghost-busting gobbledygook." Harrison kept driving without looking at her.

"Fine, be skeptical all you want. But our profession is real, and so is paranormal phenomena." Charmaine gave a sniff to punctuate her words.

"Spirits are the least of your worries. Now you got the Dawson family mad at you." Harrison glanced into the rearview mirror at Jessi. "Smarting off won't work with them."

"We didn't do anything to them. They got themselves caught, busting into the place and getting into a family fight," Charmaine protested, trying out her argument with a less threatening listener.

"You really think they'll blame each other? Keep dreaming. The way they'll see it is you two messed up a lucrative gig." Harrison waved to a private duty security guard parked on the wide driveway leading to the historic home. The man nodded back.

"Curtis and Troy tried to kill their own cousins. Sheniqua was just as ready to throw down, too. We got caught between the battling burglars. Hell, we're the only ones who were at the place legally," Charmaine said.

Harrison pulled alongside Charmaine's Cruze. He shifted into park, engine still running, and turned to her. "Don't lay that line of horse shit on me. The old lady covered for you because... I don't know. I'm guessing you've got enough dirt on her that she's going to stick by you two. For now at least."

"Or maybe she's telling the truth, and we're doing the job she hired us to do and nothing more. I suggest you look into why her son ended up with a dead friend in his living room," Jessi retorted.

"Nick didn't have a motive for killing Tanner," Charmaine said a bit too quick. She pressed her mouth closed when Harrison and Jessi stared at her. "I mean, they were friends."

"Nick, eh? You're so close to Sir Nicholas that you know what he's thinking. Interesting. Tell me more." Det. Harrison squinted at her.

"We've had interviews with the guy," Jessi put in. "He doesn't strike me as the violent type. Plus, he'd known the victim for some time. They seemed on real good terms."

"Hmm, about that quote friendship. I heard it was more intimate," Det. Harrison said with a side glance at Charmaine.

"Tanner Gladstone was gay, yeah. He had a thing for Nicholas Villiers, but the feeling wasn't mutual. From what I could see, Tanner had accepted they weren't going to be more. Nick is into girls," Jessi said.

"Women," Charmaine said. "Let's not normalize calling grown women 'girls'. It devalues our work and our perspectives as intelligent people with skills."

Jessi sighed as she rolled her eyes at Charmaine. "As I was saying. Nick Villiers lacks motive based on our professional observations and interviews with other principals of our case."

"We'll dig out the real nature of their relationship and any motives sooner rather than later." Det. Harrison waved a hand at no one in particular.

Charmaine frowned at him. "Meaning?"

"Your little game won't work. All this talk about women versus girls, and professional observations? Distractions."

"In other words, bullshit. He's being polite about calling us out," Jessi said with a chuckle.

"I'm going to figure out what's going on." Det. Harrison said.

"Good for you. Bye-bye and thanks for the ride." Charmaine got out and slammed the passenger door as hard as possible.

The solid construction of the cop car meant it didn't even rattle the frame. Or maybe she was too weak. Either way, her exit had less scornful impact than she intended. Which made her even more annoyed. She hit the remote on her keychain to open her Cruze. The door locks clicked open, but she didn't get in. Instead, Charmaine leaned against the car and waited. Jessi stayed behind with Harrison. After a few minutes of fuming, Charmaine stood straight and yanked her driver's door open.

"Let's go," she called to Jessi.

Jessi waved goodbye to Harrison, said something muffled by the closed car windows, and got out. She walked toward Charmaine as his car pulled away. "I was smoothing out your bad diplomacy so I could milk him for intel."

"Intel? You've been watching too many bad thriller movies," Charmaine retorted and got behind the wheel.

"You noticed tension between him and Rathborne back there? NOPD and the Jefferson Parish Sheriff's department don't always play nice. Pretty stupid the way different cop departments fight each other. Just gives gangstas an advantage."

"Whatever." Charmaine started up the engine and turned the Cruze onto the road.

"Well, it also gives us some wiggle room. Play both sides against each other. Not too much. Harrison ain't stupid. I rubbed it in how Rathborne and his guys saw a bunch of black folks and assumed we're all the same. Before you interrupted, he told me Shenqiua and the others will be charged, but Mrs. Villiers didn't seem thrilled about it." Jessi buckled her seat belt.

"Okay." Charmaine drove on, eyes on the road ahead.

"Look, get out your hurt feels because Harrison thinks your boyfriend is a murder suspect. The stakes are too damn high. What if the police start thinking you're lover boy's accomplice? Hey!" Jessi yelped when Charmaine made a sudden sharp right into a parking lot.

Charmaine hit the brakes and ignored stares from two guys coming out of a convenience store. A woman frowned at them through the glass walls of the store. "Oh fuck off, lady. I'm in a mood."

"What the hell?" Jessi let out a slow breath.

"We don't have even one good reason Nick would kill Tanner. And he's not 'my lover boy'. If he's in anyway part of something funky, I'll help take him down with a smile on my face. Got it?"

Charmaine kept both hands on the steering wheel. She gazed straight ahead.

"You need to..." Jessi's voice trailed off at the hard look Charmaine gave her.

"If you say it," Charmaine began, then blew out a grunt.

"Right. Work out your stress whatever way you need to, sis. Just not by driving up through the wall of a Pack-N-Go liquor store," Jessi said in a controlled voice.

Charmaine released her grip on the wheel. She shook her head and laughed. "My insurance rate would go way too high anyway."

Jessi joined her in laughing. "Whew, girl. I thought my life was on the line there for a minute. You really got a thing for Nick Villiers? I'm just asking. Don't decapitate me."

"Relax. I'm still thinking straight." Charmaine looked straight into Jessi's skepticism. "My judgment isn't screwed up over a fine body, silky bedroom voice, and... Okay, maybe I got a little invested in seeing him as innocent."

"Hey, it happens." Jessi's cell phone chimed and she took it out. She read a text, answered it, and shoved the phone back into her jacket pocket. "Artie says he's got more background on the family. Let's go to his office. I'll drive."

"I'm fine," Charmaine protested, but Jessi had already left the car. She huffed with irritation when Jessi jerked the driver's side door open. "Jessi."

"C'mon. Out. Faster than me giving you directions. Plus, you can continue your mood without getting us both killed." Jessi pulled Charmaine from the seat. When Charmaine glared at her, Jessi gestured for her to walk.

Charmaine marched around the front of the car mumbling. She got into the passenger seat, put on the seatbelt and glared at Jessi. "Happy now? You're in control."

"Yeah. I'm thrilled. Now shut up. I do my best crime solving when I drive."

"Oh pu-lease," Charmaine blurted.

Still, she kept quiet for the twenty-minute drive to the Lakeshore campus of the University of New Orleans. Charmaine had to admit that Jessi was right. In short order, Jessi found a parking space. She whipped out a permit and hung it on the rearview mirror.

"I don't have to circle looking for a spot like the rabble," Jessi quipped. She winked at Charmaine with a grin.

"The perks of doing the head of a department," Charmaine murmured. She ducked a playful swat aimed at her head.

"Don't knock it until you've had to fight rush hour in the rain to get here," Jessi replied. "Besides, at least my guy hasn't killed somebody."

"So funny." Charmaine squinted at her. "I finally get to meet the old dude."

"Yeah, so mind your manners."

Jessi pointed a finger at Charmaine. Then she led the way into the three-story building. They entered the Midlo Center for New Orleans studies. Jessi explained along the way about the library and extensive documents related to New Orleans history.

"Historians and researchers from all over come here to get information. Very big time," Jessi said with pride.

"Wow. My turn to ask if you're stuck on this guy." Charmaine whispered as a group of people walked toward them.

"Just concentrate on why we're here," Jessi replied. "And be cool."

"Don't worry. I'm won't show out in front of your boyfriend," Charmaine teased.

Jessi let out a snort of disgust as she pushed through the glass door. She waved to a young woman seated at a desk, who nodded back. Charmaine noted how the woman sneered behind Jessi's back.

"His office assistant," Jessi said looking back. "She made a face at me, right?"

"Yeah, not a fan." Charmaine glanced over one shoulder. The woman continued to track their progress down a hallway. "Competition for Dr. M.'s affections?"

"Don't know, don't care," Jessi replied. She stopped at a door, knocked once, and pushed through.

Dr. Arthur W. Marigny stood and took off his glasses. Charmaine suppressed a giggle when he actually sucked in his stomach at the site of Jessi. Still, he wasn't half bad looking for a middle-aged professor. He stood at least six feet tall with brown hair mixed with gray that somehow didn't make him appear old. His brown herringbone wool jacket and solid brown slacks completed his distinguished academic image. Handsome and loaded down with letters after his name. Nice package.

"You didn't have to come in, but I'm glad to see you." Artie beamed at Jessi. "This is your famous sister. Great to meet you."

Charmaine took his offered hand. "Hello, same here. I've heard a lot about you."

"All good," Jessi put in with a grin. She pinched one of his cheeks, which made his smile get bigger. "Now to business."

"Of course. Have a seat. I have refreshments after your ordeal with the police. Cold or hot?" Artie went to the corner of his office. He looked at them expectantly.

"Coffee please," Jessi said

"Nothing for me, thanks." Charmaine raised both eyebrows as Artie poured a cup for Jessi. He took great care to make sure Jessi was properly served before he sat down with them at a small table.

"So, babe. What do we know?" Jessi sipped from the UNO mug. When Charmaine mouthed the word "babe" at her, Jessi favored her sister with a death ray glare.

Charmaine cleared her throat to ward off a giggle. "Yes, Dr. Marigny, we're very interested in the Villiers line."

"Right." Artie drew himself as if preparing to address a grad school class. "What I have is as much a history of New Orleans."

"Don't get sidetracked into a discourse on the difference between the Spanish and French colonial influences in Louisiana," Jessi said.

"You know me too well," Artie said with a crooked grin. He looked at Charmaine. "My bottom line student."

"I'll bet," Charmaine replied with a smile. She felt the blast of heat from another fiery glance from Jessi.

"The Villiers family goes back over two hundred years in Louisiana. They settled in what was the old Attakapas Region, near what is now St. Martin Parish. Nicholas Fuselier de la Villiers is recorded as one of several commanders at the Attakapa Trading Post. In his case, from 1719 to 1722, he licensed merchants in the area. His sons became prosperous merchants. The family acquired land in what was to become St. Martin and Evangeline Parishes. Fascinating history."

"Not all of which we need to know right now," Jessi warned.

"Message received." Artie gave Jessi a pat on the thigh.

When his hand lingered as he looked at her, Charmaine cleared her throat loudly. "I think something warm would be nice actually. So chilly today."

Artie jumped up. "I have hot chocolate. Let me pour you a cup. Hot water on the ready always. Not everyone wants coffee. I have tea as well."

"Hot chocolate sounds wonderful," Charmaine said, with a side glance at Jessi.

"Don't worry about it being instant. I assure you the taste is fantastic." Artie spoke with his back to them as he busily fixed a mug.

"Lovely," Charmaine said. Then she lowered her voice. "Quit sending him erotic vibes or we won't get anything done."

"I didn't do anything." Jessi shrugged. "I can't help it if he's deprived at home and I woke him up."

"Then shut him off for a minute. Geez," Charmaine mumbled. Then she plastered on a smile when Artie faced them again with a steaming mug.

"Here we go. Sip and pronounce judgment." Artie handed the mug to Charmaine with a flourish.

"Thanks." Charmaine sipped, then blinked in surprise. Rich chocolate flavor flowed down her throat. "Damn that's good."

"I knew you'd approve. Now, where was I?" He turned again to his desk, found his tablet computer, and sat down again.

"Three hundred years ago in atta-something," Jessi replied dryly.

"Yes. To summarize, the Villiers family fortunes have fallen and bounced back three times over the generations. The money they now enjoy can be traced to lucrative land deals related to the oil and natural gas industry." Artie shrugged. "Not as interesting I'm afraid."

"Yeah, they're stinking rich. We're more interested in personal stuff," Jessi said.

"We read somewhere there were several suspicious deaths, talk of mistreatment of slaves and servants," Charmaine said with a glance at Jessi.

"Hmm, yes. I spoke to a friend of mine. Martha Harding does more of what I call historical gossip. A joke between friends. Anyway, there are references in early letters to an ancestor who had a separate family. A beautiful woman of color gave birth to six children. Their surnames were Villiere"

"Many white planters had mistresses and children with them. We're interested in..." Jessi stopped when Artie held up a palm.

"Yes, murder. But the two are related in this case." Artie smiled with satisfaction when Charmaine and Jessi leaned forward with interest. "In a happy coincidence, Martha is writing a book on family scandals. Many times, the domestic dramas of rich and influential families affected history. I have to concede Martha's interest isn't totally lightweight in nature."

"What's the story?"

"In 1803 or so, Alexandre Villiers de la Claire caused a family crisis by giving land to his eldest son born from his affair with a woman of color, a beautiful plaçage. Martha even sent me a picture of her oil portrait. Part of a private collection." Artie held up his tablet to show them the oil painting from an old art book. A lovely woman of color dressed in an elaborate ball gown gazed back at them from another era.

"Wow. Dude opened up the checkbook after getting a look at her, huh?" Charmaine let out a long whistle.

"Theirs was a true love match. Fortunately for him, Alexandre had come of age when his scandalized mother found out. Unfortunate for his legal wife, a seventeen-year-old girl from a prominent family. Basically, she was advised to suck it up," Artie said.

"Probably because all the men had mistresses, and were cool with the status quo." Charmaine shook her head with sympathy when Artie flipped the image to show Alexandre and his bride, Georgina.

"She's cute, but she's no Jessamine," Jessi said bluntly.

Artie blinked with surprise. "How do you know her name?"

"Here, on the page with the picture," Charmaine broke in, then rushed him on when Artie squinted at the screen.

"Georgina might not have had the charm of Alexandre's mistress, but what she did have was a fortune and a powerful family. Her father, grandfather, and uncles were willing to brush off a mistress or two. As long as Alexandre followed the rules. Be discreet, and most of the family money stayed with his legitimate heirs." Artie turned the tablet around to scroll through more pages.

"Except he gave a son property," Charmaine said.

"Deeded to the child's mother that he would gain control of once he reached age twenty. Apparently, Georgina had a temper like her father. She gave her husband hell, with support from her mother-in-law. But neither of them could fight male dominance. Here's the thing, the illegitimate son died of some mysterious illness, followed by his mother." Artie looked from Jessi to Charmaine, his dark eyebrows raised.

"Let me guess. There were whispers of murder. Are you saying sweet little Georgina, the southern debutante, did the deed?" Charmaine asked.

"Not personally. She had someone do it for her. The Villiers family history is mighty bloody." Jessi gazed at Charmaine. "You sure know how to pick 'em."

"Something I should know?" Artie's hazel eyes sparkled with curiosity.

"No," Charmaine replied when Jessi's lips parted. She stood and held out her hand. "Thank you so much for the research. I'll be in touch if I need any more background, but this might just be enough. Jessi, we'd better get going."

Jessi gave Artie a look. She stood, went to him, and planted a kiss on his cheek. "Thanks, prof."

"I was hoping we'd have lunch together. It's not often I deal with the contemporaries of the old families of Orleans Parish. They're a closed bunch." Artie came to his feet fast. "Sassafras won't be crowded yet, as it's only eleven."

"We've had a rough night and lots of work. But thanks. Maybe another time. C'mon, Jess." Charmaine smiled at him and pulled Jessi toward the door.

"I didn't know we were in such a hurry, but okay." Jessi exchanged another look with Artie before Charmaine pushed her out into the hallway. "Damn, Charmaine."

"Don't be talking about my love life to your man," Charmaine strode off.

Jessi jogged a few steps before she caught up to walk beside her. "He's not 'my man'. We have an understanding."

"And what's with that crack about my judgement when it comes to men? Like you of all people can talk. I can list five of your worse mistakes without even straining. Starting with Dayshawn when you were in high school."

"Ouch. Now that was unnecessary. Besides, the teen years don't count. I'm just saying, the family pedigree for your..." Jessi broke off at the scowl Charmaine gave her. "Nick's family creeps me out, and I regularly chat with dead people."

"Yeah, well passing judgment based on family is something neither of us should be quick to do." Charmaine pushed through the doors that led outside. Bright sunshine worked to sweep away the dark subject they'd been discussing. She breathed in the crisp early November air and let it out.

"True, but still..." Jessi went to the driver's side despite Charmaine's grumbling. "Oh just get in. I'll get you home fast."

Charmaine got into the Cruze. She glanced at the digital clock in the dashboard just as a bell tinkled on her phone. The looked at the calendar alert. "Shit. I have to shower, change, and get into the clinic. I have a two o'clock appointment. And my clinical supervisor is going to ask why I didn't come in this morning."

"Hey, that's a part-time gig anyway." Jessi guided the car through student traffic.

"Which I'd like to keep for the regular income, thank you very much. And I also happen to love being a therapist." Charmaine dropped the phone in her lap. Then she closed her eyes as she massaged her temples. "This case."

"Let's wrap it up and let the Villiers folk deal with Det. Harrison." Jessi made a rude gesture at another driver. She got a horn blast in response.

"The ghosts are still trouble at Magnolia Grove. Our job was to stop the thefts and clear out the ghoulies." Charmaine opened her eyes and heaved a deep sigh.

"Getting pulled into a nasty murder ain't exactly healthy for us either. The sheriff in Jefferson Parish would love to take us down to keep scandal away from the Villiers. They've got power and he's an elected. How much you wanna bet they contributed to his last campaign? Nick and company got it all figured out."

"Jessi, Nick wouldn't..." Charmaine's argument died away. The cold reality of Jessi's point sank in.

"Look, we can claim that we solved the thefts. I'll go in and make a big show of getting rid of the spirits. Then I'll wrap it up and invoice Miss Ann." Jessi gave a nod.

"Miss Marguerite," Charmaine replied, eyebrow raised.

"Same difference," Jessi snapped. "Besides, that will give me one last chance to squeeze info out of Georgina."

"Be nice to her. After all, she kind of helped us out the other night."

"That heffa had fun scaring everybody. She wasn't doing it to help us, trust me. I'm going to get more answers this time."

Charmaine picked up her cell phone again and tapped a text. Her finger hovered over the send button for a few seconds before she touched it. "I'm going to meet with Nick."

"You gotta be joking," Jessi said with force. She let out a loud hiss. "Charmaine."

"One last time. I have questions." Charmaine looked out of the window instead of back at Jessi.

"Oh, sure. And you figure he's going to open right on up and tell the whole truth, nothing but the truth, so help him God."

"If I can tell he's lying, then I'll have an answer. Plus, I want to know what's happened to Kadeem," Charmaine replied.

"Ah yes. He's the other likely candidate to be thrown under the bus. He's perfect. Not only did he have inside knowledge working for the Villiers Company, but he's related to the thieves. Hmm, maybe we're off the hook." Jessi slapped Charmaine's shoulder.

"Or he could be another victim." Charmaine looked at Jessi. Both went quiet for the rest of the ride.

****

Charmaine managed to get through the rest of the day. As usual, she rallied when her client came in. The young woman tore at Charmaine's heart, but she kept her professional face on. Her story of abuse as a child brought back memories from Charmaine's own early years. The difference between them was Latrisha's psychosis was real, not psychic ability mistaken for mental illness. Charmaine was careful to look for the difference. So far, she hadn't met anyone like her or Jessi. She spent most of their first hour trying to convince Latrisha to take the medication prescribed. Once her new client left, Charmaine lost her burst of energy. She couldn't stop frequent yawns. Paperwork required by insurance companies and Medicaid could cure the most severe case of insomnia. When she left the clinic at five o'clock, Charmaine had to fight fatigue to stay alert for the drive home. When she got inside, she dropped onto her sofa. An hour-long nap revived her. She got dressed for her dinner date with Nick. He'd moved back to New Orleans. No need to hide out since the cops knew where to find him. She drove to Upperline Restaurant. The same waiter that had served them before met her at the entrance. They went up the short flight of stairs to a less crowded section.

Nick stood as Charmaine walked toward him. The waiter pulled out a chair for her. Nickmade a fuss over making sure she was confortable. With a nod to the waiter, he sat down again. "I hope this means you don't think I'm a killer. You probably wouldn't want to share dinner rolls and sweet tea with me otherwise."

"So, we're skipping the small talk." Charmaine glanced at him and away to look around the room.

"Under the circumstances." Nick tried a smile but failed. He fidgeted with the butter knife on the white table cloth. "Listen, I know how it looks. You've probably heard some things about me, about Tanner and..."

"Was he your lover?" Charmaine said. Several heads turned in their direction. She looked at them hard, and they turned away.

Nick cast a quick glance around them as he cleared his throat. "You might want to talk a bit louder. I think that couple in the corner missed out on the drama."

"Sorry," Charmaine started, then stopped mid-apology. "Hold on. No, I'm not. I'm guessing you and your mother knew exactly what Ms. Yolanda Dawson's thug nephews were doing. Did Tanner stumble on the truth and the secrets behind your deal? Or was he in on it?"

"I don't know what the hell..." Nick blinked hard. He took a long drink from the tumbler in front of him. "I didn't know anything about the thefts. We wouldn't have hired you to find out about them. It doesn't make sense."

"Maybe you wanted us to uncover the truth. You couldn't turn in Yolanda's relatives. She knows too much about you and your mother. So, you had to stop her from robbing you blind. Hiring us to get rid of the ghosts was just a cover. You know what? I don't think your mother really believes in them."

"Good God, you give us way too much credit for being clever," Nick shot back with a bitter laugh.

"Devious is the word I'd use," Charmaine said.

She stopped when the waiter approached. When he left, Charmaine leaned close to Nick. He swallowed hard as he looked into her eyes. Charmaine fought against the magnetism that pulled her body to his. Nick's subtle, yet seductive scent thrown in with his good looks worked on her resistance.

"I didn't try to use you, not to cover up family crimes. What we felt, skin to skin, tongue to tongue, and more, that was real. I miss you."

Charmaine slowed her breathing and cleared her mind. She rested one palm on his right knee. Then slid her hand up higher to stop on his mid-thigh. The elegant tablecloth concealed the movement from everyone else unless they walked up to the table. Nick's leg trembled a bit. Lust pushed aside, Charmaine listened. Really listened.

"Dinner is almost here," she said after another thirty seconds. Then removed her hand. The heat from his muscular flesh still burned from the tips of her fingers and spread up her arm. "We'll go to your new place. Let's take dessert to go."

"Let's cancel the order and/or get them to pack it up for us," Nick said. His voice thrummed deep as he moved closer.

The waiter walked up and placed salad plates in front of Charmaine and then Nick. "Ranch for the lady and sensation dressing for Mr. Villiers. Your entrees will be out shortly. Can I get anything else? More tea, ma'am?"

"No, I'm good. Thanks." Charmaine gave the waiter a polite smile and started on her salad.

"Yes, you are. I still say we can skip..."

"You'll need nourishment to fuel the night ahead of you, Mr. Villiers," Charmaine quipped. She felt a flush of triumph when Nick gasped.

Charmaine savored every minute of lingering over her meal. The rainbow trout smothered in a sauce that included crawfish tails and crabmeat tasted wonderful. That wasn't the reason she took her time with each forkful. She enjoyed the delicious sensation of teasing Nick until he squirmed. By the time he paid for dinner, Nick seemed ready to grab Charmaine right there. He would have no doubt agreed if she'd suggested they race to the parking lot and have sex in his Mercedes SUV. Still, she made him wait. By the time he fumbled with the keyless entry to his spacious flat in the Warehouse District, Nick had trouble controlling his breathing. They started peeling off clothing before the door closed.

"Make sure it locks," Charmaine said. She laughed when Nick yanked his expensive sweater over his head and threw it on the floor.

"I don't care."

Nick grabbed her buttocks with both hands and lifted against his pelvis. Both were down to underwear only as he ground his hips against her. Their foreplay increased to a frenzy until they were naked and writhing together on a sofa that must have cost thousands.

"What will your housekeeper think if we leave traces of sex all over the furniture," Charmaine whispered, then bit his ear lobe.

Nick groaned deep in his throat. "She'd better get used to it. Getting inside you on my sofa is now my favorite."

Hours later Charmaine won a mild battle Nick waged to make her spend the night. She finally extricated herself from his embrace. Showered and dressed, she gave him a playful trail of kisses from his mouth down to his bellybutton before she left.

Forty minutes later she arrived at her cottage-style home. Jessi's SUV sat parked on the street. Scotty's new Range Rover sat in the other half of her double driveway. When she entered, Charmaine followed their voices to her kitchen, their usual war room. Jessi sprawled back in the chair at Charmaine's breakfast table. Scotty juggled a mug of beer with his cell phone. He gave a short wave by way of greeting and kept talking.

Jessi gazed at Charmaine. "Well?"

Charmaine shrugged out of her black leather moto jacket. She dropped her designer purse onto the small desk in a corner where she paid bills. Then she faced Jessi, hands on both hips.

"He's lying.

10.
Trick Questions

The next morning, a Thursday, dawned bright and clear. Charmaine stood at her kitchen counter nursing a second mug of Louisiana medium roast with chicory when Jessi padded into the kitchen. After downing six beers, Jessi had decided to spend the night with Charmaine. Scotty took his assignment to find Kadeem Hardy and left around one in the morning. He'd cautioned them to be careful as if it was necessary.

"Morning, late sleeper. Grits still hot."

"The hell you talkin' about? It's not even ten o'clock yet. Done lost your mind." Jessi continued mumbling as she shuffled around in Charmaine's extra slippers. She got two eggs from the refrigerator. Seconds later, they were frying sunny-side up in a small skillet.

"Hope you didn't drink all the coffee."

"My house, my coffee. Remember? And don't walk on the back of my slippers. Tearing my stuff up." Charmaine gave her a swat on the backside and then sat down. "I got us some croissants from my fave place on Royal Street."

"You up running the streets getting donuts at the crack of dawn. That rich white boy got the power," Jessi teased.

Charmaine frowned at the reference to her night with Nick. "Ain't got nothing to do with it."

"I'm not complaining. Hmm, these smell delish. Will go great with my eggs," Jessi replied. She picked up a croissant and saluted Charmaine with it.

"He knows more than he's telling." Charmaine went straight to what had troubled her sleep.

"Nah, you mean he's a bold-faced liar who may also be a murderer. The guy was his friend, maybe even in love with Nick. I'll bet he lured the poor sucker into a death trap." Jessi kept eating as if talk of murder with breakfast was no big deal.

"Nick may be all you say, but he's not stupid. He wouldn't kill Tanner and leave the body at his house. Doesn't make sense." Charmaine wrapped both hands around the mug to warm off the chill of their grim subject.

"Let me ask you something, and don't get all pissed off." Jessi's fork of runny yellow egg mixed with grits poised over her plate.

"Go ahead." Charmaine drank a coffee.

"Did you fall in love with Nick Villiers, I mean the real deal? Not a good sexing that made you like him better than the next guy. I'm talking planning a future together kind of love. The 'I wanna have his baby' thing." Jessi's voice held no trace of joking.

"No," Charmaine replied. She stood and crossed to the coffee pot. Even though the mug was still half full, she poured in more.

"You answered too quick, girl. Shit." Jessi dropped her fork and heaved a deep sigh.

"Jessi..." Charmaine stopped. Her sister knew her better than anyone. Scotty came in a close second, though he'd never have asked such an intimate question.

"You didn't have to sleep with him to get information," Jessi said.

"I go to bed with men to have sex. Period. Mutual desire and respect with a partner who is single. Sex doesn't have to be dirty, forbidden, or a means to an end." Charmaine let out a huff of air.

"You mean a commercial transaction like my former profession? Hey, some argue that a woman has a right to sell her services. Don't start," Jessi said fast to cut off Charmaine's protest. "Having a right doesn't mean it's a good idea. No matter how you dress it up, sex work is a dangerous, dirty biz. Being an object with some dude grunting and squirting all over you is demeaning. Oh sure, sex work activists try to spin it a different way. But any prostitute will tell you they want out as soon as possible."

Charmaine sat down next to Jessi again. "But you and Diamond have gone back to it before."

"Short answer, money. We both made a lot of cash, still could. We know a woman who has a nice setup. Safe, girls keep a big cut. High-end stuff. Politicians, fat doctors, even a few professors." Jessi grinned at Charmaine. "Not Artie. I really did meet him when I started school."

"Okay." Charmaine pursed her lips.

Jessi slapped her on the arm. "Shut up. And don't try to change the subject. Nick is lying. But about what?"

"If only I could read people like I'm reading a newspaper. Something about Kadeem, and snatches of being worried." Charmaine frowned in concentration. She mentally ran through her impressions from the night before.

"He could be intentionally blocking you. Hey, it's possible," Jessi added when Charmaine raised both eyebrows at her.

"Or distract me with sex." Charmaine tapped a forefinger on the side of her mug.

"Either way, you better kiss him goodbye. Consider last night your farewell fuck."

"Oh my God, Jessi. The things you say," Charmaine spluttered as coffee sloshed down the front of her cotton T-shirt.

"Hell, I've had my share of those. You know, one last freak for the road. Then adios, sucka." Jessi waved a hand over her head.

Charmaine laughed so hard, she had to put down the mug before the rest of the coffee ended up in her lap. Jessi took full advantage of her stage. She jumped up and performed a version of an erotic dance.

"Stop it," Charmaine finally gasped. She swatted Jessi with a dish towel. Both collapsed into giggles.

"Feel better about letting Nicky boy go?" Jessi said when they'd calmed down.

"So, that was your strategy. Distract me from the pain of giving up more nights with Nick. Well, you don't need to worry. I'm good." Charmaine looked at Jessi.

Jessi gazed back at her for a few seconds and then nodded. "Okay. Gotcha. What's our next move?"

"Like I said, from the snatches I picked up, Kadeem is somewhere in Gretna," Charmaine said. She pictured the small city across the Mississippi River south of New Orleans.

"Makes sense. They've got family over there." Jessi looked at Charmaine. "You didn't say, but I'm guessing he's still alive."

"I think so." Charmaine bit her bottom lip. "I hope so. Talking to the dead is your department.

"Speaking of which, Georgina wouldn't come out to play when I went to Magnolia Grove yesterday. Not that I had much time to work. Yolanda threw me out. Like her kin getting arrested was all my fault." Jessi clicked her tongue in disgust. "She should blame them for being dumb as a sack of rocks."

"Mrs. Villiers went along with you being kicked out?" Charmaine got up and washed out her mug.

"She wasn't there. Hey, I just thought of something. Yolanda still has a job." Jessi's arched brows pull together.

"Mrs. Villiers doesn't have warm feelings about Yolanda, but she doesn't fire her. Proof of our theory?" Charmaine starting cleaning up dishes, but her mind worked through the Villiers case puzzle.

Jessi nodded. "Yeah. She's definitely got something on them. Only thing that makes sense. If we find out what..."

"Then more pieces may fall into place. Like how all of it connects to Tanner ending up dead."Charmaine was about to lay out more theories when her cell phone rang. She cut off the blast of a bluesy R&B tune when she answered it. "Yeah, got it. No, I can do it. Scotty... okay. Fine."

"Let me guess. Scotty found Kadeem," Jessi said.

"Like I knew he would, and yes, Kadeem is breathing. I can't wait to hear his explanation for what the hell is going on." Charmaine glanced down at her T-shirt. "I gotta change."

"Another guess. Scotty says you shouldn't go see Kadeem by yourself. I agree. With Kadeem and Yolanda's family, no telling what you'd be walking into." Jessi pointed a finger at her.

"Yeah, yeah. I'm sick of these guys jerking me around just because I gave them a little bit of heaven." Charmaine chuckled.

"Girl, get the hell outta here with that mess. Hey, serious though. Watch your back." Jessi's expression turned serious.

"I'll be with Scotty." Charmaine formed a pretend pistol with one hand.

"Nuff said. I hope y'all don't end up in a street battle though."

"We'll be all right. What are you going to do?" Charmaine wiped the counters as she talked.

"First, I'm gonna warm up the rest of my breakfast in the microwave." Jessi got up with her plate.

"Oh yeah, at least your priorities are straight," Charmaine quipped.

"Then I'm going to turn in this mid-term paper. Finally, I'm going to call on my Shadow Squad to get some intel." Jessi put her plate in the small microwave, set it, and turned to face Charmaine.

"Your who?"

"My Phantom Posse," Jessi went on, warming up to her topic. "I've been developing a spirit network for the past year. Makes sense, right? I figured, why wait until I'm in a neighborhood to find the ghosts in the know. So far, I have seven sources from the other side. They see a lot." Jessi nodded with satisfaction. "Lucas has been a big help."

"Your..."

"He's not my ghost boyfriend. He lacks a very important qualification." Jessi shrugged and held up a middle finger.

"I'll bet he's working on it. I've read about spirits who have sex with the living. Then there are legends about incubus. Except Lucas isn't a demon." Charmaine considered the flaw in her premise.

"No, he's not. Will you focus?" Jessi snapped. "I have to show up at that stupid job Artie got for me."

"Don't knock legal employment. Beats looking over your shoulder all the time," Charmaine put in.

"Whatever. Then I have a class. I'll go back to Magnolia Grove this evening, once Yolanda gets off work. I got the go ahead from Mrs. Villiers."

"Good. Speaking of our client, she emailed me this morning."

"Another early riser," Jessi joked.

"Yeah. She says the spirit activity has greatly decreased, and she'll no longer need our services. So today is to be your wrap-up visit to deal with the ghosts." Charmaine held out her cell phone for Jessi to read.

"You believe her?" Jessi removed her plate when the timer on the microwave pinged. She blew steam from the hot food as she sat down again.

"Girlfriend has bigger issues what with an employee dead, another one missing, and her son a suspect." Charmaine loaded the dishwasher. "A few missing doodads have probably dropped to the bottom of her list."

"Especially if she thinks we're about to pull family skeletons out of the closet. Hey, you think she knows about you and Nick?" Jessi tested a forkful of grits. Satisfied, she downed a mouthful.

"Who cares? Just find out as much as you can from that Georgina. And don't let her cause more trouble for us," Charmaine said. She headed out to her bedroom to dress to leave again. "And start the dishwasher on your way out."

"Yes, mother." Jessi rolled her eyes at Charmaine's back as she left.

****

Scotty sat at a table in the fast food restaurant where he and Charmaine had agreed to meet. Just off the busy Westbank Expressway in Gretna, cars whizzed by in a steady stream outside the glass front of the main dining area. Scotty waved to her from a corner table when she entered. He was dressed in a heavy black denim jacket against the chilly morning. The early lunch crowd, or late breakfast diners, sat scattered around tables. At just after eleven in the morning, the place wasn't crowded.

"Traffic bad?" Scotty pushed a mug of coffee toward Charmaine after she sat down.

"Not too." Charmaine scanned the dining room.

"Food's okay. Nice waffles. At least that's what Brian said." Scotty gave a subtle jerk of his head to their left. Two men talked as if they didn't notice Charmaine or Scotty.

"You think we need that much back-up?" Charmaine felt a twinge of anxiety.

"Best to be safe now than sorry later. Especially when it comes to Kadeem's crowd," Scotty replied.

His calm tone and relaxed posture helped settle her nerves. "If you say so."

Scotty hunched forward and spoke low. "We have the advantage. I'm pretty sure Kadeem has no clue we've found him. Plus, I hear he's scared."

"That's what worries me. If he's scared, then we've got danger coming at us from all sides. The police in two parishes would love to jam me and Jessi up behind this crap." Charmaine tried the coffee, found it lukewarm, and wrinkled her nose.

Scotty motioned to a waitress, and the young woman scurried over. She poured steaming coffee. He thanked her and waited until they were alone before speaking. He leaned across the table. "I thought Harrison was cool. I mean, for a cop. He follows the facts."

"Yeah. Well, the fact is, Jessi and me keep landing with both feet in the middle of murder cases. Look, let's just get this over with. I'm eager to get out of Jefferson Parish fast as possible." Charmaine downed a gulp of coffee to fortify herself.

Scotty gave an exaggerated sigh. "I need to give you tips on making friends with local law enforcement."

"Funny man."

She followed him out of the restaurant. After checking to make sure she'd locked her car, Charmaine climbed into Scotty's Range Rover. The two men Scotty had recruited to be private security strolled out five minutes later. They got into a black Ford Explorer. With a barely perceptible nod, the man Scotty had called Brian pulled into traffic.

"Brian and Ray will meet us there. They'll be parked down the street from the duplex where Kadeem is holed up." Scotty drove along, taking several turns. Then drove back south in the direction they'd just left.

"Great. With fancy GPS in this thing, you're lost." Charmaine squinted out the window as they passed the same discount store again.

"I'm seeing if we're being followed." Scotty's gaze flickered to the rearview mirror inside and out.

Charmaine's heart sped up. She sat stiff, afraid to look around in case they were being watched. "And?"

"All clear." Scotty nodded.

"Same here, bruh," a deep voice rumbled through the Range Rover's speakers.

"Damn. Give me some warning. Scared the shit outta me." Charmaine let out a loud breath, hand on her cheek.

Scotty laughed. "Blue tooth connection is a beautiful thing."

"Arrived at scene. Stop transmitting," the voice rumbled again.

"Message received," Scotty replied and ended the call.

"Wait a minute. That's cop jargon." Charmaine looked at the speakers as though she could see the man talking.

"Ex. Military police. Brian worked for the Houston PD for twenty years, too. Got hurt; retired on disability." Scotty continued driving.

"Hey, how old is your buddy anyway?" Charmaine frowned.

"Don't be an age bigot. He's forty-eight, and I'll take him over two twenty-four-year-olds any day of the week. He's solid muscle, got hella experience and he's armed." Scotty drove into a neighborhood of houses close together.

Charmaine raised both palms. "I'm golden with him then. Are we close?"

"Yeah, number 2346. No parking close by. That might be a good thing though." Scotty expertly parallel parked on a cross street. "We'll have to walk about a block."

"He'll see us coming." Charmaine took a felt hat out of her large purse and jammed it on her head. Then she put on sunglasses. "This will help. Plus, he's never met you."

"Hopefully Kadeem is still distracted on the phone." Scotty hit the electric locks opening the doors.

"Oh, so you're psychic now," Charmaine quipped to cover the return of her jangled nerves now that they'd arrived.

"Nope. Reverse phone number lookup using the address. His cousin inherited the house from his grandmother. Lucky for us, he was sentimental and kept the number." Scotty tugged on his jacket with the New Orleans Saints football team logo.

"And you know he's on the phone because..." Charmaine scanned the neighboring houses.

"I had a friend call pretending to look for the cousin to give him a prize. Nobody can resist getting a freebie." Scotty grinned at Charmaine. Then his expression turned serious as he placed a hand on her forearm. "We're ready, and we got your back. Concentrate on your objective and let us handle what comes up. And no, I'm not expecting any serious issues."

"Right. Let's go."

Charmaine inhaled and let out the air once her leather boots hit the pavement. She started at the sound of Scotty turning on the Range Rover's alarm system. Despite Scotty's six foot three muscular presence, Charmaine felt exposed as they walked along. They didn't pass anyone, which didn't surprise her. Most were probably at work. A chilly day meant anyone with the day off would most likely prefer to stay inside. Charmaine couldn't decide if the lack of people was a good sign. A lot of fellow pedestrians would have made her see threats all around as well. Scotty must have picked up on her paranoid vibes. He looped his arm through one of hers seconds later. They walked along like a couple visiting friends. Scotty kept up a stream of small talk for the short walk that seemed like forever to Charmaine. When Scotty pulled to the path leading to the front door, Charmaine tugged him back.

"We gonna just walk up and ring the bell?" she whispered. Her head swiveled left and then right as she talked.

"If we break in through the back door or a window, the guy could shoot us," Scotty replied in a level tone.

Charmaine started to respond, but Scotty had flattened his bulky frame against the front door. He gestured for her to make herself visible by standing three feet back. Then his pressed the button on the frame. She heard the series of musical chimes.

"Lord, please don't let him start shooting because of nerves," Charmaine murmured. She pushed away the image of a bullseye painted between her eyes. The tan and green curtains to her left twitched aside. She waved though she couldn't see anyone. Fifteen seconds later the sound of a series of clicks and clacks signaled locks being opened. Scotty eased away as Charmaine moved in close to the door. The moment it cracked, Scotty pushed his way in. The force shoved Kadeem across the foyer. He stumbled against the wall but pushed upright again.

"Gun," Charmaine blurted out.

Scotty had already jammed Kadeem's wrist against the jagged edge of a table. Kadeem yelped as his fingers released against his will. The pistol dropped onto the beige carpet, bounced, and slid well out of his reach. Charmaine pushed the door closed with one foot. Then she crossed to scoop up the pistol.

"Don't be so damn stupid. You don't want the police responding to shots fired, do you? I'm guessing not," Charmaine hissed at him.

"He's alone," Scotty said before she posed the question. "We made sure."

"Oh, so they sent you to kill me Must be a sweet payday for you," Kadeem said. He clenched his teeth against the pain of Scotty's strong grip on his injured arm.

Charmaine crossed to a window. The Ford Explorer still parked down the street helped ease the tightness in her chest. "I'm here to try and help you, fool."

"You're hired help for the Villiers, and the Hulk here attacks me soon as I opened the door. I'm feeling loved already," Kadeem spat.

"Look, bruh, I'm gone let you go. But trust and believe I will take you out if you move wrong. We ain't here to hurt you. She's telling the truth." Scotty spoke in a level voice.

Kadeem's chest heaved as he breathed fast, eyes still wide with fear. "Then give me my gun back."

"Man, be serious," Scotty said with a grunt.

"Okay. Okay." Kadeem swallowed hard. "What y'all want?"

"The story, Kadeem. The whole story. Look, I'm in this shit storm just like you. The cops think I had something to do with Tanner ending up cold in Nick's house. The way I see it, we're both dead meat the rich folks are willing to throw to the dogs. They don't care which one of us ends up on trial for killing him. With your cousins locked up, won't take the Jefferson Parish Sheriff long to find you. We don't have time to play." Charmaine spoke fast and to the point.

Kadeem blinked at her hard. Then he directed a gaze at Scotty. "They won't talk."

"You don't seem too sure of that," Scotty drawled. When Kadeem flinched, a terrible grin made Scotty even fiercer looking rather than affable.

"Your folks have given up their own brothers and sisters over less serious crimes. We're talking murder. I figure they're negotiating who to give up as we speak." Charmaine tapped the fashion wristwatch on her right wrist with a forefinger of her left hand. "Tick-tock."

"Yeah, and then you could turn me in to clear yourself of a murder beef." Kadeem licked his full lips as he gazed from Charmaine to Scotty and then back again.

"NOPD has a call out to other LEO's with your description. We came to talk instead of making a call to them," Scotty answered before Charmaine could reply.

Charmaine didn't say anything, content to let the silence stretch. In the quiet, she heard voices. For a few seconds, she wondered if Scotty had gotten it wrong that Kadeem was alone. Then sounds of a bell and applause sounded familiar. A television game show droned on a room away. She centered her attention on Kadeem. His dark gaze bounced back and forth from Scotty to Charmaine. She picked up on words playing across his mind like closed captions on a movie screen.

"The bottom line is, you don't have anything to lose. Keep up the debate and we walk. By the way, your cousin and his girlfriend have been gone a long time. No telling what they're up to right now. We could let you deal with 'em all by yourself." Charmaine stood with her legs apart, hands on her hips, to strike a "don't try me" pose.

"Shit." Kadeem scrubbed a large palm over his closely cropped hair. "Shit."

"How did you get caught up, man? C'mon," Scotty prodded.

"Tanner and Nick. I shoulda known them rich white dudes would burn me first chance. They—"

"We don't have time for you to hit the replay button," Charmaine snapped to head off his rant. "Start with the night Tanner was killed."

"We was partying. Booze, drugs, girls, guys... it was a buffet up in there. No different from what we usually did. Tanner is rubbing on some guy. I knew he was mostly trying to get Nick's attention. That was some twisted shit between them. Tanner pretended he didn't care Nick wanted no part of him. Nick sorta enjoyed yanking his chain. A power trip ya know?" Kadeem gave a snort. "I didn't care. It was all golden. Here I'm in fancy penthouses and shit. Some of their vacation cabins look like mansions."

"Yeah, yeah. That night," Charmaine interrupted again to get him back on track.

"I seen it building up to a head for a long time. Between Nick and Tanner I mean. Tanner numbed up on a mix of drugs like always, watching Nick when he thinks nobody is looking. Nick goes to a bedroom with like three women. I'm letting this crazy redhead blow me. It was wild." Kadeem's eyes glazed over as he remembered. "All of a sudden, I hear yelling, girls screaming, furniture turning over. Tanner and Nick are swinging hands at each other. Then Gee showed up wanting his money."

"Wait, back up. Who?" Charmaine blinked at him.

"Greg, but we call him Gee. He claimed I didn't pay enough for the party favors. Just a misunderstanding. It's all a little hazy. I'd been blowing smoke and drinking, plus the chick ain't never stop working on me. Man, my head was swimming. Greg talking fast. Her head going up and down in my lap. Shit got real when Gee pulled out his piece and one of his boys pushed his way through the front door. I'm trying to talk some sense to Gee when Tanner comes stumbling in crying about Nick owes him. The others got scared and scatter, shots are fired, and Tanner ends up on the floor." Kadeem dropped onto a lumpy sofa along one wall. He seemed to have run out of steam.

"You weren't even at Nick's place." Scotty looked at Charmaine and shrugged. Then he kicked Kadeem's leg to prompt him. "Hey, keep talking. How did Tanner's body end up at Nick's place?"

"He wasn't dead. Nick and Tanner wanted to run before the cops got there. We heard sirens. No way we had time to clean up the drugs, the blood, and... one of the girls was passed out in a corner.

Overdoes maybe?" Kadeem blinked up at them as if they had the answer.

"So, y'all left. Didn't wait to see if the girl needed help or was still alive. Where was this?" Charmaine gazed at him with a scowl of contempt.

"Flat in one of the buildings owned by Tanner's uncle. Or maybe one of his brothers. It's going to be rented out, but the other units need to be finished. Holding company, so it wouldn't be traced to them if things went wrong." Kadeem waved a hand. "Report was somebody broke in to party."

"Did you bother to check on the woman y'all left behind?" Charmaine wanted to take a turn kicking the man.

"Hell, we had bigger problems. Besides, street hoes know the deal. Occupational hazard. Tanner was bleeding, but the wound didn't look serious. I helped patch up cousins all the time after drive-bys," Kadeem said.

"I can't even..." Charmaine huffed out a short breath. "Go on."

"Tanner was more worried about Nick. He blubbered on and on, kept trying to get Nick to hug him, to admit they belonged together. I left to get some bandages, peroxide, stuff like that. Like I said, I figured I could patch him up." Kadeem sprang to his feet. He looked at Scotty. Then he started to pace in a circle. "I didn't have nothing to do with him ending up dead. I wasn't even there. Look, I can maybe find the receipt. Wait a minute. I'll bet that all-night drugstore has me on their security tape. When Tanner ended up dead, I was nowhere around Nick's place."

"Your story is Tanner was alive when you left, but dead when you got back." Charmaine looked at Scotty. "Why not just explain all this to the cops?"

Kadeem skidded to a stop three feet from Charmaine. "Bitch, you crazy?"

Scotty crossed with so much speed that Kadeem had no time to blink. He yanked Kadeem close until their faces were inches apart. "Call her a bitch one more time. Go on, so I can smash them yellow teeth down your throat."

Charmaine moved fast to stand next to Scotty. "C'mon, relax. Besides I've been called worse by a better class of dude. I won't break."

Kadeem stumbled when Scotty shook him loose. He smoothed out the wrinkles of the pull-over sweater. A lump still showed where Scotty had gripped the fabric into a ball in one massive fist. "Thank you. Acting all crazy up in here."

"If you punch him in the mouth, he won't be able to tell us more," Charmaine replied in a cool voice. She wore a hard smile. "Then again, we might have all we need already."

"Yeah." Scotty took a step toward Kadeem again.

Kadeem scuttled away until he flattened his body against a far wall. "Hey, hey, I can clear myself and you."

"Humph. We could get police calls for that date. Find out the address of the property. They'll be able to place you there using fingerprints and maybe DNA," Scotty said.

"Find the drug dealer you cheated to confirm you're a drug trafficker, and an accessory to murder," Charmaine added.

"Gee won't talk. He's married to my cousin and he..." Kadeem's voice died away. His Adam's apple bobbed as he swallowed hard.

"Greg-married-to-your-cousin is pissed about his money, his drugs, and I'll bet this wasn't the first time you shorted him." Charmaine didn't need to guess. She read it all in Kadeem's fevered thoughts. They swirled around his mind like a whirlpool.

"Plus, you the reason he's jammed up with a murder," Scotty added.

"Listen. Listen to me." Kadeem pushed away from the wall to stand straight. "Tanner had a pill problem. Plus he liked synthetic weed. Plenty of people knew about it. What if his drug dealer followed us and killed him?"

"The dealer you hooked him up with, Kadeem." Charmaine shook her head.

"Even if that's what happened, then the dealer will want to shut you up. He won't go after the rich white dude. Too risky. But you?" Scotty shrugged with a smile as if the idea pleased him.

"After all, you're the one who didn't pay up," Charmaine said, piling it on.

"Nah, nah. I ain't goin' down by myself. You and your sister, y'all been screwing Nick. I'll tell them all about it." Kadeem gasped at the scowl Scotty turned on him. "Wait, I didn't mean... man, I'm stressed to shit. Lemme just..."

"Shut up," Charmaine hissed.

She spun aside to get clear of a window. Seconds later a crash from the back of the duplex made them all jump. Footsteps followed. Kadeem stood frozen in place, his mouth stretched wide in a silent scream. Scotty pressed his back against the wall to be invisible to the person coming down the hall. A black sleeved arm appeared first. Scotty took advantage of the guy's focus on Kadeem. He grabbed the arm, twisted hard, and jammed a booted foot into the intruder's instep. The gun went flying at the same moment the man cried out.

Charmaine would later swear she heard bone cracking. Yet in the midst of the action, they had no time to reflect.

A teenager, no older than eighteen it appeared, panted between moans of pain. He lay rolled into a ball on the floor. When Scotty turned, he suddenly jumped to his feet and lunged. Scotty whirled to the side and put him in a choke-hold until his body went limp.

Charmaine rushed forward and slapped Scotty's muscular arms. "Scotty, don't kill him."

Scotty let the guy sink to the dingy carpet. "Nah, he's just out. Pressure point."

"Let's get out of here in case someone heard the fight and called 911," Charmaine said. She scurried to a window and looked out.

"Wait, you can't take off and leave me behind when they tryin' to kill me," Kadeem croaked. On his knees, he cowered in an attempt to scoot behind the sofa out of sight.

"No worries. You're coming with us. First, you gonna change your pants." Scott pointed to the wet stain on Kadeem's crotch. He took three long-legged steps then dragged Kadeem to his feet.

Charmaine wrinkled her nose as she looked at Scotty. "Then we'll have breathing space to figure out what to do with you."

"Oh God." Kadeem gaped from her to Scotty and back again.

"Too late to get religion," Charmaine retorted.

****

Jessi arrived at Magnolia Grove around three thirty in the afternoon. Luckily the truculent housekeeper had the day off. Mrs. Villiers told Jessi she'd be in later. So, the groundskeeper, a man in his late fifties, let Jessi into the house. Mr. Sammy Perkins smiled often as he walked Jessi from her SUV in the parking lot. Jessi joked he seemed in good humor for a man who worked in a haunted mansion owned by murder suspects. He let out a belly laugh.

"I do my job, collect my pay and head home before dark to the grandchildren. My formula for staying safe and sane when it comes to this place." Mr. Perkins' chocolate brown face split in half by a wide grin. "You holler when you're done, little miss."

"Thanks, Mr. Sammy." Jessi grinned back at him.

He waved as he strode off to other tasks. Jessi wandered down the central hallway after he was gone. She peeked into the formal dining room but moved on. A tickle up her spine guided her. She paused at the bottom of the grand staircase. Jessi looked up to the second-floor landing. Ten seconds ticked by and she continued on. The ladies' parlor was opposite the formal dining room. She entered and glanced around, standing very still to focus. The only movement visible came from the draperies pulled back to let in light. Stirred by air from a vent, the delicate cream lace shivered. A movement to her right confirmed Jessi's sixth sense.

"Good afternoon, Georgy, old girl," Jessi said.

Georgina Turnbull Villiers sat in a chair holding a fan. The floral fabric of the upholstery showed through the transparent figure. Still, the outlines of her peach taffeta gown could be seen. She snapped the decorative fan closed.

"Address me as Miss Georgina or Mistress Villiers, or don't speak to me at all," Georgina snapped. "Your station in life does not permit such familiarity."

"Stuff a sock in it grumpy old bat," Jessi shot back. She strolled in and sat across from Georgina in a matching chair. "I'd offer to fix us a cup of coffee or tea, but you can't partake. Tsk, tsk. Another drawback of being dead."

"You seem very careless with your attitude, young woman. Have you forgotten I have something you want very much?" Georgina lifted her chin as she stared away from Jessi. "I can carry my secrets to the grave, you know."

"You're already in the grave." Jessi waved a hand.

"What I mean is..." Georgina screwed up her face when Jessi chuckled. "The devil take you then. I won't utter another word."

"Georgina, you're stuck to this house because you were murdered here. Well you claim. Could be a lie to get attention." Jessi shrugged.

"How dare you." Georgina huffed and puffed into incoherence.

"I've been able to find out a lot more without you. Talk or don't talk. Makes no diff to me." Jessi noticed a crystal bowl of chocolate covered mints. "Hey, I love these."

"So, you don't care if Nick and Tanner Gladstone had an unnatural friendship," Georgina replied. She glared at the bowl and it moved two inches from Jessi's reach.

"Old news." Jessi leaned forward enough to grab a mint. She popped it in her mouth.

"Or that Laura and Nick are plotting to shut out Evelyn from the family coffers. Evelyn and her husband are planning the same for them." Georgina sniffed. "I know the details and how it relates to that poor boy's untimely death. Not that I approve of homosexuality. In my day, men performed their duty to provide heirs. What they did on 'business trips' to the city was kept discreet."

Jessi did not let her interest in the connection show. Instead, she maintained her casual pose. "Tanner threatened to tell the world Nick swung both ways. Ho-hum. Figured it out days ago. Not that anyone would care. Lunch time gossip that would lose steam quick."

"Tanner wouldn't tell something that would harm him more than Nicholas. No, the secret was much bigger." Georgina grinned when Jessi glanced at her. "Ah, I have your attention at last."

"Almost two hundred years ago, one of you killed the child and his mother over land," Jessi tossed out. Her gambit worked.

Georgina gasped, one hand over her heart. "How did you... You couldn't possibly know."

"Don't you love this modern information age?" Jessi unwrapped a second mint, popped it in her mouth, and grinned.

I don't as a matter of fact," Georgina grumbled.

"I'm not surprised family ghosts still float around here. If there is a heaven, and I'm not convinced, you folks wouldn't get in. I don't believe the afterlife or other religious stuff. So, there must be some other reason you can't move on." Jessi tapped one forefinger against her jaw.

"This is my home. I have a perfect right to be here," Georgina replied with starch in her tone.

"I think you'd like to rest. You don't like the modern age, and those spirits upstairs aren't your friends." Jessi played her last and best card.

Georgina's mouth trembled. "Haven't I suffered enough? You come here to torture me. Those cretins that prowl in the attic are no fit company for a woman of my breeding."

"I have a way out for you, a method that will ease your transition. I can't say to what. Obviously since I'm still alive. But a change might be nice." Jessi kept her tone casual. "Of course, I would set the ticket price for such a journey."

Georgina swiped her eyes with one hand and stiffened her spine. "What I know in exchange for some kind of witchcraft? Certainly not. I'm a good Christian woman."

"Don't be so dumb," Jessi said.

"I know about you people. The fact that you speak to spirits tells me you have an unholy alliance with Satan. You're no different from that evil woman, Marie Laveau. Oh yes, I know all about your kind." Georgina snapped the fan open again. It fluttered as she worked it.

"As opposed to your murderous relatives, who gotta be roasting in hell for all the shit they've done. Yeah, right. You can judge me." Jessi let out a snort. "I don't believe in magic. But science... We're all energy, and there is some force tying your energy to Magnolia Grove. We don't have all of the answers, but there are promising lines of research. In the meantime, think of it as a treatment for what ails you. Not magic. Definitely nothing tied to a mythical demon."

"My older brother was quite the man of reason. Of course, father ended his studies because Bartholomew had obligations." Georgina gazed off as though looking into the past.

"Spill the dirt if you want out," Jessi said, cutting into Georgina's thoughts.

Georgina's expression turned mischievous. "Oh bother it all. I want to tell you just so that noxious Marguerite will twist in the wind."

"Georgy, I don't care what anyone else says. You're a gem." Jessi winked at her.

"Stop calling me that ridiculous name," Georgina said and shook a finger at Jessi. An impish smile tugged at her lips until her frown dissolved.

11.
Disorderly Conduct

"Something about a will. That's it? Three hours hanging out with dead people who should know all the secrets and nothing but vague gobbledy-gook." Charmaine threw up both hands.

Jessi jammed fists on her hips. "Like you did so much better. Kadeem is full of crap and not much else. Damn sure ain't no useful information."

"Keep quiet," Scotty said, his voice a quiet rumble in the dark.

"Yeah. Y'all talking loud enough to wake the dead." Diamond whispered. She covered her mouth with both hands. Muffled snorts came as she smothered her giggles.

The other three turned in concert and shushed her. And so began what Charmaine called their most insane witness interview ever. They crouched down behind a massive marble tomb in the Metairie Cemetery on Ponchartrain Boulevard. Two massive security poles provided pools of brightness, but most of the cemetery lay in shadows. The lights only made the shadows look more menacing. Despite the name, the one hundred and forty-five-year-old cemetery was located in New Orleans. Resplendent final resting places held the remains of numerous distinguished figures. None of which impressed Charmaine and company in that moment. They had more pressing concerns.

Scotty's friend from the Gulf War Vets group owned the company that provided security. He'd let them in with assurances they weren't hanging out to do a drug deal. After all, there weren't that many legit activities one would perform in a cemetery after dark. Unless of course, you were a detective who used ghosts as confidential informants.

"Trespassing, desecrating graves, criminal mischief," Charmaine mumbled. She hugged herself, hoping the hand warmers in her suede jacket pockets would penetrate her chilled body.

"Hey, don't sweat. Plan B is Donnie will step in to back us if the police show." Scotty's teeth flashed a smile at her.

"I feel so much better," Charmaine mouthed.

He was about to reply when the swish of leaves and keys jingling made them all freeze. A circle of white light played along the ground, then up the sides of several tombs. A gruff voice sounded.

"Hey, Scotty and friends. It's me, Donnie. For God's sake, don't shoot me or nothin'," he said in a good-natured voice.

Scotty stood first with a grunt. "Hey, man. Lucky for you I'm not trigger happy."

Donnie shared a brother-man half hug with Scotty as the two laughed. "Word, bruh. How y'all doin' out here? Listen, no need to worry or anything. I told the grounds manager some ghost hunters are shooting a film. Gave him the cash you supplied. He's solid. You got until midnight."

"Hopefully we can finish filming by then." Scotty turned to Jessi.

"Right. Five hours is more than enough time. We'll be long gone by then." Jessi made a show of hoisting her camera.

"Fancy outfit you got," Donnie said, pointing at it.

"Full spectrum HD camcorder with UV and IR sensitivity capable of recording light not visible to the human eye," Jessi recited.

"Right." Donnie frowned in puzzlement at the camera.

"Anyway, thanks for helping us out, man. We really appreciate," Scotty said and slapped his pal on the shoulder.

"No prob, bruh. Remember, I get discounted advertising on your hit show." Donnie smiled at him and nodded.

"We have to sell it to the Supernatural Channel first. You know how it is. We gotta get quality footage and pitch to the executives," Charmaine said.

"Right, right. Hey, there's always going viral on the internet as a back-up," Donnie replied, his eyes bright with excitement. He was about to go on when his two-way radio beeped followed by a female voice. He turned to reply.

Five hours?" Charmaine looked from Scotty to Jessi, then at the digital display on her smartwatch. "Oh hell no."

"It's going to feel like five hundred years if you keep bitchin' and moanin'," Jessi clipped.

"Hey, guys. Gotta go to another site. Some drunk tourists are stumbling around the pet cemetery yelling, 'Here kitty, kitty.' Damn, they must think it's Mardi Gras or something. My guy is at the main gate. Just be sure to text him when you're on your way out."

"Sure thing. We won't make the guy work too late." Scotty slapped palms with Donnie.

"Naw, bruh. He normally patrols six to overnight anyways. Peace." Donnie waved and then left.

"Charmaine shook her head. "Indie filmmakers pitching a ghost hunting reality series. Sounds more sensible than what we're really doing. And more stable."

"We got paid for this case," Jessi reminded her.

"Yeah," Charmaine conceded. The image of several bills marked "paid" made her feel somewhat less irritable.

"Now we get to find out what Mrs. Villiers and her crazy kids have really been up to." Jessi squinted into the dimness that surrounded them.

"The Villiers family has several dozen wills on record. They stretch back at least two hundred years, not counting the ones in France. I wish Georgina could have narrowed it down a tad." Charmaine followed Jessi's gaze, saw nothing and leaned against Diamond for warmth.

"But you do know the time period, sort of. If she knows about it, then it's probably a will Georgina's husband made or one of his parents... maybe his grandparents. She was murdered, so that may be why she doesn't know more." Diamond scrolled through one of her social media feeds as she talked. She didn't notice the other three gaping at her.

"Damn. That actually makes a lot of sense," Charmaine said. She stood straight and stamped her fur-lined leather boots on the ground. "We could be sitting all warm and cozy in the Orleans Clerk of Courts archives room. Sure beats trolling a cemetery for spirits that may or may not cooperate."

"Yeah, on a night with forty-two-degree temps," Scotty added and glanced at Jessi.

"Look, my sources say at least three Villiers ancestors haunt this place. The family moved the one that died back in 1807..."

"Yes, we know. When the prestigious cemetery opened, they moved him here for a grander burial site. I'm sure he appreciates lying next to his fancy friends." Charmaine snorted and nudged Diamond with an elbow.

"You too crazy, girl," Diamond said, still following the antics of her buddies online.

"My dead sources are more help than your live one. Kadeem got nerve trying to dictate terms in his position. Y'all should have introduced his scrub ass to rock and hard place," Jessi shot back.

"Brian and Ray aren't going to let him feel comfortable, trust me," Scotty replied.

"Oh, Scotty put a scare in him, too." Charmaine bounced from one foot to the next to fight the chill.

"Yeah, well—" Jessi's head jerked to her right and swung the camera up.

"What?" Charmaine peered in the direction Jessi faced.

"I think they're here," Jessi murmured.

"I'm out. I don't do chats with dead dudes," Scotty said. He walked backward along the concrete paved path in question.

"Um, I'll be with him." Diamond skipped a few feet to catch up with him.

Charmaine frowned at them over her shoulder. "Y'all supposed to be our back-up."

"We gone be your back-up over there, under the light. By the big statue of the Archangel Michael." Diamond pushed up against Scotty.

"C'mon, Scotty. You faced down insurgents in Iraq and tracked terrorists over here." Charmaine turned to confront them.

"Uh-huh, live ones. But I'ma let y'all handle the ghost thing. We need to talk later about how you know so much about my work. Yell if you need me." Scotty didn't move to follow her.

"I don't believe this." Charmaine huffed in exasperation.

"Hey, you better hurry up or you'll lose Jessi," Diamond cut in.

"Wha…" Charmaine spun away from them to find Jessi moving fast toward some invisible target. "Shit."

Jessi walked with confidence. She looked through the camera lens a couple of times, but then seemed not to need it. Charmaine jogged toward her, still cursing under her breath. She had to zig-zag between rows of elaborate tombs topped by crosses and angels.

"Jessi, stay in sight." Charmaine tried for the loudest whisper she could muster to get her sister's attention. Per usual Jessi paid her no mind and kept barreling ahead.

Charmaine stumbled over the feet of Jesus. The stream of cuss words died away when she looked up at the statue. After a mumbled apology, she scrambled forward in the direction Jessi had taken. Minutes later she saw a green light dancing in the dark. She dashed toward it, skidding to a halt on wet grass.

"Can we have no peace in this wretched modern world?" a hollow voice echoed.

"Obviously not, Waldo. You've been asking the same damn question since eighteen seventy-six," another voice piped up in a plaintive tone. A sigh that sounded like a breeze followed.

"Yeah, a little variety would be nice," a high childish sounding voice added.

"Well excuse me for being out of sorts, Violet. I'm trapped in this awful place with a sorry lot for company. More than enough reason to complain," the first hollow voice replied.

Jessi cut into their back and forth. "I'm not out here freezing my cute ass off to hear bickering y'all. So, I'll ask again. Where is Ferdinand Nicholas Valliere buried?"

"I do admire said derriere though," the second voice that had spoken said. "One advantage to these times is the revealing way women dress. Not all those fussy layers to peel away."

"You see? This is a small sample of what I have to suffer constantly," the complainer groused.

"You are being somewhat crude, Claude," Violet put in.

"Okay, I'll assume y'all don't know anything. Excuse me while I go elsewhere and make a deal with more helpful spirits." Jessi turned to walk away.

"Wait, stop. You really can help me get out of here?" the irritable ghost blurted out.

"Jessi." Charmaine stepped forward into what felt like a fog. The sensation of ice cold droplets of water made her shiver.

"Walk around, please," came a snappish voice.

"The clumsy lady who just walked through you is my sister Charmaine. Meet Claude, Waldo, and Violet."

Charmaine shuffled to her left. "Sorry, uh, I can't see... Kinda awkward not knowing where everybody is."

Jessi snapped the viewfinder shut on her camera. She let it hang from the shoulder strap against her chest. "I'm working here, Char. And you're messing with my process."

"Could y'all excuse us a moment? Please? Just a few..." Charmaine took a guess which way to go and pushed Jessi several feet west. "You're an atheist."

"This ain't the time for a debate on religion," Jessi shot back.

"Any ritual to help a spirit cross over involves prayer. Sincere prayers from a person of faith, which excludes you. Lying to these, er, people could have serious consequences. You know as well as I do that they stick together, no matter how much they get on each other's nerves. If it gets out we can't be trusted—"

"My friends and I have developed a process of energy transference. We're not talking about waving incense and muttering nonsense phrases to non-existent entities." Jessi jerked her arm free of Charmaine's hold.

"We're surrounded by angels, the Virgin Mary, and even Jesus. Don't be talking blasphemy. We've got enough trouble already," Charmaine hissed and glanced around.

"Listen to yourself. You're being ridiculous. I used my modified device to defuse an attack by 'ghosts'. Which proves what Logan and I developed is effective," Jessi replied, referring to her physicist friend.

"Okay. You've transferred a spirit, it worked?" Charmaine crossed her arms.

Jessi cleared her throat. "We haven't found a willing subject yet."

"You mean a spirit dumb enough to be your lab rat who might end up who knows where?" Charmaine kept her voice low.

"Excuse me, but there need not be a rigid dichotomy between science and religion. Scholars have long argued that God is the master scientist." A mellow baritone voice floated from somewhere, or everywhere.

"While you were debating, we found Ferdy for you," Violet chirped.

"I've asked you not to use nicknames in reference to me," the dulcet voice replied. "Run long now, Violet."

"I'm almost as old as you, jerk. And don't forget it," Violet said, her voice deepened by outrage. A swishing sound followed seconds later.

"She stomped off," Jessi explained to Charmaine as she jerked a thumb toward the retreating spirit.

"I apologize for my young friend. Being eternally thirteen annoys her to no end. I am indeed Ferdinand Nicholas Villiere. What a pleasure it is to meet you," Ferdinand said. "I must say, I'm flattered two such lovely ladies took the time to..."

"You might want to get down to business," the irritable ghost broke in. "He can go on for decades."

"Not true. Besides, we all have plenty of time on our hands," Ferdinand replied, a trace of petulance in his tone.

"Look, guys, we're not crazy about hanging around in cemeteries late at night. So, we should get right to the point," Jessi said.

"Thank you," Charmaine muttered. A movement, the outline of a hand, caught her eye. "Hey, I think I just saw—"

"Not now, Charmaine," Jessi snapped. She switched her attention back to the ghostly newcomer. "Your mother was Jessamine Baptiste, correct? Mistress to the wealthy Alexandre Villiers who lived in New Orleans around... well a long time ago."

"Correct. My sweet mother, an upright woman of great intellect, owned a cottage in Tremé. Although I believe that name came later." Ferdinand seemed on the way to a long lecture, but Jessi broke in.

"She was murdered, and so were you, because Alexandre left you part of his land holdings," Jessi said.

"Such delicate family matters," he said with a gasp and prepared to hold forth.

"I apologize for my sister's curt manner. She tends to be too direct at times. Please don't take offense." Charmaine aimed her comments at a space she thought he might be.

"Please. We ain't sippin' tea on the veranda," Jessi cut in.

Charmaine lifted a hand at Jessi. "As you've probably noticed, modern social and business discourse is handled in a much more accelerated fashion. At least this setting offers some level of safety to discuss sensitive topics." Charmaine put her counseling techniques to use.

"Yes, but still..."

"It's been ages, man. Everyone involved has crumbled to dust," the second ghost interjected.

"He's right, Ferdinand. No harm in speaking plainly," the complainer said, less annoyed and now interested.

"You just want to know his business," Violet added.

Charmaine jumped at the voice just over her shoulder. "Crap!"

"She's sitting on top of the stone tomb behind you," Jessi said to Charmaine.

"Keeping secrets is so pointless after generations have been born and laid to rest. What could it hurt to talk about it all now?" the second ghost replied.

"Might even help prevent another injustice," Jessi said. "Your family has a habit of solving problems with various methods of murder."

"You may be able to break the cycle," Charmaine said, ever the social worker.

"Hmm, I care not at all about the Villiers side," Ferdinand said in a mild tone. "I never got a chance to marry, to have a son of my own because of father's other wife."

"Still, your mother was a devout Catholic. She believed in forgiveness, charity, and family," Charmaine said.

"Hey, everything okay?" Scotty yelled. His voice moved closer.

"We're fine. Give us another fifteen minutes or so," Jessi shouted.

"No problem. Finish your business," Scotty said. His voice faded because he was already putting distance between them.

"You brought reinforcements. Is he your suitor, Mademoiselle Jessi? I had hoped you were free to entertain—"

"Are you joking?" Waldo ghost choked out. "I would think the amorous escapades of your family had caused enough disasters."

"He's horny even in death," Violet said and giggled.

"Most unsuitable talk from a young lady," Waldo replied.

"You'll be sent off if you continue. I have long said we shouldn't encourage the child to engage with her elders," the irritable ghost said.

Ferdinand ignored his squabbling companions. "How will I profit if I provide you with the information you seek?"

"Well, um, we can help you move on." Charmaine looked at Jessi.

"Not interested." Ferdinand flipped the fingertips of one hand in dismissal of the offer.

"Don't be selfish, Ferdinand. Some of us want to go toward the light," the irritable ghost said.

Charmaine spun toward his voice. "Whoa, tell us about your experience trying to crossover and what stopped you."

"Not now, Charmaine," Jessi clipped.

"I want the property that was stolen from my family returned. Sixteen arpents along what you call Canal Street should be ours. Give or take ten," Ferdinand said.

"A what-pent?" Jessi squinted at him and then Charmaine.

"Arpent was a system of measurement used back then, roughly an acre I think," Charmaine replied. "I remember from reading the documents Artie sent us."

"Have you lost your ever-loving mind? That's some of the most expensive real estate in the city. Hell, the damn state. There are luxury hotels, office buildings," Jessi ticked off fingers as she stammered into coherence.

"Monsieur Villiere," Charmaine said and faced the direction of his voice.

"Call me Ferdinand. After all, you're going to re-store a fortune to my family. By the way, my mother adopted Villiere as a variation of the Villiers name. Drove father's widow and children to distraction. Still, it's recorded on numerous official documents easily found in archives. Along with the works of two noted authorities on New Orleans history, I can give you the names." Ferdinand paused to take a deep breath.

"You're jumping way ahead without considering the huge challenge. That property has changed hands numerous times for two centuries." Charmaine turned to Jessi, who stuttered outrage.

"Crazy," was all her sister managed to get out.

"You underestimate me, my dears. I can direct you to land transaction records. The Villiers family sold the property, profiting handsomely I might add. That land was given to me and my twin sisters by our father. You can easily prove it should have belonged to us. Then my family could sue to get the value we should have received] if reclaiming the property is no longer possible."

"But." Charmaine stopped and searched for a more cogent response. She had nothing.

"You'd be willing to let murders ago unavenged over land." Jessi crossed her arms.

"The Villiers miscreants have been killing each other for years. I do not give a jot or tittle about their spilled tainted blood." Ferdinand sniffed.

"We're standing in a cemetery negotiating an impossible deal with ghosts," Charmaine blurted out, arms pinwheeling in frustration.

"Complex, actions requiring deftness in the law and historical research, yes, but not impossible," Ferdinand said mildly. "Not with our guidance. Several impeccable legal minds are buried here. They will be glad to help. We get quite bored, you know. Scaring vagrants and rogues prowling the streets fail to amuse after a hundred years or so."

Charmaine burst out laughing. Jessi gaped at her, speechless, but Charmaine couldn't help it. Tears dripped down her face, and she gasped for air. Rustles like wind told her the ghosts were likely staring at her. Yet Charmaine had to fight for twenty or so seconds to get under control.

"Don't let me stop you from having a damn party out here." Jessi glared at Charmaine for several seconds. Then she gripped her upper right arm and shook Charmaine hard once. "Get your shit together. We need to work this out."

"No, you're right. I, uh." Charmaine waved a hand. She stifled the last giggle. She wiped her eyes with the sleeve of her jacket, hiccupped and let out a slow breath. "I apologize."

"Ferdinand, tell me this priceless information that will help us solve the case," Jessi said.

"Not until you both agree to advance my family's claim. By the way, my siblings went back to mother's family name of Baptiste. And no wonder. Those people have truly soiled the Villiers name. I'm shocked father's spirit is resting given what they've made of it," Ferdinand replied.

"Look, there is no—"

"Deal," Charmaine blurted out. "We'll provide the information needed to help the Baptiste family."

"What in the hell?" Jessi hit Charmaine on the shoulder.

"What your family decides to do is up to them. But we'll provide historical and current information to help them review their options. We can't guarantee they'll take action. Nor can we guarantee they'll succeed," Charmaine said.

Jessi thought for a few minutes before she nodded. "Yeah. Exactly. Anyway, unless you give us the information we can't even do that much. What we need is tied to finding whatever evidence you claim to have."

"Maybe, I would wager the villainous Villiers are devising ways to make a great deal of trouble for you lovely ladies." Ferdinand shrugged translucent shoulders. "But if you're willing to take the chance."

"Damn it," Jessi muttered.

"You have more at stake is what Ferdy means," Violet added in a too cheerful tone.

"Oh shut up. It's past your bedtime by about one hundred years," Jessi hissed at her. She huffed in anger when Violet tittered.

Charmaine cut in before Jessi could give in to venting rage at a baby spirit. "Like I said, we agree to your terms."

"Hey, y'all. I hate to interrupt. I mean, really, really hate to." Scotty appeared with Diamond beside him. Both darted nervous glances around the darkness. "But an NOPD cruiser has circled twice."

"My guess is they're about to decide they need to investigate." Diamond nodded, the voice of experience when it came to attracting the notice of cops.

"Get your friend to distract them somehow. We're wrapping up," Jessi said.

"Right."

Scotty did not pause to question her. Seconds later he was gone. So fast that Diamond was left behind. She let out a tiny cry at the empty space he'd left. Then she stepped close to Charmaine.

"Are they here?" Diamond said in a too loud whisper. She mouthed "What?" when Charmaine rolled her eyes.

Jessi crossed her arms as she faced the handsome young spirit. "Okay, Ferdinand. Spill the tea."

****

Two days later, after much midnight oil had been burnt to a crisp, Jessi and Charmaine sat across from Mrs. Villiers. They'd agreed to meet at the headquarters of VSI, Inc. Evelyn had insisted on being present, though her mother had convinced her not to call their lawyer. Evelyn's assistant Garland Evans came in with a tray of refreshments. His curious gaze swept around all of the women, no doubt in hopes of getting a clue. He made a great show of setting up the cups on a polished oak buffet along one wall. He handed a cup of tea to Mrs. Villiers. Evelyn got up and poured herself a cup of coffee.

"We're good, thanks," Jessi said into the silence of no one offering them anything.

"What do you want?" Evelyn sat down at her desk. She put the cup down untouched.

"We have evidence that one of your ancestors fathered six children at least with his plaçage," Charmaine began to go on. She stopped when Mrs. Villiers interrupted.

"We know what the word means. He had a mulatto mistress installed in a cottage. They bred like rabbits, those women. Not even worth a footnote in our family's history," Mrs. Villiers said with a smile.

Evelyn laughed. "The word common perfectly describes the practice and the women who took part. Many prominent families have the same history. No one cares. You've wasted my morning."

"We have reason to believe Alexandre Villiers left property to his children. They were prevented from taking possession. There are historical and legal documents. I think the attorney we talked to mentioned something called precedence." Charmaine raised an eyebrow at them.

"We think y'all decided to shut him up," Jessi said.

"Even if you could trace these alleged descendants, which I doubt, proving they own land that's changed hands dozens of times would be hard to say the least." Evelyn relaxed against the rich leather of her executive chair. She took a sip of coffee.

"You see I was right. We don't need our attorney here," Mrs. Villiers said to Evelyn. She turned to Jessi. "You've been paid well, and I'm pleased with the results. Not perfect, but we haven't had an incident in days. Though I do think you stumbled onto solving the thefts. Still, it's the results that count."

"Mother has convinced me not to sue you for conning her out of hundreds. You're welcome." Evelyn raised her cup to them in a salute and drank again.

"We can locate members of the Baptiste family who still live in New Orleans. They might not agree once they see Alexandre's will, letters from Madame Villiere to him and more," Charmaine replied.

"Good luck to them. You two are entertaining. I admit that having you clomp around playing detective irked me for a while. But my husband helped me see the humor in the situation," Evelyn said. "Increased tour bookings are an added benefit. So, I'm smiling as the profits go up."

"Evelyn still doesn't believe in ghosts, or that they haunt Magnolia Grove. We know differently though, right my dears? I'm grateful we had this little chat." Mrs. Villiers looked at her daughter.

"I agree, Mother. Thank you, Joliet sisters, for giving us fair warning about a possible nuisance lawsuit. We'll be prepared. Let's see, the family name is now Baptiste." Evelyn put the cup down and wrote on a notepad. "Very helpful."

The office door swung wide as if orchestrated to be on cue with Evelyn's final words. Her executive assistant wore a blank expression, though his thin top lip curled a bit. He stared at Charmaine first and then Jessi. He didn't need to say anything. Evelyn stood and came around the desk. Mrs. Villiers continued to pay more attention to her tea than the surroundings.

"My assistant will validate your parking. Good-bye." Evelyn wore a chilling smile that radiated she'd call security if necessary.

Jessi stood. "We're not done yet."

"I've spoken to the police chief here and the sheriff in Jefferson Parish. So, you might want to re-think your position." Evelyn turned her back on them to return to the wide desk.

Charmaine followed Jessi out of Evelyn's office feeling like the losing team exiting the field. Garland extended a copper colored token that they could give the parking attendant. Jessi brushed past him with a venomous serving of side-eye. He gave a satisfied grunt when Charmaine took it. For the fifteen-minute drive to Charmaine's house neither spoke. Jessi parked her SUV behind Charmaine's Cruze. Once inside her cozy kitchen, Charmaine let out a long breath as though she'd been holding it the entire ride. Jessi let out a lot more.

"Those shady bitches." Jessi threw her large tote bag onto the kitchen table. The slim laptop inside it made a solid thunk as it landed.

"Don't break up your stuff and mine throwing a tantrum. And by the way, they're right. We have no connection between Tanner Gladstone's murder and family dirt from a couple of hundred years ago." Charmaine yanked open the fridge and took out a half-pint bottle of apple juice.

"We can't let them beat us, Charmaine. There's some deep shit going on." Jessi banged her way around the kitchen as she fixed a fresh pot of coffee.

"I have three appointments at the clinic. Oh, and mama called. She still wants us to visit her, get to know her new husband." Charmaine glanced at a cute clock on the wall, a red rooster. "I've got enough time to finish the file on this case and see my first patient."

Jessi whirled around spilling coffee grounds on the counter. "What the hell are you talking about? We have a possible murder suspect stashed away. The police might be drafting up our arrest warrants for killing a rich white dude. And you're acting like life goes on."

"I'll get Scotty to cut Kadeem loose. He didn't offer us anything we can use to figure out who killed Tanner," Charmaine replied.

"Real humane. Toss the dude to the circling pit bulls so they chew him to pieces."

"We're not running a bodyguard service. Kadeem should go to the police, tell them what he knows and hope for the best. I hate it as much as you, but Mrs. Villiers and Evil Evelyn are on point. We did what they hired us to do. We got paid. End of case." Charmaine stared out over her small patch of backyard. Pale November sunlight splashed across her forlorn looking patio furniture. "I'm going to fix up the patio. I'll put some money in savings first though."

"You're forgetting something. They're gonna offer us up as suspects right along with Kadeem. Hell, they've probably already done it. Yolanda will tell them you met with him more than once." Jessi leaned against the counter, arms crossed tightly.

"We talked to a lot of people. If Kadeem, no make that when Kadeem talks to the police, because they're going to find him, his story will steer the cops away from us. Nothing he said about what happened to Tanner has anything to do with me or you. Remember?" Charmaine nudged her aside. She swiped up the coffee grounds with a paper towel into her cupped hand. Then she dumped them into the kitchen trash.

"Yeah, I guess."

"I mean, maybe we're overthinking it. A dealer killed Tanner. The thefts from Magnolia Grove aren't connected to the murder." Charmaine drained the bottle of apple juice and threw it into her recycle basket.

"I'm still curious about what Georgina and Ferdinand said about the family skeletons though," Jessi insisted.

"Digging into their ancient gossip won't pay. I say we let the police clean up the mess. Some lady wants us to lift a family curse or something. I could call her back. I think she's got us mixed up with that voodoo priestess on St. Philip Street." Charmaine finished the job of making coffee. "Not that we're hurting for money with the check from Mrs. Villiers."

"Yeah, murder pays well," Jessi muttered.

"Don't start. We didn't kill anybody, and for all we know, Kadeem's whole story is a lie. He could be trying to hide his part in Tanner ending up dead."

"Maybe the Baptiste family can fill in more blanks." Jessi spoke more to herself than to Charmaine.

"Oh hell, Jessi. Let it go." Charmaine started to say more, but the doorbell cut her off. She strode off to the front door. "I've got better things to do, and so do you."

Charmaine couldn't make out Jessi's reply as she entered the hallway. Her heart thumped when a shadow loomed through the curtains. Someone seemed impatient to get in. Not a good sign given recent events. She thought of a tactic favored by thugs. Bullets flying once a door is answered. So Charmaine froze. She tiptoed to the peephole. Det. Harrison's profile appeared. She exhaled in relief, then realized he represented a different kind of threat.

Det. Harrison stepped back to give her a better view. "I see both your cars parked in the drive."

"Damn it," Charmaine whispered. She took a second to recover then opened the door with a slight smile. "Good morning, detective."

"Good morning to you. May I come in?" Det. Harrison smiled back.

"Hmm, sure." Charmaine glanced up and down her street. "No SWAT team nearby?"

Det. Harrison marched past her when Charmaine unlatched her storm door and stood aside to admit him. "Funny. I have news."

"Sounds better than 'You're under arrest'," Charmaine quipped as she shut and locked her doors. Jessi scowled at him when they entered the kitchen.

"Show me some paperwork, otherwise get out and be ready to hear from my lawyer." Jessi slurped coffee and smacked her lips at him.

"No need. I was invited in. Besides, I'm not here to search your house or accuse you of anything. We made an arrest in Tanner Gladstone's murder. Drug dealer related to the same crew who were stealing from the Villiers plantation." Det. Harrison eyed both as if gauging their reactions.

Charmaine clapped her hands together. "Congrats on a job well done."

"Thanks. Though we do have some loose ends to clean up." Det. Harrison sat down at the breakfast table uninvited. "Coffee smells good."

"Yeah, make yourself at home. Maybe I should run out and get you some beignets to go with it." Jessi glanced her disapproval at Charmaine.

"That would be nice, but don't go to any trouble." Det. Harrison flashed a grin at her. A good-natured laugh followed when Jessi gave a snort of scorn.

"You're in a good mood." Charmaine put the mug in front of him.

"Getting a killer off the streets always brightens my day, Ms. Joliet. Anyway, we caught up with Kadeem Hardy. Well, he strolled into the Fifth District station. Guess he got tired of hiding." Det. Harrison brought the deep blue mug to his lips.

Charmaine sat next to him. "Yeah, you see we—"

"I'm not interested in anyone who helped him hide. Though my boss would call it obstruction of a criminal investigation. Hardy was a suspect at one point." Harrison lowered the mug to gaze at Charmaine.

"Something we would never, ever do," Jessi said before Charmaine could reply. "What loose ends?"

"The bullet wound didn't kill him. Weird that a street gangsta would shoot the guy and then strangle him. Not usually how they operate. They rain down more bullets to get the job done. And why mess his face up? Kinda looks like somebody tried to delay identification"

"Hmm." Charmaine cleared her throat.

"Another thing. It doesn't look like he got shot at Nicholas Villiers' place." Harrison's dark eyebrows pulled into a solid lined frown. "Almost like more than one person was involved."

"Right, a gang. Never know what's on the mind of a thug these days. Sad." Jessi let out a dramatic sigh.

"Yes. A drug deal gone bad for such a clean cut rich guy." Charmaine pondered Harrison's facts. Det. Harrison's deep voice cut through her musing.

"Any theories?"

"No, nothing comes to mind," Charmaine replied fast. Too fast judging from the look Harrison gave her.

"Like you said, rich kid runs up on the wrong street dealer. Kadeem should have known better than..." Jessi's voice trailed off.

"Finish your thought," Harrison clipped.

Jessi returned his hard stare without blinking. "He should have known better than to get himself caught up with rich boys who like hood thrills. The Nicks of this world always get off."

Harrison studied them both in silence for a few beats. Then he nodded once, stood, and buttoned his wool jacket. "Case closed. At least for me. The rest is up to the DA and defense attorneys."

"Yeah." Jessi wore a frown.

"By the way, stay out of cemeteries at night." Harrison's cool tone contrasted with his threatening scowl.

"How did you know?" Charmaine pressed her lips together.

"Now that I know you two, I take note of certain unusual calls. Especially if it involves a graveyard." Harrison stabbed a finger at Charmaine and then aimed it at Jessi.

"Thanks for the advice," Charmaine said before Jessi could make a joke at his expense. The last thing they needed was Harrison pissed off enough to dig deeper.

"Y'all have a nice, quiet day," Harrison rumbled. He tipped an imaginary cap to them both before he strolled out.

Charmaine followed him, locked the front door and returned. "That's that."

She met Jessi's defiant grimace with an equally stubborn one. Then she heaved a sigh and started thinking of ways to keep Jessi out of trouble with the cops.

12.
Curiosity Kills More Than Cats

Two days went by with life going as normal. At least that's what Charmaine wanted to believe. Jessi gave up trying to punch through that particular veil of denial. Once her big sister decided life was roses and whipped cream, nothing could convince her otherwise except cold hard facts. Jessi had none. Only hunches and intuition.

So, Jessi turned in her last midterm paper, way past due. Dr. Patton, the teacher, cut her slack after a tale of family woe. A sick great-aunt who didn't exist. But whatever. Ends justifying the means and all that. Then Jessi tried to buckle down for looming finals coming up. Yet her thoughts kept bouncing from art history to New Orleans history. The tale of two families intrigued her way more than what Degas got up to in the Vieux Carré.

Which is why she stood on the steps of a home in Metairie on a bright Monday morning. Gloria Baptiste-Edwards had agreed to meet with her. With help from Arthur and Diamond, Jessi had dug through fading records and scoured phone books. The twists and turns of the prolific Baptiste clan had been stunning. Yet she'd managed to narrow her search. Born in nineteen forty-five, Mrs. Edwards was retired. She'd expressed enthusiasm when Jessi called.

The front door opened to reveal a gray-haired woman dressed in a pink sweater over gray slacks. Her alert brown gaze traveled down Jessi's outfit and back up to her face again. "Yes?"

"Mrs. Edwards, we spoke on the phone about your family genealogy, and—"

"Come in. It's cold out there," Mrs. Edwards broke in. She unlocked the storm door to let Jessi in. "Wind will cut right through you. But of course, young people don't feel it the way us seasoned citizens do. My friend Barbara hates that moniker. Says it makes us sound like some fast food menu item."

"Yes, well..."

Jessi glanced around expecting to see lace doilies, a collection of dolls, and too many cats. She was surprised to find none of those. Though cozy in hues of beige, emerald green, and earth red, the interior looked modern. Floral patterns of upholstery contrasted with more contemporary patterns on throw pillows, and two ottomans. Framed prints on the walls included abstracts and landscapes.

"I prefer it to senior citizens. I mean, what does that condescending phrase really mean? Senior." Mrs. Edwards turned to face Jessi. "I'm rambling, which probably makes you regret coming. You'll decide I'm a silly old lady with too much time on her hands."

"No, ma'am." Jessi fixed a smile on her face to hide that she was thinking exactly that.

"Such a polite young woman. But you're right to think so. Terrible habit I've picked up since I retired from Michoud." Mrs. Edwards waved at Jessi to have a seat. She settled on one of three chairs that matched the sofa.

"NASA? Like in the movie Hidden Figures?" Jessi gaped at her.

"Yes, an engineer. Rare for Blacks in the sixties, even rarer for black women. But you mentioned something about Creoles in early Louisiana." Mrs. Edwards sprang up. "Oh, I made coffee and donuts. No store-bought stuff. I even grind my own beans."

"Don't go to the trouble." Jessi sniffed the enticing perfume of southern home-cooked treats. Her stomach growled like an angry lioness, giving her away.

Mrs. Edwards grinned. "No trouble at all."

Seconds later, they were seated in Mrs. Edwards' breakfast nook. Jessi savored the rich flavor of homemade beignets. "You should sell these. You'd clean up."

"Between volunteering at St. Ann's on the Hospitality Committee and working eight hours a week, I don't have time." Mrs. Edwards winked at her. "My eight grandchildren love them, and my Italian cream cake."

"Eight, huh?" Jessi dipped her donut in more powdered sugar. "Want to adopt one more?"

"You and your sister are welcome any time." Mrs. Edwards raised her dark eyebrows when Jessi blinked hard.

"You know about us."

"Private investigators who also look into the supernatural. More sophisticated than ghost hunters though. You've been involved in at least two murder cases."

Jessi wiped her fingers or a napkin as she cleared her throat. "Well involved might be one way to put it."

"You weren't accused." Mrs. Edwards sipped from her rose patterned china cup. "I know how to use the Internet, dear."

"Yeah." Jessi sighed at how the information age helped and screwed up her job.

"Don't worry. I wouldn't have agreed to see you if I was concerned. Of course, my granddaughter Angela said I shouldn't. But her twin, Andrea, is like me. Risk taker. So, fire away." Mrs. Edwards looked at Jessi with a twinkle in her eyes. "I couldn't resist when you mentioned the Villiers family."

"You were the only Baptiste I called who knew the connection," Jessi replied with care.

"The only one who was willing to admit knowing the connection. It's amazing how family secrets can survive for so long. You see, the emotion behind fear is strong. Survival." Mrs. Edwards nodded.

"I don't get it. After so much time, it shouldn't matter," Jessi said.

"What is only whispered about when the children are asleep over the years is lost. People die, memories fade. Unless there are letters or records kept." Mrs. Edwards smiled.

Jessi stopped in the act of getting a third beignet. "Which you have?"

Mrs. Edwards picked up their empty saucers. She came back with a china pot that matched their cups. She poured more coffee for them both and sat down again.

"My great-grandmother was a remarkable woman. She managed to save three family Bibles. Emilia, my older sister, inherited her love for history. Well, bless her heart, she was eccentric. Stuck on documenting the family tree. She found church birth records that linked us to the Villiers family. How much do you know?"

"Alexandre Villiers had a mistress. He fathered four of her six children." Jessi started to mention Ferdinand but decided against it. No need to freak her out.

"Yes, she had two sons when they met, which attracted him as much as her beauty," Mrs. Edwards said. Chewing on a donut stopped her from going on.

"Most guys run from a woman with kids," Jessi prodded.

"Hmm, but having children proved a man's virility in those days. And his legal wife had problems giving birth. Then she had two girls. Their son died before his fifth birthday. Men prized sons to inherit."

"That's so Henry the Eighth. But an illegitimate son couldn't inherit, let alone one born of a Black mother," Jessi said.

"Ah, but this was early Louisiana, and Creoles didn't see these things in the same way Americans did. Back then racial boundaries were different. As more whites from other parts of the country arrived here, they were shocked. There was slavery and racism, of course. But many white Creole men gifted property before and after their deaths to women of color and their biracial children. As our state became more 'Americanized', the culture changed." Mrs. Edwards shrugged.

"And laws were passed to enforce racial division."

"In an eighteenth-century lawsuit, a white Creole widow wrote a letter supporting the case for a Black woman. The white woman's own son tried to take land his father had left the mistress and their children. Just one example," Mrs. Edwards said.

"Wow." Jessi's mouth hung open.

"Wow indeed," Mrs. Edwards replied with a laugh. "But the culture shifted over time."

"Yeah, all very interesting history. But I don't see how it's gonna help me figure out who killed Tanner Gladstone.

Mrs. Edwards set down her cup with a thump. "How is that connected to the Villiers family?"

Jessi gave Mrs. Edwards the condensed version of why they were hired. The older woman peppered her with shrewd questions. All the time, she played the cultured southern hostess without missing a beat. Ten minutes later, both women sat thinking over the facts.

"I'm not surprised their connection wasn't mentioned. The Villiers family name carries a lot of weight in Orleans Parish," Mrs. Edwards said after a time.

"Yeah. Well, at least my history professor will be happy. I'll bet Dr. Marigny will want to call you, even have a look at your family records." Jessi sighed. "But my sister is right. Ferdinand's death has nothing to do with the present."

"Our family has passed down the story of how he was murdered. Then her other son disappeared."

"Ferdinand didn't mention a brother," Jessi murmured.

"Who?"

"Nothing, I meant. Your ancestors didn't leave behind any letters about another child dying," Jessi replied.

"We have birth records. Jessamine was pregnant when Ferdinand died mysteriously. She grieved herself into an early grave less than a year. Her pregnancy was difficult. Her health never recovered." Mrs. Edwards sighed over the old family tragedy.

"Wait, she died in childbirth?"

"Complications of childbirth. Keep in mind there were no antibiotics in those days. From what we heard, sounds like she developed an infection. Even the common cold or a small cut could lead to death for healthy people. Just imagine being sickly under those conditions."

Jessi blinked fast as she mentally reviewed what Georgina had told her. "But we heard she was murdered. I'm confused."

Mrs. Edwards gasped. "Who told you she was murdered?"

"Hmm, well we read some old journal or something, a letter maybe." Jessi rushed on to change the subject. She wasn't about to try and explain talking to dead people as a way to solve crimes. "Nothing more than gossip. Vague really. You mentioned what sounds like way more reliable written accounts."

"What I have is a combination of family oral history and documents. For instance, birth and deaths recorded in Bibles passed down. We also found records in the archives both Tulane and UNO. But some stories were too dangerous to put on paper." Mrs. Edwards bit her lower lip. "Even after two hundred years almost, some of my family members say leave the dead buried."

"Like you said, the Villiers have power."

Mrs. Edwards waved a hand. "They can't hurt us in any material way. Remember I said Jessamine had two sons before she set up house with Monsieur Villiers?"

"Yes, and used a variation on the spelling of his last name. Girlfriend had guts." Jessi grinned.

"She wasn't just a pretty face and a good figure. Jessamines's first 'husband' never married. A much older man who was thrilled that he'd fathered children. He left her three properties. Her two sons kept their name and their property. I guess the Villiers mob didn't see them as threats. Their families benefited from their business skills."

"Okay, but I still don't..."

"Back to the second Villiers son born on the other side of the blanket," Mrs. Edwards cut in. "Family stories say that Monsieur Villiers somehow managed to take his infant and pass him off as the offspring of his white wife. Which is why she had to die."

Jessi sat with her mouth open for several seconds before she recovered enough to speak. "But Georgina is, I mean, I read in letters his wife was a bit nuts, paranoid. Most didn't believe her when she kept saying she was being poisoned. What's more, the records say her child survived."

"Only a few months after she died. And the servants whispered that it was another girl. The midwife, a free woman of color, was paid handsomely to sign off on papers saying the child born was a boy." Mrs. Edwards wore a pleased grin at the stunned expression on Jessi's face. "Bet the high and mighty Mrs. Marguerite Villiers wouldn't want that to come out."

"Damn right. But still, it's all ancient gossip. Nobody in their fancy social circles would care. Not really." Jessi wiped powdered sugar from her fingers on a napkin. She slipped the strap of her bag over one shoulder and stood. "Thanks for a peek into juicy drama, but I'm gonna have to hear my sister say she told me so."

"She can't when you tell her about the will of one Henry James Turnbull written in eighteen-thirty." Mrs. Edwards nodded slowly as Jessi sat down again.

****

The next day Jessi and Charmaine met up for lunch at Scotty's place. The bar was mostly empty, but Scotty had added a limited menu to increase income. The room for dancing had been transformed. Charmaine enjoyed a small bowl of red beans and rice. Jessi opted for a chicken salad sandwich. Yet neither of them paid much attention to the food.

"Y'all, Bernard is gonna start feeling something ain't right with his cooking," Scotty said and pointed at their untouched plates. "He's real sensitive. Not to mention it's getting cold."

"You gotta hear this story." Jessi pulled Scotty by one arm, forcing him to drop onto the chair beside her. "Daddy Turnbull heard the stories that one of the Villiers kids was Black, okay biracial, which was a big thing. So, he wanted to keep his family 'pure'."

"Give me a break," Charmaine blurted out and gulped diet cola.

"I know, right? Anyway, he made them swear the whispers weren't true. His family had all the money by that time. A financial downturn in eighteen twenty-two left the Villiers pretty much broke.

The Turnbulls, Georgina's kinfolks, held onto their coins. Anyway, this dude wrote into his will that no descendant with even a drop of color in his veins could inherit." Jessi sat back and crossed her arms.

"Your theory being?" Scotty prompted after looking from her to Charmaine and back again.

"Tanner Gladstone found out, and he was blackmailing the family. Get it?"

"Aw c'mon. Way corny, Jess." Scotty laughed.

"Anyway, Tanner had to go." Jessi drew a finger across her neck. Eyes closed, her head flopped to one side in high melodramatic style.

"Excuse me, but there is a major problem with your theory. Tanner didn't need money. He had his own fat trust fund," Charmaine said.

"Maybe so." Jessi stared down at her sandwich but didn't touch it. "But he loved being a top executive at their company. Or maybe he used it to make sure he stayed close to Nick. He had a thing for him."

Charmaine dabbed her lips with a paper napkin. "Doesn't add up. Okay, okay. He liked his career, but unlike us broke folk, he didn't need it."

"Yeah, but—"

"And the fact that he was allegedly crazy in love with Nick means he'd be more than willing to keep the family's secrets. He wouldn't do anything to hurt Nick. Not that some old will would put it in jeopardy," Charmaine said.

"I was thinking along the same lines, Jessi. Sometimes the obvious and simple answer is the one. Like Harrison said, drug deal goes bad. Rich kid ends up dead. End of story. Moving on."

Scotty rested an arm on the back of Charmaine's chair. The action earned a scowl from his employee Rochelle. She hoped to turn their business relationship into a more personal one. She headed for their table.

"Y'all need anything else?" Rochelle stared at Scotty's arm. Then she transferred her gaze to Charmaine, a stiff smile on her pretty brown features.

"No, we're good," Charmaine said. She leaned a little closer to Scotty and beamed at her. "Tell Bernard he makes gumbo as good as any southern grand-mama."

"I'm sure he'll be thrilled," Rochelle said in a dry tone. "Scotty, I wanna go over the employee applications we got. Now that I'm managing the restaurant, we need to hire somebody to take my place."

"Congrats on the promotion," Jessi said. She raised an eyebrow at Scotty.

"More long hours with the boss, but whatever it takes to make things happen," Rochelle said.

"I'll get with you later," Scotty broke in before Charmaine could reply. He pointed to a young woman. "Uh, that new waitress is trying to get your attention."

Rochelle glanced over her shoulder and faced him again. "Right. But we really need to get on interviews today."

"Okay. Whatever. Go take care of business," Scotty's voice held an edge that didn't seem lost on Rochelle. She strode off. "Don't say it. I know."

"Why the hell? You know she's got a hot thang for you," Charmaine whispered. She eyed Rochelle, who darted side looks back.

"The old saying about good help being hard to find is true. Let alone finding help that won't steal from you or hire their shady friends. Try finding someone with management skills and the pool gets even smaller. Rochelle keeps this place humming and profitable. Emphasis on profit. She knows her stuff. We had a real talk, so she knows where we stand."

"Yeah, well her mouth said one thing. But her panties are still smokin' for you, bruh," Jessi retorted. She gave a cackle when Scotty winced.

"Whatever, back to the case. Or lack thereof. The Villiers lied to keep their grubby hands on a fortune. I'm no lawyer, but I doubt anybody would care," Charmaine said.

"Find out." Scotty studied his employees across the space as if making sure things went smoothly.

"Huh?" Charmaine and Jessi said together.

"Find out if anybody cares. Look, I gotta go. Shit load of stuff to do." Scotty said. "Let me know if I can help. Though I'll have my hands full for a few days."

Charmaine gave him a sisterly thump on his big bicep with a fist. "You've done enough. Thanks for sitting on Kadeem for us."

"No prob. How much trouble is he in?" Scotty unfolded his tall frame to stand.

"It's a thin case to get him for dealing. You can bet he's singing the 'I-didn't-know-he-was-gonna-buy-drugs' song," Jessi replied.

"Yeah. The cops know he didn't shoot Tanner. They could have trouble finding evidence he was an accessory," Charmaine added.

"Which leaves Nick on the hook?" Scotty exchanged a glance with Jessi.

"Stop with the silent messages and signals." Charmaine stabbed a forefinger at them. "I'm open to all theories."

Scotty held up both palms. "I'm gone. Tell me what you find out."

"Uh-huh." Charmaine squinted at him when he blew a kiss and strolled off.

"He's right, sis. We're back to the Villiers folks possibly having a motive to kill Tanner." Jessi took a bite of her neglected sandwich.

"You're not going to let this go. Are you?" Charmaine looked at Jessi, waiting for her to swallow her mouthful.

"I'm just saying. I don't like folks tryin' to play me. I got a street rep to maintain."

"Oh please." Charmaine rolled her eyes and started back on her lunch.

"I might also add Joliet Investigations got a nice PR boost when we helped solve murders before." Jessi winked at her. "Sure, it was rough for a minute, but it paid off."

"You're out of your everlasting mind," Charmaine blurted.

"I'm talking big picture results," Jessi said and licked mayo from one thumb.

"We almost ended up victims, then murder suspects, and the cops still think we're guilty as hell of something. You know what that means? I'll tell you what it means. NOPD will look for any excuse to lock us up. Even if it's for a crime we didn't do. Cops don't care how they get you or what they get you for. Not once they're set on getting you."

Charmaine peppered Jessi with her points at top speed.

Jessi shrugged as if being in the bullseye didn't bother her. "Then we'll just have to keep proving them wrong. And get paid doing it. According to you, Harrison isn't one of those kinds of cops."

"I better run outside and look up for flying pigs. You're defending the police," Charmaine retorted. She broke off a chunk of French bread and nibbled it.

"No, I'm defending Harrison. He's got a permanent stick up his ass, and no imagination, but he seems straight. He doesn't like having his pet theories blown up, but he'll accept evidence that proves them wrong. Grudgingly. With a lot of bitching." Jessi laughed. "Which is kinda fun to watch."

"Well, as long as you're having fun," Charmaine drawled.

Jessi leaned forward. "If Tanner's death wasn't a drug deal that goes real bad, then it's more complicated. Georgina and Ferdinand—"

"Ghosts," Charmaine cut her off.

"They're as good as live people when it comes to informants," Jessi protested. "Better even. They can pop up in places, listen in and not be seen."

"Uh-huh. They also tend to be a bit unhinged, still traumatized by their own deaths. Georgina sounds nutty if you ask me. Ferdinand is bitter. Plus, he didn't even know he had a brother. Georgina didn't know about the second baby boy," Charmaine pointed out.

"True. But we wouldn't have found out about past family murders, the Baptiste family, or the rest without them," Jessi countered.

"Okay, so how are you going to find out?"

"Huh?"

"There has to be a strong reason they'd kill to keep their ancestor's little secret. Money and status would have to be at stake, in that order. What's your plan?" Charmaine savored the last slice of smoked sausage in her bowl.

"You're gonna just throw me out here by myself," Jessi said, waving the sliver of dill pickle that came with her sandwich.

"You're the one convinced there's a connection. Your baby, your footwork." Charmaine drained her glass of diet cola. "Here's my money for lunch. Gotta run. One of the social workers is on vacation, so I'm seeing her clients."

"Okay, fine. I'm up for the work. Though I don't know where I'll start." Jessi picked up the last half of her sandwich.

"Treat it like a skip trace." Charmaine picked up her leather cross-body bag.

"Ugh. Sounds like a lotta sweat, hours poking through old papers. I've got final exams, and—"

"Whine, bitch, moan." Charmaine smirked at her and waved goodbye.

"Go on then. Like I need you. I bet I uncover more in ten minutes than you could in ten days," Jessi called after her. When Charmaine didn't look back, she sighed. "Crap. I could use her help."

****

Two hours later Jessi manned the front desk in the student services department. Her job, part of her student aid package, meant she rotated between offices. She answered the phone and scheduled appointments. To her annoyance, the day had not wound down.

"No, you need to call the registrar's office. Okay, wait a minute." Jessi hissed in disgust as she put the phone down. "Geez, Look it up yourself, moron."

Diamond sat at a table a few feet away. "You're supposed to be helpful to your fellow students."

"They're in college. We all know they can read. Every one of 'em has a smartphone with at least two search apps." Jessi hit the button again and read off the number. "Oh yeah, you heard me? Well hoo-hoo, your wittle feelings got hurt. I'm tore up about it." She dropped the handset onto the cradle, ending the call.

Diamond looked shocked for a millisecond before she giggled hard. "You gone get fired."

"Whatever. Tell me what you got so far." Jessi left the desk and crossed to stand over Diamond.

Her friend's mouth turned down. "I'm not the detective, so I shouldn't be doing all this work to track down clues. Keep this up and I'll demand a paycheck."

"Consider this an internship. Me and Charmaine didn't know anything at first. You gotta start somewhere," Jessi replied as she looked over Diamond's shoulder.

"Hey, I didn't say I wanted to be a private investigator. I'm going to be a paralegal." Diamond swiped through pages on the touch screen before her.

"Exactly, and you'll be ahead of the pack because of me. Paralegals do tons of research," Jessi replied. "Now go."

"I'm gone help you out this time, but be on notice. I'm charging for any future assignments."

"We don't have much time. Mrs. Shaffer will show up any minute. Spill." Jessi poked Diamond's shoulder with a finger.

Diamond forgot her complaints and grinned. "Digging into rich people's biz is fun. Court documents show there was a fight over who would run the company in the nineteen forties. Somebody named Kathleen Ackerson in Falls Church, Virginia was on the board, and she objected to the decisions being made. She made a move to get a majority stake."

"Nope, not interested. I..." Jessi started to say more but stopped. "Wait, scroll back."

"What?" Diamond swiped back to a previous page on the screen.

"There, that's it. Ackerson is a Turnbull descendant. Let's do more digging. I smell a nasty family fight." Jessi smiled down at a puzzled Diamond.

13.

What's One More Murder Between Friends?

Mrs. Villiers, Laura, Evelyn, and Nick sat around the formal parlor of Magnolia Grove. Charmaine studied each in turn. The females of the family seemed at ease. Nick fidgeted with his tumbler. The whiskey sour that filled his glass was soon gone. He jumped up seconds later and went to the antique table that served as a bar. Once he'd refilled his glass, he sat down again.

"Notice he can't look you in the eye," Jessi said low to Charmaine.

"His best friend is dead, the cops interviewed him, and mommy is displeased. He's got more on his mind than me mad at him," Charmaine whispered back. She was about to go on when the door opened.

"Well, well." Jessi strolled over to the newcomer.

Elliot Forstall looked at Mrs. Villiers first. Then gazed around the room. "Good evening everyone."

"So, y'all figure you need a lawyer," Jessi said.

"I advised them not to have this meeting at all. But since they ignored my caution, my being here is the best alternative. Ms. Joliet, Mrs. Villiers tells me that you've been paid for your services. The case is over." Forstall raised a dark eyebrow at Jessi and then at Charmaine.

"Yes, well—" Charmaine searched for some diplomatic response. Failing, she glanced at Jessi.

Jessi backed away from Forstall. She adopted a wide-legged stance near the marble fireplace that dominated one wall. "Thanks for telling us what we already know. You should be worried that your clients wanted to hear what we have to say."

Forstall kept his impassive face, yet the telltale twitch of a jaw muscle showed his annoyance. "Just get on with it."

Charmaine cleared her throat. She checked for the nearest exit in case they'd need a fast getaway. Since Jessi would be in charge, Charmaine felt certain they would need it. A tumble of voices distracted her. Each Villiers babbled internally. What they were thinking winked on as an image in Charmaine's head. She tried to follow the stream of words but went cross-eyed in the attempt. Nick's silk-like baritone cut through the chaos.

"Are you okay?" He stood close to Charmaine, one hand under her left elbow.

Charmaine blinked several times as she looked up at him in confusion. She hadn't noticed him move in her direction, or heard anyone talking. Mrs. Villiers and Evelyn glared at them. Laura kept her gaze on Elliot Forstall, as though waiting for rescue.

"Not acceptable, Nicholas," Mrs. Villiers said. Her thin lips pressed together into a tight line.

"Stop thinking with your..." Evelyn let the rest remain unspoken. Her expression of scorn completed the thought.

"Yeah, Nick. Pedal your cheesy charm someplace else. We ain't buyin' no more." Jessi looked at Charmaine.

"You intended to find out what I knew, maybe throw me off if I got too close to the truth." Charmaine gazed at him.

Nick took his hand from Charmaine's arm and stuffed it in his pants pocket. "Ridiculous. I tried to help you satisfy Mother's demands. I never believed in the whole ghost business. But if you make money catering to nervous superstitious elderly ladies, fine."

"I kept close watch to make sure you didn't con large sums from Mother," Evelyn added.

"Any recreation Nick enjoyed with you was his little bonus," Laura said with a sneer. "Not that we could have stopped him. Nicky has large appetites."

"Including a taste for a buffet of party drugs," Jessi snarled. "Which led to his best buddy ending up stone cold dead on his million-dollar hardwood floors."

Elliot Forstall broke in before any of his clients could answer. "A poor choice of associates isn't a crime."

"Tell that to Tanner," Jessi replied.

Mrs. Villiers rose from her chair. She clasped her hands together into a ball. "You're saying he's here? T-Tanner."

"For God's sake, Mother. There are no ghosts, and these two are fakes. Like those voodoo shops in the French Quarter that dupe gullible tourists." Evelyn stood and put an arm around her mother's shoulders. She whispered close to Mrs. Villiers' ear until the older woman sat again.

"I must insist that you stop playing on the fears of a vulnerable woman. You two are flirting with a petty fraud charge. Based on your past, I don't think you'd like the police involved." Elliot Forstall stared at Jessi and then turned to Charmaine.

"You're wrong. We called the police," Charmaine clipped. She gave Nick a heated side-eye before she crossed to the door.

"We did?" Jessi blurted out. Then she recovered when Forstall's dark eyebrows bunched together. "I mean, we did."

"Detective Harrison at first refused to get involved. But about an hour ago, he changed his mind. I sensed it." Charmaine looked around the room.

"Of course you did, Ms. Joliet. And Elvis just entered the building," Evelyn said. She looked at Forstall. "We're done here."

Forstall nodded. He took a long envelope from an inside pocket of his suit jacket and handed it to Charmaine. "This is for you."

"What's it say?" Jessi squinted at Forstall as though not willing to take an eye off him.

Forestall spoke without waiting for them to read the document. "It's a cease and desist letter. Contact Mrs. Villiers again and we'll press criminal charges. We'll also file a civil lawsuit if you continue to spread false rumors about this family or VSI, Inc."

Detective Harrison stuck his head through the door and looked around. Mrs. Villiers put a hand on her chest as her mouth fell open. As if deciding he was in the right place, the detective opened the door fully and walked in.

"The guy outside showed me in. Guess y'all don't have a new housekeeper yet." Harrison strolled in.

Evelyn left her mother's side to approach him. "I suppose you're psychic as well, Detective Harrison. We need you as it happens. They claim to have damaging information about our family and want money or else."

"That's a lie," Charmaine protested. "We didn't ask for money. We only want the truth."

"Now that the police are here to observe your tune changes." Evelyn looked at the detective again. "I won't make an issue about what they charged our mother so far. She hired them because she truly believes in spirits."

"What bull," Jessi said with heat. "What you want is to bury what really happened to Tanner Gladstone, cover up another Villiers family murder. Y'all can't let one generation pass without a murder. Ask 'em about it. Go on."

"You read old letters from over one hundred years ago and think it's proof. You're the only one here full of bull." Laura stood as well. "Evelyn is right. We want these women out of our house and our lives. In return, we'll generously agree not to press charges."

Jessi spun to face. "Detective Harrison—"

Harrison held up a palm, and Jessi stopped. "I don't care about dry bones in the family closet, okay? I've got enough death and destruction right now to keep me busy."

"I agree. These two are wasting your time and ours," Evelyn said with a curt nod of satisfaction.

"We appreciate how the NOPD and sheriff's department have conducted their investigation so far. Of course, we'd prefer the details be handled discreetly. Poor decisions were made," Forstall said, his voice pitched deep. Nick blushed red when the lawyer gave him a sharp side glance. "But the fact is, taking a killer off the streets is the top priority."

"Still, we would be grateful if you could avoid more distress for poor Tanner's grieving family," Evelyn added with force. "They've been through enough."

"They don't give a shit about justice, 'poor Tanner', or his family. All they care about is keeping their dirty secrets. I can give you an earful..." Jessi followed up with a few expletives.

"Magnolia Grove is haunted for a reason. The sins of our ancestors are why the spirits won't rest here. A psychic told my mother years ago," Mrs.

Villiers whined. She covered her face with both hands.

"Mother, the last thing we need is to hear such superstition. Laura, help talk sense to her," Evelyn said with exasperation as Mrs. Villiers teetered on the edge of hysteria.

Laura ignored her to blast back at Jessi. "Not everyone leads the kind of trashy life you do, Ms. Former-Stripper-Slash-Hooker."

"You get paid for getting on your knees, too. The only difference between us, is you married to your trick. Screwing his friends on the daily is your hobby." Jessi waved a forefinger in the air as she talked.

"You don't know anything about me, Bourbon Street prostitute," Laura shot back.

"Your mouth just wrote a check your ass can't cash." Jessi advanced toward Laura.

Charmaine grabbed Jessi's arm to yank her back as Laura shouted more insults. Evelyn demanded that Charmaine and Jessi be arrested. Then threatened to sue them for harassment, slander and fraud. Nick yelled for everyone to calm down, though he kept well out of the fray. Laura put up her fist in a comical fight stance. Charmaine would have laughed if she hadn't been wrestling with Jessi. Harrison stood in the middle between the Joliet sisters and the Villiers women, arms stretched out. He looked like a wrestling referee trying to stop a wild free for all.

"Everybody quiet," Harrison said.

Charmaine used the brief shocked silence on both sides to push Jessi against the fireplace. "Get some damn chill. Getting locked up will be a disaster."

"I wanted him to see how crazy they are," Jessi murmured low.

Charmaine glanced at the pandemonium her sister had caused. "Job done."

"Looks like they might be winding down. Watch this," Jessi whispered. She had a wicked gleam in her dark eyes.

"Wait, no." Charmaine wasted her breath.

Jessi spun around to shake a fist at Laura. "Bitch, you tried it. Like the whole city doesn't know you're a ho."

"I'm not going to take crap from a filthy—"

"What part of shut the hell up confused you people?" Harrison's voice boomed like thunder. He glared at each one of them in turn to further make his point. Then tugged on the wool blazer he wore over a tan dress shirt.

"Calm down. Everything is going to be fine," Nick said to his sisters and mother.

"You sound sure." Jessi looked at him hard, eyes narrowed to slits.

Nick ignored her and turned to Harrison. "Thanks for such a quick arrest of Tanner's murderer. We've lost someone who we cared about very much. Both our families are relieved at least you caught his killer."

"Let me know if we can assist you or the DA. I can't imagine they'll need any more statements from Mr. Villiers or his family. But contact me if you do," Forstall said. His tone made it clear he expected his clients to be left alone.

The detective transferred his intense scrutiny from Nick to the lawyer. Harrison's steady gaze caused the lawyer to fidget. "Oh yeah, I can almost guarantee you we'll have more questions for them."

Forstall cleared his throat and took a step back. "Which brings us to the reason for your visit."

Evelyn guided her mother back onto a chair. Then she looked at Harrison. "I hope you've come to tell us the police have found more of our family heirlooms."

"We have. We found six items at an antique dealer in Denham Springs, Louisiana. She also happened to have a meth lab out back. But that's not why I'm here," Harrison replied mildly.

"Excellent work. Um, you say there's something else?" Forstall looked at Evelyn, then back to Detective Harrison.

"Pretty convenient you're all in one room," Harrison said. He seemed in no hurry to reveal why he'd shown up.

"Like a low budget mystery movie. All the suspects called together to hear the detective lay out the facts." Nick seemed to have regained his usual poise. He sat in a French Louis XV style chair and crossed his long legs. "Except we already know whodunit."

Forstall eyed the detective with a wary expression. "So why are you here?"

"Yes, yes. We have a corporation to run, not to mention guests arriving here for the weekend. Get on with it." Evelyn waved a hand like the queen, and Harrison a butler moving too slowly.

"Okay," Harrison drawled, giving her a sour look. Still, he paused and looked at everyone again. "The drug dealer didn't kill Tanner Gladstone."

"Aw snap," Jessi blurted out.

"But, but..." Forstall's questions seemed to dissolve on his lips as he gaped at the detective.

For his part, Harrison seemed content to let silence stretch out in the room. Tension rose with each tick of the Edwardian mahogany clock on the mantel. Jessi sidled up to Charmaine until they were shoulder to shoulder.

"That's impossible," Nick burst out at last. He swallowed hard when Harrison said nothing. "We were there when the guy came in, like... it was a home invasion kind of thing. Kadeem will tell you."

"Glad you mentioned Mr. Hardy. He's another one of Mrs. Dawson's nephews." Harrison looked at Charmaine.

Charmaine felt pressure building in the room. She whispered a prayer of thanks her telepathy hadn't kicked in. With the tsunami of emotions swelling, getting reception from everyone would likely make her pass out.

"Yes," she murmured.

"Keeping it all in the family." Harrison nodded as he rubbed his chin.

"Honestly I don't see how..." Evelyn's voice trailed off when she looked at the lawyer.

"Which turns out to be the key, doesn't it? He's related to Yolanda Dawson. His cousins burglarize this place with directions from her on what to take. You folks don't fire her even though you know what she's up to. Because she's got something on the family." Harrison looked up at the ceiling as if deep in thought. "Wonder what's worth thousands in hush money?"

"Lies," Mrs. Villiers stammered. "Don't believe what she says."

Harrison pivoted to cross the room. He stopped in front of Mrs. Villiers. "What part is a lie?"

"Anything that implies my clients had knowledge of a crime," Forstall broke in before Mrs. Villiers replied. He shot a warning glance around. Nick and Laura pressed their lips together.

Evelyn placed a restraining hand on her mother's shoulder. "Right."

Harrison walked in circle examining his surroundings, or so it seemed. "Hmm. I'll get back to the thefts in a minute."

"He's really into this detective reveals the killer act," Jessi stage whispered. She smothered a giggle when Harrison glowered at her.

Charmaine shushed her. "We know the bullet wound didn't kill Tanner."

"Last time I tell you anything about one of my cases," Harrison grumbled at her. Still, he appeared placated by the effect of the revelation. He looked at the Villiers clan. "Gee, y'all don't look shocked. Not even a teeny bit surprised?"

"No, because they..." Jessi bit off her sentence at his dark look. "Sorry."

Harrison straightened his spine. The effect made him look even taller than his six feet. "Greg, alias 'Gee' Parker, the dealer in question, says he was paid for the drugs. That part is true. But he got an extra few thousand to ambush Tanner."

Jessi broke the heavy silence that had descended. "Why?"

"He didn't know why, and he didn't care. He's a thug willing to do whatever for the right price. Problem is, Kadeem's cousin bungled the job. Lucky for us cops, most criminals are dumb. Doesn't make them any less dangerous though." Harrison continued his circuit around the room until he stopped in front of Nick. "But Kadeem knew the answer or at least part of it. Tanner stumbled on a family secret that you folks couldn't afford to let get out. He's not here to tell us about it. Kadeem doesn't know the details, by the way. So, don't send somebody to kill him."

"This is too much," Evelyn said. "Elliot, I want to file a formal complaint with the police department. We're also going to file a defamation lawsuit."

"Slander, his allegations aren't in writing," Forstall replied. He cleared his throat and held up both palms when Evelyn gave him a murderous glare. "Let's all collect ourselves."

Evelyn raised her fists in frustration. "Do something, man."

"Detective, unless you have solid evidence I caution you not to spread these specious speculations." Forstall gave Harrison an "I'll see you in court" scowl.

"We can fill in the details," Charmaine said. "Over two hundred years ago a Villiers ancestor paid for someone to be murdered. The victim? Ferdinand Villiere, the illegitimate Black son who was about to get a fortune from his father. Well, Alexandre's wife wasn't having it. The young man was killed, and his mother died almost a year to the day later, under mysterious circumstances."

"How do you know all this?" Mrs. Villiers had one hand over her heart.

"If you say ghosts told you, I swear..." Harrison huffed out a grunt.

"Research, and we found the Baptiste family descendants," Jessi put in.

"We're detectives after all," Charmaine continued. "Your killer great, great and about a dozen more greats, grandmother didn't stop there. You see, Ferdinand's mother gave birth to another boy. That dude was a baby-making machine."

"Charmaine." Jessi put a hand on her arm.

"I'll stick to the subject," Charmaine said aside to her. "Anyway, turns out the plan to kill the second son failed. Alexandre Villiers, your ancestor, slipped the baby boy into the family after he killed his white wife. He got two for the price of one. Revenge for losing the true love of his life, and the heir his legal wife couldn't give him. That's what you couldn't afford to get out."

Laura looked at her siblings. They seemed too stunned to move, so she stood. "What a fascinating tale. Which no one cares about in the twenty-first century."

"Don't be so sure. Hector Turnbull heard the rumors that wouldn't go away. One of his granddaughters married a Villiers. Marrying a wealthy Turnbull saved your family from poverty after the financial crisis of eighteen-twenties. Turnbull wrote his will to exclude any child found to have 'a drop of black blood'," Charmaine said.

Harrison let out a second grunt. "I gotta say she's right. Nobody would care about an old will now."

"The Turnbull descendants would be thrilled. For the past ninety years or so, they've been trying to get control of Villiers and Sons, Inc. Two lawsuits and a couple of attempts to gain a majority stake based on what we found. Not to mention Tanner knew someone..." Charmaine looked at Laura, who hissed. "Has been dipping into business funds."

"Which would be more than enough reason to challenge your control of a multi-million dollar company," Jessi added.

More than one person shivered at the sudden chill in the room. A muted rumble sounded in the distance. Mrs. Villiers cast a wide-eyed glazed look around, her mouth working like a goldfish in a bowl sucking air.

"Sounds like a thunderstorm brewing, so let's wrap this up." Harrison rubbed his hands together. "Either somebody cranked up the A/C or there's a cold front coming through. Anyway, Mr. Villiers is coming with me to answer some questions."

"You can't take her outlandish story seriously," Laura shouted.

"Lady, I don't care about a set of dusty facts from way back in the day. All I know is, Tanner Gladstone met up with Parker to pay him."

Charmaine broke in. "Tanner met up with the dealer to pay him, because Kadeem shorted him for the drugs. I mean, that was the cover story for why he shot up the party, right?"

"I don't know what you're talking about." Nick's voice came out as a strangled croak.

Harrison spoke to Charmaine though his gaze remained on Nick. "You're saying Parker's farfetched story is true. Gladstone found out the real deal, so he paid Parker money not to kill him. We know this because we got video at an ATM machine with Gladstone withdrawing the cash. Parker with was with him. Then Gladstone confronted Nick, and he does the job himself."

"No- no. I never." Nick panted as he cast a panicked glance at Forstall.

Jessi jerked Charmaine aside. "We got a problem."

"Shh... this is getting good." Charmaine tried to pull away, but Jessi's grip tightened.

The clock and vases on the fireplace mantle rattled. The room seemed to darken in an odd way. Yet sunlight shone outside through the windows. Rustling began like hundreds of dry leaves swirling in the wind. Hissing followed that was so loud, Charmaine looked down to check for giant snakes at her feet. She realized listening to Jessi might be a great idea.

"Georgina didn't know about the baby. You just broke that bit of news to her, and she is one pissed off poltergeist." Jessi talked fast as the mayhem around them increased.

"Do something," Charmaine yelled to be heard over the roar of an angry ghost.

Jessi let out a hiss. "I left my bag in the Jeep."

"Please tell me you're joking. You didn't come into the most haunted mansion in Louisiana without your gadgets."

Jessi hunched her shoulders against what felt like a gust of wind. Yet nothing moved in the room. "I'm gonna go get what I need. Hang on till I get back."

"Aw hell, Jess. I'm that one that pissed her off," Charmaine cried.

"Hit the siren on your phone. The high-frequency sound might slow her down," Jessi yelled back before she dashed toward the door.

"Might?" Charmaine asked the empty space where Jessi used to be.

Meanwhile, the others huddled together in the center of the room. None of them paid attention to Charmaine or Jessi. Then Harrison's head jerked around. She couldn't hear his attempts to speak, as if cotton had been stuffed in her ears. Charmaine fumbled to get her cell phone out of her bag. Freezing fingers didn't help. Detective Harrison got two feet when he yelped. Brocade fabric from the draperies of a window hugged him like a living thing.

"Jesus be a fence, my co-pilot and take the wheel." Charmaine improvised a prayer with every Black gospel song she could recall.

Jessi fell through the wooden doors. She huffed with the effort of fighting against a strong force. Her mouth worked, but the chaos caused by an enraged ghost drowned out the words. Charmaine tried screaming, but couldn't hear her own voice. Looking away from Jessi, Charmaine concentrated on her cell phone. She had to tap in her security code twice. Then she had to swipe through two pages of apps before she found the siren.

"Please open. Please open," Charmaine chanted as she fumbled to hit the right icon to activate it.

Five seconds of terror later, the blast of a virtual air horn pierced the room. The draperies fell away from Harrison. He swung out at the air for a few seconds before he realized he was free. Although the unnatural movements decreased, inanimate objects continued to vibrate.

Across the room, Jessi raised both arms. She held what looked like flashlights in each hand. She swung her devices in opposite arcs. "I command you to cross into the spirit realm."

Vases, portraits on the walls, the draperies, everything stopped shaking. The rustling noises faded away in seconds. Nothing but the whimpering of four women, and the sobs of Nick remained.

"I never wanted him to get hurt. He was my friend. I just meant for them to scare him." Nick snuffled. He wiped his nose on the sleeve of his thousand dollar suit jacket. His breath hitched. He mumbled too low for Charmaine to make out the rest of his words.

"Lord, please forgive our many sins. I repent. I'll go to confession and do whatever penance Father Richard says I have to." Marguerite Villiers groveled on her knees before a large porcelain figurine of a woman.

"Mother, get up." Evelyn struggled to pull Marguerite to her feet but failed.

Laura pushed her disheveled blonde hair from her eyes. She staggered a few moments. "Nonsense. The caretaker must have mistakenly turned the AC fan up too high. Or the security alarm came on. Or both. A windstorm."

"Laura, please." Her mother clutched the edge of an empire styled marble end table.

"I told them it was a bad idea," Laura squeaked when the crystal flower vase closest to her wobbled.

The doors swung wide, which made everyone gasp in horrified anticipation. The groundskeeper walked in. He gawked at them in alarm. "Y'all okay? I heard a bunch of yelling, so I called the police. I didn't know what the hell was goin' on up in here."

Two Jefferson Parish deputies strode in, hands on their service pistols as if ready to draw. Two more followed seconds later. Fifteen later minutes, an ambulance arrived and everyone had been checked for injuries. Mrs. Villiers moaned about chest pains. Her head bobbed from side to side. A new housecleaner, a short Hispanic woman, bustled in. She took a dust cloth from a pocket of her apron to pat Mrs. Villiers' sweaty face as paramedics strapped her onto a stretcher.

The female paramedic turned to everyone. "We can allow one family member to ride with the patient."

A chorus of voices from the Villiers children greeted her pronouncement. Detective Harrison watched them shout each other down as the debate raged. All four deputies stood at the perimeter of the room observing. They seemed poised to prevent anyone from leaving.

"I don't need this shit," Harrison muttered and pulled a large hand over his face. Then he strode over to stand in front of Charmaine. "Do your thing."

Charmaine blinked at him. "Huh?"

"Tell me who stays and who goes. I can't let a possible murderer just ride out of here." Harrison nodded in a due west direction. "The airport is too damn close. They'd be whisked off to anywhere in the world in no time."

"Yeah, and I'll bet this crowd owns a private plane," Jessi agreed. She looked at Charmaine. "Well?"

"I can't tap my forehead and... Okay, okay. Too much damn pressure." Charmaine panted as performance anxiety gripped her by the throat.

"Give me a minute." Harrison glanced at a deputy and gave a signal the man apparently understood.

"Everybody quiet," the man barked in a deep, commanding voice.

On cue, his fellow officers closed in on the Villiers children in tight formation. Their voices died away. The Hispanic housekeeper clutched the cloth in her hand and whispered in Spanish. She went quiet as a deputy got closer to her.

"Better?" Harrison murmured aside to Charmaine.

She nodded. Nick, Laura, and Evelyn stared wide-eyed at the deputies. Evelyn radiated outrage at her treatment given her social status. Laura grappled with using her looks to charm the deputies, including the lone female officer. Through it all, Nick focused on Charmaine.

Seconds ticked by as tension clogged the atmosphere. Charmaine turned her back on them and pushed Harrison to a far corner. "You're not going to believe this."

"I'm ready to believe in leprechauns and sparkly vampires to sort through this crazy situation." Harrison towered over her with a look of expectation.

"They all knew about the plan to get rid of Tanner, but Laura killed him. Nick called her over his place in a panic when Tanner showed up. She went into a rage when Tanner drunkenly taunted her about having an affair with her husband," Charmaine said. "Evelyn is the least likely to run though. Too much at stake."

"Holy shi—" Harrison straightened his shoulders until he looked even more intimidating. He spun around. "Mrs. Harmon, in the ambulance. You two, go with the deputies."

"Our attorney will have something to say about..." Laura looked around, but Elliot Forstall was gone.

"Looks like your guy took the first chance to bounce outta here. Girl, that ain't good news," Jessi quipped.

"Charmaine." Nick started toward her but stopped when Charmaine shook her head.

"Nice knowing you, Nick. I hope it all works out." Charmaine crossed her arms tight against her frame.

Nick stammered out protests and Laura wailed in outrage as they were led away. Charmaine caught a snatch of Evelyn's thoughts as she followed her mother to the ambulance. She had already begun to plan her complete takeover of VSI, Inc. Jessi tapped one of Harrison's broad shoulders. When he faced her, Jessi smiled and took a bow.

"You're welcome."

"You and your sister got a whole lot of explaining to do, so don't think you're going home either, Ms. Joliet," Harrison put in.

"Aw hell. Absolutely no gratitude," Jessi cried.

"Right, like me thanking you for putting out the fire that burned my house to the ground. After you torched it," Harrison tossed back.

"You kidding me? We handed you another win all wrapped up like an early Christmas present. We even saved everybody from the crazy ghost." Jessi held up her modified Tasers to reinforce her arguments.

Harrison grunted. "Two flashlights. One is leopard print, the other some pink flowers. Cute."

"But—"

"A freak windstorm shook the house. Or maybe an eighteen-wheeler got lost and rumbled too close. Maybe plumbing rattled. Whatever my final story is, you two better go along with it. Dump talk about spirits, goblins, or any of that spooky crap," Harrison cut her off.

"I take a scientific approach. I don't deal in superstition like Charmaine," Jessi said.

Charmaine clamped a hand over Jessi's mouth. "Yes sir, Detective Harrison."

"Good. Otherwise, I'll ask questions you don't want to answer, like how and why you found Kadeem Hardy. Don't complicate my life." Harrison stabbed a forefinger at them.

"We understand. Don't we, Jessi?" Charmaine kept her hand on her sister's mouth. Jessi nodded.

"Then let's roll up out of this creep show," Harrison muttered with a look around.

****

Two days later Charmaine sat in her small home office. A mug of strong coffee and the comforts of home felt so good. Signed into the clinic's secure server for staff, she entered notes on several cases. Pale afternoon November sunshine brightened her entire house and yard. A definite improvement from the gloom that seemed to permeate all things tied to Magnolia Grove.

"We're coming through," Jessi yelled down the hallway, having used her key.

Footsteps announced that Charmaine's solitude would be interrupted by more than one. Scotty and Diamond followed Jessi in to her surprise.

"Don't you people have lives?" Charmaine signed out, closed the screen and exited the application. Before any of them could answer, the kitchen doorbell sounded.

"I'll get it." Diamond scurried out and returned seconds later with Detective Harrison in tow.

"Put away the stolen goods and drugs. It's the po-leece," she chirped.

"Cute." Harrison looked downed at Diamond. His frown made him look like a disapproving school principal.

Diamond's gleeful expression faded under his stone-faced scrutiny. "You're not here to arrest anybody, are ya?"

"Gotcha," Harrison's scowl melted into a grin. "Unless you do have drugs and stolen loot."

"Nah, we cleared it out. As you can see from the luxe lifestyle we have from ill-gotten gains," Charmaine joked. She waved her hand around at the room.

"Yeah," Harrison replied. "Just like the grand stuff I buy with my huge cop's salary."

"What's up, man?" Scotty shared a dap with Harrison.

"My world has settled down. Laura Villiers is expensively lawyered up, and her family is in the process of doing damage control. As you predicted, several members of the extended family have already swooped in. Not that I care. It's the DA's pain in the ass now." Harrison's relaxed smile confirmed his mind was at ease.

"The Turnbull faction is forcing an audit of how the corporation has been run. Every decision, expenditures, employee qualifications, the works."

"You don't think an old will with a racist clause could be enforced? I mean, seems pretty much a stretch," Diamond said.

"I called Mrs. Edwards. A group of Baptiste descendants have hired a lawyer. He's going to advise them on what to do about their land claim. I hope they win big." Jessi held up both hands with fingers crossed.

"Sounds like the Villiers branch won't have time to run the family company anyway," Scotty said.

"I predict the Baptiste family will be offered a settlement." Charmaine's tone was subdued as she thought about her former lover. Nick wasn't evil, more like afflicted with fatal character flaws.

"Laura and the rest will be busy fighting criminal charges for months. The DA's office is having fits sorting through who did what. She's going to be charged. The question is, with what. Maybe manslaughter or second-degree murder. The rest could be booked on accessory or obstruction, maybe both." Det. Harrison shook his head. "Glad it's his problem."

"Nick will put his energy in staying out of jail. If I know them, Mrs. Villiers and Evelyn will scramble to keep any part of the family riches they can.

"They're getting hit from all sides," Harrison said.

Scotty glanced at Charmaine. "You okay?"

"Why shouldn't I be?" Charmaine brushed hair from her forehead. She returned his searching gaze with a steady one of her own. He nodded, satisfied with her response.

"So, that is that, as my grand-mama used to say," Harrison said, breaking the charged silence. He rubbed his hands together.

"Right. On to the next action-packed case for the Joliet Sisters." Diamond grinned. She snapped her fingers. "Hey, I can be your Watson, you know chronicle your case files in a blog. Set up a Facebook page. Maybe get a book deal!"

"Oh geez no. All of you, take a vacation from investigating. Say ten years. I'll be ready to retire by then." Harrison switched to grouchy cop in a flash.

"Aw c'mon. We gonna make you famous," Charmaine chimed in with a wink at Diamond.

"Yeah man. You'll go down in history. I can see the headlines. Detective Uses Ghosts to Crack Tough Cases." Jessi grinned at him.

His laid-back mood gone, Harrison wagged his head from side to side. His melodramatic reaction inspired Diamond to tease him even more, to the delight of Scotty. Jessi threw in a few suggestions for lurid blog headlines. Harrison boomed about confidentiality and protecting police investigations. Charmaine turned to Jessi, pulling her aside.

"Hey, what do you think it means, that I could hear ghosts for a minute?" She frowned at her baby sister.

Jessi shrugged. "Usually a psychic has one ability. Even more weird is you developing one out of nowhere. I told Logan and the others at school about it. We're going to do some research."

"I hope it doesn't mean we've stirred up the wrong forces." Charmaine chewed on a thumbnail, an old habit from childhood. She caught herself and stopped to avoid ruining her manicure.

"Don't start with the religious superstition. And don't be tellin' Rev. Grab-Yo-Money our business either." Jessi squinted at Charmaine.

"Bishop Sykes cares about—"

"Whatever. Just keep my name out your mouth when you talk to him. Maybe your God wants you to have another gift." Jessi slapped Charmaine on the back, then joined the others.

"Hey, I hadn't considered..." Charmaine's angst began to dissipate. Maybe she wasn't a tool of Satan after all. "What's everybody doing for dinner? I can whip up a big pot of my famous spaghetti and meat sauce real quick."

"You mean add Louisiana hot sauce to a jar of store bought stuff and throw in some ground beef," Jessi quipped.

Charmaine got into a spirited back and forth with Jessi. Scotty and Diamond chimed in. Harrison declared he could use a semi-home cooked meal, which brought hoots of laughter. For her part, Charmaine enjoyed their banter with good humor. Intended or not, they'd become a team. They would no doubt end up tackling another strange case together. Charmaine laughed when she imagined Harrison's future pained reactions. She went into the kitchen to start their meal, enjoying the noise made by her outlandish crew.

About the Author

Mix knowledge of voodoo, Louisiana politics and forensic social work with the dedication to write fiction while working each day as a clinical social worker, and you get a snapshot of author Lynn Emery.

The author of over twenty novels, she is currently working on the next mysteries in three series. Learn more at:

www.lynnemery.com

www.ingramcontent.com/pod-product-compliance
Lightning Source LLC
Chambersburg PA
CBHW030647120726
47905CB00001B/103